# UNDER FIRE

While police forces across the country are investigating a series of fires, a complex of offices in Cloughton is burned down and two bodies are found in the ruins. One victim was an Asian woman, the other a white man. DCI Benny Mitchell and his team soon learn that the fire was deliberately started, but they don't know if it is the work of the serial arsonist. Could the fire be a copycat arson attack, designed to mask the real crime, or racially-motivated murder? Or are Mitchell and his team dealing with an incident involving family dishonour and revenge?

# UNDER FIRE

# UNDER FIRE

*by*

Pauline Bell

**Magna Large Print Books**
Long Preston, North Yorkshire,
BD23 4ND, England.

British Library Cataloguing in Publication Data.

Bell, Pauline
     Under fire.

          A catalogue record of this book is
          available from the British Library

          ISBN   978-0-7505-2996-9

First published in Great Britain 2007 by Constable,
an imprint of Constable & Robinson Ltd.

Published in Large Print 2008 by arrangement with
Constable & Robinson Ltd.

Magna Large Print is an imprint of Library Magna Books Ltd.

Printed and bound in Great Britain by
T.J. (International) Ltd., Cornwall, PL28 8RW

For Maurice H. T.
with thanks for many kindnesses

# Prologue

The arsonist in his red anorak had been walking briskly to keep warm. He had never had reason to pass along this road before and he slowed now, looking around him with some curiosity. Here was where, more than a century ago, rich mill owners had lived. Had there been, he wondered, any other way, in nineteenth-century Cloughton, of acquiring enough money to buy one of these near-mansions?

Huge they certainly were, but not so grand now. The young man stopped to examine the fine building opposite. It was still well kept up, its garden trim, the shrubs neatly pruned and the paintwork recent and smart. Further along, though, several of the houses were for sale and he knew from the local paper that the prices being asked were less than their present owners had paid for them. The local joyriders had discovered that the wide stretch of smooth tarmac in front of them made a splendid racetrack. The lads had been thwarted when the council had closed the road to through traffic by means of a row of concrete bollards at the end nearest the centre of town – a solution to which the residents too had an ambivalent attitude. It made life as inconvenient for them as for the unwelcome marauders, and the ugly stumps did nothing to improve the view.

Across the road from the row of still-stately houses a narrow shelf of rock was all that separated the pavement from a precipitous drop to the centre of Cloughton below. The light was beginning to fade, but the arsonist could still make out the rising slope beyond the town, and, for a moment, he watched a bus tacking its way up the other side of the valley. The view was spectacular and deserved a proper spot from which to admire it. An iron-framed, slatted-wood bench had been provided for the purpose, originally as a tribute to a certain Geo. C. Greenway. This man, so he had been told, had owned the most thriving of the woollen mills. The profits from it had provided alms-houses and a huge orphanage which now housed one of Cloughton's two grammar schools. Availing themselves of the bench at present was a selection of the Cloughton youth. They might have been ex-joyriders, but, from their quiet and watchful demeanour, he suspected they were the local druggies.

Whoever they were, he frowned at the litter they had dropped, kept his distance from them and admired the clean austerity of the chunks of rocky cliff below him and the wind-battered, leafless, puny silver birches. Raising his eyes, he made out, just discernible in the dusk against the grey-blue sky, the Greenway Tower, a tall chimney that was the philanthropic Mr Greenway's folly and status symbol. It seemed unhappy and out of place, rearing up, slender and much decorated, from the shabby, scrubby hillside with its rough tussocks and stones. Perhaps he should put it out of its misery, burn it down. He considered the idea for a moment. Did he feel a sufficient urge to take the risk? No, he wouldn't set a fire tonight. The dry leaves blowing round the bases of the rocks would have made good kindling but there wasn't time to make a plan.

A good plan was essential. He had still been attending junior school when he set his first fire. He'd been found out, of course, and claimed it was an accident – or at least a miscalculation. It had been neither. He had planned it deliberately and carefully and his calculating had been, for a nine-year-old, pretty accurate. He had made mistakes, though. He hadn't known that petrol and paraffin evaporated at very low temperatures. He had taken his time putting a match to it so that the vapour had risen to produce an oxygen-gas mixture that had exploded into a fireball.

These days he worked quickly and usually

started his fire from a distance, using a cord or paper trail. That first time, he had regretted the painful charring of the fingers of his left hand more because it had betrayed him than because of the discomfort. Afterwards, his classmates had nicknamed him 'Lucifer' and he'd encouraged them, proud of this mark of their esteem. But later, the boys who despised him because he wasn't good at games had shortened it to Lucy. That had made him angry.

He couldn't remember a time when fire had not fascinated him. When he had been barely old enough to go to school, he had stolen boxes of matches from the pockets of his parents' smoker friends and smuggled them into his bedroom. In the safe time during the family's favourite television programmes, he had happily singed tiny holes in his bedroom carpet or watched paper flaring up on a metal tray.

Since then he had always carried matches. He patted the pocket they were in now. Fire burned up rubbish, left things clean, somehow. He liked things clean – and tidy. When his life silted up he felt out of control and panic-stricken. He shuddered at the memory of having to share his bedroom with his younger brother whenever visitors stayed overnight. He would find, at bedtime, toy cars scooped up from the floor and dropped in a higgledy-piggledy heap on the top of his chest of drawers – his brother's response to being told to tidy away his belongings. It infuriated him – no, it hurt him, frightened him even. Each time, he would put the cars back in Thomas's toy box, arranging them neatly in rows.

A shiver interrupted his reminiscence. It had become extremely cold and quite late. Time he set off back to the house. On an impulse, he crossed the rocky shelf and clambered down into a sheltered hollow beneath a jutting and slightly overhanging chunk of millstone grit. He felt in his pocket for the box and opened it. Feeling a frisson of pleasurable excitement, he breathed in the rising scent, half salty half smoky, of friction-ignited phosphorous. With its pointed peak dancing, a small oval flame appeared, teetering on the end of the matchstick.

For a moment it looked vulnerable but then, tiny as it was, it took firm hold of the scrap of wood and began its inexorable work. Fine lines of dark brown charring ran down towards his fingers. He saw the first tiny wisp, just a suggestion of smoke to the eye. He breathed in and it caught at the back of his throat.

When he felt the heat uncomfortable on his hand, he blew. His breath was stronger than the little bobbing yellow ball. It denied this embryo fire the fuel and oxygen that would have allowed it to grow, to fulfil its beautiful, destructive, intoxicating potential. The smoky puff of its dying protest took its revenge on him. His half frozen nasal passages stung and tears trickled

He knew better, nowadays, than to throw the remaining splinter of wood on the ground. That was too dangerous a habit to get into. Taking out the box again, he stowed the remnant carefully inside.

## Chapter One

At the end of the second week in January, Detective Constable Caroline Jackson, dressed in thin cotton trousers and a short-sleeved cotton vest, sat at a table on the pavement outside a small café.

She was not cold because this was Cairo. She was not bored because a fellow Englishwoman, seated at the next table, was providing her with entertainment. Her compatriot's attire, brief shorts and a sun top, seemed to offend the café proprietor even more than her own uncovered arms. Caroline hoped he could not translate the woman's conversation. 'There's nothing here. Absolutely nothing! The shops are shut every afternoon and the cafés...' The woman's vocabulary proved inadequate and her hands gestured her disgust. 'Well, this coffee's diabolical and I've looked all over for a vanilla slice. There isn't one to be had.' Her companion nodded sympathetically.

Caroline stopped smiling and wondered whether her own attitude to her surroundings was any less reprehensible. She too hated the extremely strong Turkish coffee, served in mercifully tiny cups by their host, Cavill's friend from his university days.

She sipped orange juice from the tall glass in front of her and looked forward to her return to England. Cavill's friend had politely regretted that this was a flying visit that left no time to show them the marvels that they had read about. Caroline was undismayed, doubting that the Sphinx and the pyramids would compensate for the filth, the heart-rending, often mutilated beggars and the police at every street corner, not only armed but seeming to take pleasure in brandishing their guns. She had thought that the Egyptians would make their capital city more welcoming to visitors.

Perhaps her disorientation accounted for some of her disenchantment. Cavill's concerts, the real purpose of their trip, had been given in Israel, so that this diversion to Cairo for the last few days had given her more strange circumstances to adapt to: summer weather in January, a slipped weekend with the day of rest first on a Saturday in Israel and now, here, on a Friday, and finally a Muslim after a Jewish culture.

It was all diverting and mind-broadening but Caroline was glad that she was going home later in the day. She was looking forward to being back on her own job. She had enjoyed Cavill's recitals in Jerusalem and Tel Aviv, but this time she had felt no lingering regrets for the giving up of her own musical career.

Cavill seemed to thrive on spending several days of a week in an equal number of different countries. Occasionally, when her job allowed, she enjoyed accompanying him on these trips. For the most part, though, she needed her own base and her own timetable. In spite of her musical talent, a concert career would not have made her happy. She would have resented having to wait for invitations to perform. She would have chafed at the necessity to be ingratiating, and to meet the 'right' but uncongenial people in order to be offered work.

Cavill was beyond all that now. Work poured in and he could choose what to accept. Caroline could not have submitted to the subservience that would have been necessary to achieve that enviable eminence. She got up to go and meet him, well satisfied with the decisions she had taken and the way her life was shaping. Cavill needed a base too. It was part of her respon-

sibility, willingly taken on, to provide it. She missed him when he was away, but the strength of their marriage lay partly in the variety of experience that each of them contributed to it.

Tomorrow she would be back in Cloughton, and, later in the week, cheerfully chasing villains. She set off for the cathedral where they had arranged to meet and where Cavill had not been invited to play.

Fran Mitchell had enjoyed his chilly ride from Ripon on this Sunday afternoon. It had been bitterly cold. His face was numb and his hands in their fleece and leather gloves had frozen fingers. It had been a bonus, though, to clock up the miles – a good start to the new week's training. Now, as he coasted along the main road out of Bradford and towards Cloughton, he was feeling some trepidation. He had stayed with his uncle and cousins before, of course, and they had always been most hospitable. On those occasions, though, he had come here in company with his parents and some, if not all, of his brothers and sisters. And the visits had been for no longer than a weekend.

Now, he was being wished on to them for an indefinite period. He was less sure of his welcome, anxious about being able to keep up his cycling training, about how he would fit in as a temporary family member rather

than just a fleeting visitor. There would be little kids around again. In his own family they were past that stage, thank goodness. Would Auntie Ginny expect him to be a sort of male au pair in exchange for his keep? After all, he wouldn't be going to school or to work.

He felt in a state of suspension with nowhere to belong. It would be interesting, of course, to see how a detective inspector lived when he was doing his daily work, rather than just being Uncle Benny. Fran knew he was being unfair to his aunt and, anyway, he would help her automatically. Having been brought up with five other children in his own family he was programmed to pitch in with all the tasks involved with running a large household.

He'd been lucky actually. When he and two of his sisters had been farmed out to the wider family, he had been allocated to the people he would have chosen. Now he had to present himself, however, he felt strangely uncomfortable.

He was getting quite close. In half a mile or so he would have to turn right at the hospital where his grandmother was presently a patient. All the grandchildren got on with Granny Niamh but Fran had always felt that she had a particularly soft spot for him. He was determined to visit her regularly whilst he remained in Cloughton.

Glancing at the digital time indicator on his left handlebar, he decided to call into the hospital now. Even if it wasn't the proper time, they would let him in for a few minutes if he told them he had cycled from Ripon to see his grandmother. She would soon jolly him out of his shyness and he would cheer her up with his news.

Would she be cheered by a recital of his probably unfounded worries? Well, he would go in any case.

Having carefully secured his bicycle to a railing behind the pay-and-display machine he entered the hospital building. Enquiries for his grandmother led him to a four-bedded ward, where a fellow patient suggested he should look in the TV room. Fran thought this was an unlikely refuge for Granny Niamh, but she was indeed there. The television set was switched off though and she was deep in conversation with a youngish man. Fran considered them both carefully from a position to the side of the open door where he thought he could wait without being seen until she was free to talk to him.

He was shocked to realize for the first time that Granny Niamh was an old woman and he tried to analyse her new air of fragility. Her body was still stocky, not noticeably thinner. It was something in her face rather than her manner. She paid close attention to the young man as she listened. When she spoke to him, it was with her usual brisk precision but he saw that the skin of her cheeks sagged and so did the line of her shoulders.

Her eyes were still sharp though – or maybe her ears. Without turning, she suddenly demanded, 'Well, Francis, how long has eavesdropping been your hobby?'

Fran reddened. He had certainly been listening to the conversation and, coming forward to be introduced, he regarded his grandmother's friend with some curiosity. He was disappointed when the man politely excused himself and left grandmother and grandson to their family gossip.

They were interrupted after a minute or two by the appearance of a male nurse whose upper body appeared round the half-closed door. 'Sorry. Have you seen Simon? I thought he was in here with you.'

Fran thought that the nurse's pale blue tunic with the lilac edging to its pockets made him appear effeminate and that, anyway, nursing was not a manly profession. He remembered in time that he had better not say so. Auntie Ginny's brother Alex was a nurse at Jimmy's in Leeds.

His grandmother was being helpful. 'He's only just gone. He said earlier that he would sit with Marjorie for a while.'

The nurse nodded, smiling. 'We'll miss him when he goes – Margie especially.'

'Will that be soon, then?'

'Tomorrow morning, if Mr Jones is still happy with him.'

'He'll be glad to get back to his wife. He's been worried about her.'

The nurse nodded and disappeared in search of his patient. Fran asked his grandmother, 'Who's Margie?'

'According to her, she's a friend of the Queen. Marjorie takes Her Majesty down to the hospital canteen because the royals can't get fish and chips at the Palace. Poor old soul! Still, dementia does have its compensations. She didn't have the pleasure of such exalted company when she was in her right mind. She's probably happier than the rest of us.'

Fran was still chuckling as he remounted his bicycle to complete his journey.

Detective Chief Inspector Benedict Mitchell was happy. He had driven home from work he enjoyed to a wife and children he found eminently satisfactory, through his native West Yorkshire town. Cloughton was not beautiful, but its quirky inconveniences and its rough, rather bleak setting against a Pennine backdrop appealed to him more than glittering spires or lush meadows would have done.

During the morning, Mitchell had driven to the substation further up the valley to consult a colleague. Snow had been forecast. It had not fallen, but his tyres, when he turned off the main road, had left tracks in frost as thick as snow. When he returned in the afternoon, the sun, setting behind a veil of cloud, had warmed the shades of the brown earth and dead heather and stained the white-capped horizon with a feeble pink.

An hour or so ago, when he had finally left the Cloughton station, darkness was sucking away the dusk. Now, in his own sitting room, he sprawled over more than his share of the substantial sofa, and surveyed his family complacently. This was the first day of an open-ended visit from his nephew, and so Mitchell had eaten his supper in the station canteen, leaving Ginny to settle the boy in and to produce an evening meal to suit the tastes of their young folk. Now they were all drinking coffee that he had made himself.

He had wondered how Fran would fit in with his family. At sixteen, this cousin was five years older than his own elder son. He saw that he need not have worried. The two boys sat opposite one another over the chessboard. They had raised their heads in polite greeting when he had come in, but now they were oblivious to everything but their game.

There was no reason, Mitchell supposed, why cousins had to resemble each other, but these two had no features in common, were almost perversely different. Declan, tall for his eleven years, had delicate features, presently arranged in fierce concentration. He had changed schools in the summer and had had his dark hair cut too short for his new friends to realize that it curled like his mother's. Fran too had had the good fortune to resemble his mother. He had crew-cut, fairish hair topping regular and amiable features. Neither Mitchell nor his brother would have wished their physiognomy on their sons.

Eight-year-old Caitlin sat on a stool, her long curtains of mouse-brown hair hiding her face, her head bent over a book she was not reading. She was keeping a low profile, knowing that drawing attention to herself might mean dismissal to bed. The twins had been asleep for some time, or so Mitchell hoped.

Virginia put down her book and carried the coffee tray to the kitchen, delivering over her shoulder the dreaded warning to Caitlin, 'Ten more minutes. Make the most of them.' When she returned, the chess game was over. Declan's hunched shoulders and sulky expression indicated that he had lost. His parents exchanged glances. Their eldest had still not learned to concede victory gracefully.

As Mitchell hesitated over reprimanding him in front of their visitor, Fran rescued them both. 'I've been playing since before I was eleven. Then, at my school, there was a master who was a chess ace. He taught all his tricks to anyone who was interested. I could show you some, if you like.'

Declan responded with reasonable grace and Mitchell, glad that he had held his tongue, rewarded his nephew. 'I believe there's a local club. Beardsmore, one of my constables, belongs to it. I'll get details for you. Even if you're only here for two or three weeks you'll get a few rather more challenging games in.' He glanced a warning at Declan not to sulk at the implied insult.

Fran was pleased. 'Thanks a lot. There isn't a cycling club as well, is there?'

Mitchell shrugged. 'No idea. Clement might know.'

'Is he another constable?'

'Yes. He's a detective on my team. He runs.'

Virginia turned to their visitor. 'By the way, I've moved your bike to the shed. The garage has to be kept clear. In a police house the car has to be at the ready to make a dash.' Caitlin had looked up inadvisedly and met her mother's eye. 'Bed, young lady. School tomorrow.'

'It's only the first week. We won't be doing proper work yet.' Her parents disdained to answer and Caitlin rose reluctantly. She paused to try another ruse. 'What's everyone else doing tomorrow?'

24

This one worked. Fran announced that he would spend the afternoon visiting his grandmother again. Mitchell was grateful. He had been off his patch for some days, gathering delicate evidence, and was conscious of having neglected his mother.

Fran turned to his aunt. 'What will you be doing?'

'Trying to finish two half-done articles.'

'What on?'

'One's a tongue-in-cheek piece about high-tech houses...'

'Tongue-in-cheek means you don't really mean it.' Caitlin immediately regretted this helpful interpolation.

'...the other,' Virginia continued, 'is about men's clothes.'

Fran blinked. 'What do you know about that?'

Virginia grinned. 'Oh, I have a wicked line in irony. Now, Kat...'

Turning to her father, Caitlin tried her last shot. 'You haven't told us what you'll be doing.'

Mitchell decided he would answer her. He admired her persistence. 'Who knows? In my job, you don't know at breakfast time where you're going to have lunch – or even if you'll get any.' He pointed to the door and Caitlin, reading his expression, departed with no further comment.

Virginia suggested they should watch the

news and switched the television set on. Both parents smiled as Declan quietly appropriated his sister's stool and made himself as unobtrusive as possible. Only cousin Francis had a temporary reprieve from school.

The news had already begun. '...questioning a man about a series of arson attacks throughout Yorkshire.' Mitchell leaned closer to the screen to hear the headlines above the desultory conversation. Cloughton had not, so far, been favoured by the fire raiser and so he had not impinged much on Mitchell's team's day-to-day work. At the station earlier in the evening he had heard no word of this man's apprehension, so he suspected that the television company had little more than the one fact to divulge.

It proved so. Without the man's name, any of the circumstances of his arrest or any details of what the North Yorkshire police suspected that the man might know or have done, the programmers had to he satisfied with reminding viewers of the facts they had already reported. So, there followed a composite arrangement of film already shown.

A derelict farm building appeared, well alight. The camera moved in on the blaze until the screen was entirely filled with leaping flames. The eyes of all four of them were drawn to the mesmerizing patterns and bright colours. Accompanied by a melodramatic commentary, the camera drew back and now showed a building in black silhouette, within which glowing rectangles indicated where the windows had been.

The cameraman had an eye for the piquant. His lens, roving round the fringe of the scene, focused now on a conifer, not yet fully ablaze, flames playing round the branches. Suddenly, the next tree lit up, then another until there was a wall of fire. The trees were quickly consumed and the screen darkened. Then stumps smoked against a dazzling background of the main fire. Clever work!

Mitchell imagined that the newscast's most interested viewer might well be the arsonist himself, feeding his excitement and satisfaction on this reconstruction of his achievement.

The family had all stopped talking to listen more carefully as a Channel 4 interviewer questioned an ex-fireman with a badly mutilated face. The conflagration that had caused his injuries seemed to be unconnected with the current series but his experiences were harrowing. Virginia made to turn off the set but Mitchell frowned her back into her seat. Declan was watching, eyes round, mouth open. He was at secondary school now. Yes, he might still have occasional nightmares but he had to learn to live in the real world and to pay his own tribute to those people whose bravery helped to keep him safe.

The boy turned to his father to ask, 'Do you think there'll be a fire in Cloughton?'

Virginia answered him, 'Who can tell?' Mitchell added that their fire setter seemed not to have a grudge against householders and mentioned that various commercial targets had been attacked only when their workforce was safely out of the way.

As if he had taken warning from the Mitchells' conversation, the interviewer released his injured fireman. The screen now showed a sketch map of Yorkshire. As the list of arson attacks was read out, yellow teardrops, perhaps meant to be flames, appeared at their sites. 'That was near us,' Fran remarked as a yellow blob appeared over a small disused factory in Knaresborough. Mitchell and Virginia both willed him not to elaborate and he did not.

The map disappeared and another interview began, this time with an arson investigator. He informed them that fire travelled upwards so that the site of its source would be at the lowest point of the damage. 'On the same principle, a fire on a slope travels uphill faster than to the ground below.'

Noting his uncle's concentration, Fran remarked, 'I hadn't realized that.'

Mitchell smiled at his nephew's man-of-the-world tone. 'I don't suppose you did. It's not the sort of thing you think about until something like this is in the news.' He saw that the arson expert had been replaced by a criminal psychologist and sighed.

The smug interviewer, who had prefaced all his questions with his own opinions, once more prepared to attack. 'Anyone can understand a rapist or even a sadist – there's a bit of that in all of us – but how can normal human beings like us understand someone who obtains satisfaction, sexual satisfaction from what I've read, from watching a fire?' This time it was Mitchell who got up to switch off the news.

When the household was awakened several hours later by Declan's screams, Virginia felt it quite fair to insist on her husband being the one to sort things out.

## Chapter Two

Quite accustomed to bizarre working hours and night-time calls, Mitchell's concentration at the morning briefing on Monday was not affected unduly by his attempts, in the early hours, first to soothe his elder son and then to persuade his lively five-year-old daughter that the night was not yet over. Her placid twin, his head buried beneath the sheet, had not even woken. A cooler than usual shower had been the only adjustment necessary in Mitchell's usual morning routine to compensate for his broken sleep.

Having rearranged the untidy heap of messages on his desk to an order that satisfied him, he looked up to greet his sergeant. He surveyed her approvingly as she settled herself in his only comfortable chair. Her minimal makeup and very short dark hair emphasized her efficiency. Her sensible clothes were made elegant by her wearing them. She had been widowed some years ago when her husband in traffic division had been killed by a car bomb. She was a good friend as well as a valued colleague. She and Ginny were particularly close and the families shared social activities, but he wondered now how satisfied she was with her life outside the job. He asked her merely, 'Are the rest on their way?'

'Shakila's in the foyer. Magic had a message for her–'

But DC Shakila Nazir came in to interrupt the sentence and offer her own explanation. 'There's a lad in one of the cells. I brought him in last night for selling dodgy CDs in the White Lion.'

'Has anyone ever seen a white lion?'

Shakila's look withered her chief inspector. 'Patrick Seddon. He's seventeen and he wants to become confiding about his mates.' She looked round. 'Where's Adrian?'

Mitchell shrugged. 'He won't be late if he arrives during the next three minutes.'

Sergeant Taylor asked, 'Seddon? Don't know that name – is it a first offence?'

'I think so.'

'And he's in custody for a few CDs?'

Shakila shook her head. 'No, for having dodgy mates who deal in something a bit more profitable. I thought a night in a cell might make him want to tell me about them – and he's going to if...' She glanced at Mitchell. '...if my action sheet doesn't say something else.'

Mitchell shook his head in mock despair as he appealed to his sergeant. 'When has she ever followed my agenda if she could find herself a more interesting one?' He waved her to a seat where she settled herself, unabashed, and opened her notebook.

She transferred her gaze sharply back to Mitchell when Jennifer asked, 'How are you going to manage then with your increased household?' Surely Virginia Mitchell wasn't producing yet another infant!

Noting her startled face, Mitchell replied, deadpan, 'What's another mouth to feed among my lot?' Then, relenting, he offered Shakila a brief explanation. 'Fran is my nephew. My brother and his family are emigrating to Australia. Their house was snapped up sooner than they expected. They're renting a cheap little place till all the

31

visas come through. Sean's a better Catholic than me so he has six kids. The overflow is farmed out on my sisters and me.'

He turned back to Jennifer. 'I did well getting Fran. My sister Siobhan has taken Mairead into her flat. She's next oldest to Fran and untidy. I see squalls ahead.'

A tap on the door heralded DC Clement's arrival. He sat down hurriedly, looking at his watch and pointing out defensively, 'I'm not late.'

Not in reassuring mode, Mitchell merely began his briefing. 'No dramatic tidings from Magic and the computer's thrown up nothing during the night that concerns us, except an MP.' He referred to a slip of paper in his hand. 'He hasn't been missing very long. He's a twenty-one-year-old by the name of George Varah. He's of age but he's still a student – hasn't had to look after himself in the real world. He's a sensible, hard-working lad in his mother's opinion, not likely to mess up his career for a bit of fun or his engagement by sulking over a minor quarrel–'

'Old enough to pick his future wife then?'

Mitchell nodded towards Clement. 'Right, but not, apparently, old enough to find himself when he gets lost. Varah left his London college, UC, whatever that is, for a couple of days' visit to his girlfriend's home in Cloughton. She's an Asian, a Pakistani, but

32

there's no aggro about that by all accounts, at least not from our end. When he didn't turn up last night, the girlfriend's family rang the college and then the Varah family. Neither knows where he is, so they've come to us.'

Shakila looked up from scribbling these details in her book. 'He's probably on a friend's floor, stoned out of his head and sleeping it off.'

Mitchell grinned. 'Took the words out of my mouth. I'll send a PC – Smithson, so that the super thinks we're taking his orders seriously. He can sweet talk the girl's family. The lad's almost certainly still in London. We'll leave him to the Met. Let them earn their extra screw. So…' He gave them a happy smile. 'How are you going to entertain yourselves with no work to do?'

'Go out to Egypt and sun ourselves with Caroline.'

'Go back to bed.'

'Play Cluedo with the kids.'

Mitchell held up his hand. 'From all the babble, I gather that you're glad to have some paperwork to fill in your time. In other words, you'll all be having a long breakfast. Well, watch your cholesterol levels. Jen, there's a woman in St Aidan's Hall. She wants to offer you some TICs. Can you fit that in?'

Shakila looked up hopefully but Mitchell

shook his head. 'One sergeant is quite capable of taking confessions from women prisoners without your help. Besides, I thought you'd got a young man in the cells with an offer you couldn't refuse. Adrian, can you find a minute to go down to the custody suite, see who's been brought in overnight. If they're female, blonde and under twenty-five, bring them up here. Everybody happy?'

Clement obviously was not but this was a not uncommon state of affairs. For once, though, the rest of the team had no enthusiasm for their routine day. When their CI dismissed them, even Shakila trailed out disconsolately.

By lunchtime, however, Shakila was in much better spirits. She emerged from number 3 interview room feeling pleased with herself, not least because she could now escape from breathing in smoke, sweat and other indefinable unpleasantnesses into the marginally purer air of the corridor.

As she had hoped, half a night in a cell had given young Patrick Seddon time to review his life and circumstances. He would think twice before meddling again with CDs of unknown provenance. She had further persuaded him that he would be doing a favour to the friends in the gang he was anxious to join if he shared with Shakila the secret of the source of their supply of crack.

The name of their supplier he couldn't or wouldn't tell her but she now knew that weekly supplies were handed over in a derelict warehouse a few miles down the valley. 'A Paki geezer runs some sort of junk business there but there's never nobody there after dark. Don't know if the electrics work. Monday nights we go there.'

Realizing the significance of 'we' he had looked scared. 'I don't use it. Haven't got no brass — not that much anyhow. I just keep obbo.'

Shakila considered. Should she report this news to Mitchell now? She was tempted to keep it for the debriefing where she would have a larger audience. Better to do it now, she decided. A word of praise in front of the team would have Clement sulking. She couldn't understand why he treated any commendation of others as a criticism of himself. Anyway, all the others would snub her too – to keep her humble. She took this, as it was meant, in good part.

She reached Mitchell's door, knocked on it and peered round it, as was the custom, but he was not there. Retracing her steps to the foyer, she learned from the desk sergeant that he would not be available for the rest of the day. He was probably in court, but he might have mentioned it! Never mind. It left her with a rare opportunity to choose her own occupation for the rest of the afternoon and she had a project of her own that she was anxious to pursue.

She sought out a free computer and mentally reviewed her progress so far as she waited impatiently for it to boot up. The doings of the 'Yorkshire arsonist' fascinated her. She wondered how prevalent this crime was and whether the one person touring Yorkshire, setting fire to the bits of it that offended him, was a media invention to explain an outbreak of fires lit by bored youths, each wanting a share of the publicity that they had seen their peers enjoy. If he did exist, she had frequently wondered if – sometimes hoped that – he would set a fire on their own patch.

One day recently, browsing in Waterstone's and hoping to find a suitable birthday gift for a friend, she had taken a quick look at the True Crime section. She was disappointed to find that most of the books were about criminal psychology rather than accounts of offences that had actually been committed. She had read various similar volumes, some of them as part of her police college training. Most of the theories they put forward she found farfetched. She preferred reading up cases for herself and drawing her own conclusions about why someone did what he did and whether he was to blame. In Shakila's opinion, he almost always was to blame and she was impatient with the psychologists who found feeble excuses for him.

She had been tempted though by a book on arson and arsonists and had bought it. She was unimpressed by the array of letters after the author's name and, as usual, disagreed with a good many of the great man's ideas. He asked the right questions, she grudgingly allowed, but gave a lot of wrong answers. She had set herself to find some of her own.

She glared at the screen which now, obediently if tardily, produced the list she had asked it for. She took from her bag the map of Yorkshire she had printed when she had first begun her project and added to it the two latest fires, marking the place with a red cross and adding the date with a fine line pen. In her notebook, she added a couple of observations from newspaper cuttings stored in the computer.

The trouble with academics, Shakila decided, was that they tried to fit facts to theories. Her way was better. She used common sense to deal with the facts. But then, their motives were not the same. These university people wanted to get into print. She wanted to solve crimes. She wondered how many times the learned Professor Morton had been out on the job. The amount of her hard-earned cash that she had spent on his book was out of proportion to its size. Still, it had fed her interest in its subject.

Whether or not the Yorkshire arsonist, if he existed, ever struck in Cloughton, she would not have wasted her time. She intended to rise high in the ranks of her profession and there would be other occasions when what she was learning now could be used.

She switched off the computer and spread out her notes on the table beside it. Professor Morton believed geographical locations were important. She had jotted down one of his sentences. 'Go beyond the dots on the map to understand the significance of the places he is choosing; all offenders have a choice of where to offend.'

Well, the Yorkshire arsonist had chosen Yorkshire. That wasn't necessarily where he lived, but it wouldn't be a thousand miles away either. She began to check which particular regions of the county had suffered. The first four fires, between June and August the previous year, were in the north-east – Castle Howard, Helmsley and Malton, together with Beverley which was well to the east. Then, another group from September to November were in the centre – Thirsk, Harrogate and Knaresborough, with Holmfirth, well to the south, stuck in the middle of them. In December, their man had favoured the north-west, choosing Kettlewell and Richmond.

What did that tell her? Not much for the moment. Perhaps they were looking for a sales rep who covered the area reasonably methodically. What else was possible? A travel writer? – maybe for one of those regional magazines.

The professor thought dates significant too. What could she make of those? One in June, one in July, two in August, two in September, one each in October and November and two in December?

The incidents did not seem to be happening more closely together as serial killings did. The fire setter, thank goodness, didn't seem to want to kill. He had burned a school, but at the weekend when it was empty. Then there was a café, in a park, when it was closed. Next came a block of three new houses, empty because they were only just finished and not up for sale even. A huge house had been half destroyed. It had been refurbished and extended and was intended for a nursing home, but not yet operational ... Shakila scanned the rest of the list. No, no fatalities. The actual buildings were of quite different types, having nothing in common, as far as she could see. Why had they been chosen?

Her book suggested that contact with the police who were hunting them added to arsonists' sense of adventure. Maybe that would be the next development.

Superintendent Carroll appeared in the doorway, startling her. He asked politely whether she had finished with the computer. She would not have had any choice about giving it up but she appreciated his good manners.

She stood up and slipped all her papers into a cardboard file, grateful that he had not asked her what she was working on. She decided that it was lunchtime and set off to the canteen.

Staff nurse Dorian Shaw clipped his pen on to the pocket of his uniform jacket. Having completed the necessary paperwork to discharge patient Simon Denton from the care of Ward 5 of Cloughton Royal Hospital, he made a last check in the small notebook that he kept always in his trouser pocket. Just a quick call to make to the chaplain. Yes, he would be free to play the hymns at the hospital chapel service next Sunday morning. Now he could go.

He poked his head into Margie's cubicle on his way out. 'Bye for now. I'll be back late this afternoon.' She wouldn't remember what he had said to her, but she was his godmother and he felt bad about leaving without speaking to her.

She waved an admonitory finger at him. 'Don't interrupt, dear, when Her Majesty is speaking.' With a glance at the empty chair by the bed to which Margie was respectfully giving her attention, he apologized and left, grinning to himself as he made his way down to the tiny staff cloakroom. He'd better tidy himself before his lunch with Becca.

He slipped off the blue cotton uniform jacket, routinely patting the pockets and reminding himself to return the strip of pills which he had absentmindedly slipped in there. Margie's consultant had finally taken her off them only this morning. They were good for her breathing but had certainly increased her confusion. He would love to have Margie's sharp mind restored to her but he knew it was too late for that. The mini strokes that had taken it from her were irreversible. His own opinion was that his godmother's attacks of breathlessness frightened her more than her addled thoughts. He hoped the new regime would not deprive her of the company of the Queen.

His cursory glance in the mirror over the washbasin as he buttoned his sports jacket brought him up short. The face he saw was his father's. He examined it more carefully as water gushed erratically into the basin. To a certain extent, he could blame the dilapidated mirror. At least it was the glass that was pock-marked and not his skin.

Was his a weak face? As a child he had constantly heard his resemblance to his father remarked upon. He had hoped, even in those days, that the resemblance was only physical. As he grew older, he had suspected the worst. He had battled constantly with his inability to make swift and firm decisions, knowing that this fault limited his progress both in his studies and in his career. He stared hard at the mirror. Did this face speak to everyone of an only child of elderly parents, brought up by a shiftless man who was dominated by his wife?

At least he had managed to throw off most of his mother's domination of himself. She had ruled his father for all the old man's life. Though it was only four years since his death, Dorian had had difficulty in recalling his features until brought up short just now by this copy of them in his reflection. Had he loved the old man? Had his father loved him?

He was ashamed to discover now that he could not use that debased word 'love' towards either of his parents – not compared with the way he loved Becca. You had to have some substance, a significance of some kind, to be loved. His father had been a shadow-man, hovering in his mother's vicinity, making no impact. Dorian had resented the way his mother had ruled the family, but, perhaps, she had been only what his father's fecklessness had made it necessary for her to be. And, once he had met Becca's mother, his own had seemed just a pussy cat.

Of course, he acknowledged a blood tie he had no wish to break. He had helped his parents financially when necessary and in practical ways too, particularly by providing transport. He could even say that he had been fond of them – but his father had been a failure and he should not confuse pity with love.

He blinked and became aware that his unseeing eyes had dropped to a warning on the wall against wasting water. Hastily, he turned off the tap, dried his hands and face and flicked a comb through his unruly and disappearing hair. He surveyed the result. It was still his father's face in the mirror.

He hurried off to the car park. Becca had just an hour and a quarter for lunch so he had better pick her up promptly. He knew she had been pleased and surprised by his midday invitation, expecting his shift to finish at three. She would be less happy when she discovered that lunch was a substitute for dinner tonight. Yet again, he had weakly agreed to do a split shift to accommodate absences caused by January flu.

The engine of his elderly Mini coughed and grumbled like his patients but deigned to start at the second attempt. Dorian let it turn over a few times before taxing it further, then edged the car carefully over the frosty ground towards the hospital exit, steering carefully round the hillock beside the gate. He thought the bracken that had grown over it in summer made it look, now that it was dead, like a shaggy animal in hibernation.

Waiting for a gap in the traffic, he glanced up the road and saw that his ex-patient, Simon Denton, had just left the pedestrian exit and turned in the direction of the town centre. Dorian followed, intending to offer a lift. In this small town, it would take him only a little out of his way to drop Simon wherever he wanted to be.

He was startled when a youth on an odd but expensive-looking bicycle overtook and saluted him. As he waved back, he recognized the young man who had been visiting Niamh Mitchell over the weekend. Dorian had taken to the elderly woman, even become fond of her. He had been as glad as her family would later be to learn that the test results delivered to the ward this morning were all negative. Niamh Mitchell was suffering only from the chest infection they were already dealing with and exhaustion. He hoped that he would have the pleasure of delivering the good news personally. He hoped too that the ward would not become any busier, so that they might keep her for another couple of days. She ought really to be a little stronger before she was released to exhaust herself all over again, fussing over the six grown-up children and fifteen grandchildren of whom she was so proud.

Turning back to the road ahead, he found

his way blocked by a lorry that had cut in in front of him. He watched as his potential passenger climbed into its cab. The lorry moved away, gathering speed.

Dorian was puzzled. Simon had said that he knew no one in Cloughton. No one had visited him in the eight days he had been on Ward 5. He had not seen Simon make any gesture to suggest that he wanted to hitch a lift. Perhaps a friend had come over from Leeds for him. If so, would he still be keeping the appointment that Dorian had made with him earlier this morning? He wished he knew. If Simon had forgotten the arrangement and decided to go straight back to his family in Leeds when this lift was offered, he and Becca might still have their meal out tonight, though later than they had planned. He should be off duty again by eight.

The traffic was moving on again, thank goodness, but Dorian dared not accelerate over the icy surface. Arriving finally at Becca's offices, he glanced at his watch and decided to risk parking on the double yellow lines outside.

He was both relieved and annoyed to find that she was not waiting for him in the foyer. She appeared in less than a minute, however, and he watched her descend the staircase from her office. He felt the usual lifting of his spirits, almost excitement, as he watched her progress across the vast polished floor. Her athletic stride, her sheer health and vigour contrasted so strongly with the wan faces and frail bodies of the patients he had just left. She was accompanied by a colleague, a clean-cut, equally healthy-looking young man. Was he handsome? How, he asked himself, does one man judge what a woman will think of another?

This one, after his morning's work, certainly looked fresher than Dorian felt. He licked a finger, smoothed his unruly eyebrows with it and wished he had found the time to have his hair cut. The man raised a hand to both of them, finished crossing the foyer and disappeared through a panelled door. Becca came towards him. Her eyes, he was relieved to see, had not followed her colleague. Her attention was all for himself and she had a faint air of excitement.

They spoke in unison. 'Let's have lunch at home.'

Thankfully, Dorian hurried back to the car. He found that the gods had been merciful and no ticket adorned his windscreen. Becca scrambled into the seat beside him, averting her face as she fiddled with her seat belt, then said, 'I've got something to tell you.' He had the impression that it was something that he would not want to hear. Never mind. She would not be very pleased with his news either. He replied merely, 'Snap.' She'd had her warning!

She refused to deliver her news until after they had eaten. So, he needed to be sweetened up for it. As she bustled about, preparing a pasta dish from dried penne and various jars, he tried to think of what she might want to have or do that he would deny her. Devoid of any idea, he produced from the drinks cupboard a bottle of roughish Italian red, good enough to cheer up the food but not good enough to shame it. One glass would have to suffice. It was a working afternoon. They ate hurriedly, eyes on the clock and each other, assessing the atmosphere. Neither of them wished to squander energy on a quarrel. Each of them skirted around the other's revelations, averting them with small talk. She enquired after his patients.

'We've lost Simon Denton.'

Her eyes widened. 'I thought you said he was doing well.'

'No, I mean we discharged him this morning. By the way, when I realized that our meal tonight was snookered–' She scowled. 'Afraid so. Another emergency split shift. Anyway, I arranged to have a drink with Simon when I come off.' He waited for an explosion.

She said calmly, 'You might as well, I suppose. We can eat out another night. How's Margie?'

'Still entertaining the Queen – has her as a constant companion. She's not good. The antibiotics are not improving things. Her lungs are shot at. I don't give her much longer, but she's cheerful enough.'

Becca seemed not particularly put out by this news. Dorian felt sufficiently bold to ask, 'So, what have you got to tell me?'

She made to refill his glass before she replied. He waved the bottle away. 'I've to be back on the ward at three.'

'All right, then.' She began to stack their plates and glasses in the dishwasher. 'Greystones is going on the market at last.' He was silent, watching her. She continued to clear the table, waiting for his reaction before deciding on tactics.

'Becca, we haven't got that kind of money.'

'You will have when Margie dies. You've got power of attorney now. She would never know if you borrowed some of it.'

'What are they asking for it?' The question was a mistake. Her face lit up as though he had made a promise.

'I don't know. Even if Margie did know we were borrowing from her, she'd be glad to think you had the chance of–'

'Whatever it is, it would take another fifty thousand at least to do it up.'

'You might be right but it would be worth over a million then.'

He was not sufficiently sure of his facts to argue about that. Instead, he asked, 'And what would we have left to maintain it with if everything was tied up in the building itself?'

She sighed. 'I would cheerfully starve if I could live there.'

He pushed back his chair and stood up. 'I haven't time for this now – and I'm not in the mood.'

She offered no more arguments. 'Later then. You haven't given me your news.'

'That's going to have to keep too.'

The telephone rang. Seeing that he was struggling back into his uniform, Becca went to answer it. Before she could hang up and restart their conversation, Dorian grabbed his jacket and car keys and disappeared.

In the darkness of early evening, drained by physical pain and by wakeful hours the previous night, spent planning her escape from her husband, Salma Gupte had reached the comparative safety of his warehouse. Each time he abused and assaulted her she renewed her intention to leave him. She would vow that, one day soon, she would make a careful plan to escape to a place where he would never find her. The intention comforted her even though she only half believed in it.

Today, though, he had caused her more than physical pain and she had somehow found the mental strength to act. She had left his home – she refused any longer to call it hers – at the time he would be returning from his day's work so that their journeys would cross. She had brought with her only such things as could be hidden in her clothing. Her neighbours would have been quite sufficiently surprised to see her going out alone. If she carried bags, they might guess that she had finally had enough of Mubarak's unkindness and take enough interest in her movements to work out where she was going. It was better that they didn't know.

Exhausted, she had allowed herself a short rest before working out what she should do next – and had fallen into a deep sleep. Now, she awoke groggily, wondering how much time she had wasted. The light coming through the broken blind was from a street lamp, and there was not much of that. Mubarak and his friends would have had hours to look for her. He would expect her to have fled to her family. She prayed to Allah that her mother had not been alone in the house when he hammered on the door. By now, he could well be on his way back here. It was her only other refuge. He thought that he had prevented her from making any friends who might help her.

Her head ached and dizziness engulfed her as she turned to check that the flimsy barricade she had piled up against the door was still in place. It had shifted a little and was obviously not going to prevent a furious Mubarak from coming in. She stood up carefully and went over to the window, the slight exertion making her rather breathless.

She could see very little outside. She must pull herself together and decide what to do next. Had she been wise even to come so far? Now that Mubarak's kicking had finally caused her to lose the baby, what had she to gain? He would only find and punish her. She sat on the dirty floor, her head in her hands, wondering what, if anything, she had achieved.

Then, through her fingers, she became aware of a light from behind the door, causing the wooden screen and folding table leaning against it to cast wavering shadows. She dropped her hands, blinked, looked again. Was Mubarak or one of his relatives here already, come to drag her back and take revenge? She sat still, listening. No footsteps. The light, though, was flickering and growing stronger. She noticed an odd wisp of smoke. She could smell it. She was trapped by fire. So, what? For a moment, she sat there, uncaring. At least it would keep her husband away from her and there was no baby to protect any more.

But, was this Mubarak's punishment? She could easily believe him capable of punishing her by this means. At least it meant that he wasn't up here. He wouldn't risk hurting himself. Neither, on second thoughts, would he deprive himself of her services or the pleasure of tormenting her.

Whatever had possessed her to take refuge in this tiny office on the first floor? If she'd stayed at ground level she could have broken a window and climbed out of it. Not sure whether the swirling mist was in the room or in her head, she tried to think. When she had looked out of this window a few seconds ago there had been no glow, no flames. It seemed that the fire was across the corridor, on the other side of the building. Frantically, she felt around her. Was there anything that might be used as a rope? Downstairs, where the stock was kept, there might have been real rope, or fabric that could be twisted and tied. This office was just a bit of staging to convince the tax man that some kind of records were kept – and, in any case, a search was hopeless in the dark. She must remove her makeshift barricade, open the door that was protecting her and see what way of rescue might offer itself then.

Steadying herself on a rickety table, she managed to kick away the barrier, panic lending her strength. Wrapping the folds of her chuddah round her hand, she grasped the door handle and pulled. It opened towards her, causing the screen and table to fall forward and deliver a painful blow to her knee. Immediately, flames slithered up the wall and mushroomed across the ceiling. Salma dropped to the floor to avoid them and discovered that at that level she could breathe more easily.

As she crawled out into the corridor, the window glass shattered behind her and the room filled with smoke. The fire seemed to be travelling towards her from the left. To her right, the stone-flagged floor and plastered wall offered it no fuel, at least on her side of the corridor. The cloakroom she had visited a few hours ago was just a few yards away. She would probably be singed but she might get there without any serious burns.

Did she care anyway? If she survived this, one day soon she would die from Mubarak's beatings. Her heart throbbed in her chest and she felt sick, but, in spite of her physical discomfort, her risky plan had brought a sudden change of heart. She had a chance. Someone would call the fire brigade. The men would find her in the tiled cloakroom, soaked in water, and she would tell them about Mubarak. They – or the police, or Sylvia – would find her a safe place to go.

There was thick hot smoke in front of her, but no flames, though she could hear an ominous crackling behind. With eyes stinging and running and lungs bursting, she groped her way forward until her fingers touched something. She felt fabric and then flesh and realized with horror that she was not the fire's only victim. A bristly chin told her her fellow victim was a man. She couldn't just leave him. Since she could see nothing, she pulled her chuddah completely over her face, then grasped the man's jacket. Breathless, with hot smoke in her throat burning and choking her, she managed one almighty heave that advanced them both perhaps an inch. Another was beyond her powers. She collapsed on to her fellow victim's body in merciful oblivion.

By nine o'clock on the same Monday evening, Dorian Shaw was sitting contentedly in the Woolpack, where he had few companions and those mostly twenty years older than himself. His chair was comfortably close to a real log fire and the table in front of him held that day's *Yorkshire Post*, as yet unread, and a pint of real ale.

What had promised to be a difficult afternoon had run smoothly after all. He had been able to leave his ward exactly at eight when his altered shift ended. He smiled to himself. They kept you sweet if they knew you'd do a last-minute split and the night staff had readily taken over his half-finished tasks. On his brief stop-off at home to wash and change, Becca had made no further reference to Greystones nor any complaint about his spending the evening with Simon

Denton. She had mentioned him merely to pass on his telephoned request to move their meeting to nine, half an hour later than they had previously agreed. Perhaps this morning's lorry had taken him out of town and he was having to travel back.

Becca had refused to come to this pub with him. She had, she said, plans of her own. He was glad. She had not met Simon and the night out that she had arranged with her girlfriends would put her in a better mood than a night in the Woolpack, spent resenting what he was about to do. The longer she was ignorant of that the better. He had rewarded her graciousness over the missed meal by letting her have the car and coming out to the Woolpack on the bike, in spite of the treacherous roads.

She'd been pleased and surprised that he had agreed to the request. She knew he didn't like parking his beloved Kawasaki in a pub yard where it might prove a temptation to tipsy youths with a speed addiction – maybe in both senses. No good worrying about that now, though. The Woolpack was his favourite pub, in spite of its elderly clientele – and not only for the real ale. It also carried a vast range of single malts for when you wanted either to celebrate or to drown your sorrows. He picked up the paper and read it, beginning at the back.

As he laid it down, an elderly man approached him, wrinkled and jowled about the face and neck but sprightly in his walk. 'Care for a game o' darts, mate? Me usual mucker's let me down tonight.'

Dorian glanced at his watch. Nine thirty. Dejectedly, his companion awaited a refusal. He grinned. 'I'm no great shakes. Your friend would have given you a better game, but I'd like to give you the pleasure of beating me. It's just that...'

'The missus wants you home early.'

'She isn't the missus – yet. No, I was waiting for someone. He's late, though. I suppose he might be held up in traffic if there's been an accident somewhere. He does have a mobile. He might at least have let me know.'

'Mebbe he's the one who's had it.'

'I hope not. Let's play, but if he comes in we'll have to call a halt.'

'That your bike out there?' Dorian nodded. 'Thought it must be. No one else in here's young enough or well fettled enough to cope with it. Nice job. Meself, I wouldn't risk a beauty like that in this weather.'

'I've let my woman have the car. The friend who often drives her on their girls' nights has broken her ankle.' Dorian drained his glass and stood up, ready to be humiliated for the sake of rescuing the old man's evening. He stayed another hour but Simon did not arrive. To his own great astonishment, Dorian won the game of darts hands down.

Craig Heppenstall let himself into the kitchen of his father's farmhouse, took off the garments he had borrowed from him and hung them behind the door before dropping into the chair beside the fire. Living in hall at uni, he decided, had spoiled him, with central heating and draught-proof corridors, for a return to his family home – which he had hated in the first place. He willed the last few days of the Christmas vac to pass quickly.

Not that he had any quarrel with his parents. He just hated the rigours of farm life with its money worries, physical discomfort and lack of time for any intellectual pursuits. When he had come home, before Christmas, the weather had been milder and for a day or two he had felt a sentimental attachment to the old place. Reality had bitten in together with the cold. He knew now that for him comfort was preferable to sentiment and that he would rather cultivate his mind than the earth.

He had been glad tonight to see to the livestock so that his parents could enjoy a rare night out, and the valley the farm looked down on was as pretty as he remembered – but he knew his destiny lay well away from Cloughton and farming. He went to pull down the window blinds to keep in some of the heat, pausing first to admire the silver sparkle of moonlight on the frosty dry stone walls that surrounded his parents' shaggy lawn. Beyond, the light picked out the ripples on the near portion of the dam just within the compass of the view from the kitchen window. It had not frozen over then, in spite of the cold. The cluster of buildings on the other side, in the shadow of the hill, had grown. He wondered what other ugly but useful structures had appeared in the two terms since he had last been here.

Just a minute! He halted the descent of the blind and wound it a little way up again. The windows in the largest building in that distant cluster had a strange glow, a brightness behind them that alternately grew and lessened. Was the place burning? He looked harder but could see no other evidence of fire.

As though called into being by his thought, a sheet of flame shot across the ridge of the roof, then narrowed to a thin, horizontal strip over which orange tongues danced, a flamboyant Christmas decoration. Now the windows too were flickering. He thought that the burning building was an old warehouse. If his identification was correct, then, in the days when his father was a boy, it had held bales of wool from their own farm and the ones that had once surrounded it. Now, according to the old man, it was dangerous, let go to rack and ruin, by its new owners, 'Asians or gyppos or some such!'

His father's irascible prejudices had got him in trouble many a time, but Craig agreed that the place was an eyesore. Let it burn. But, then, there were old trees surrounding it that should be saved. And, not far beyond, there was more industrial property, well maintained and reasonably in keeping with its surroundings. He reached for the phone.

The emergency operator at the Fire Service Command and Mobilizing Centre picked up, confirmed the number of the caller and took down the details he was offered. He failed to recognize the burning warehouse from Craig's description, though he knew the general area.

Craig endeavoured to be more specific. 'The first building you come to if you leave Wainwright Lane, at the corner where that big old house is – Greystones, I think it's called.'

Now the CMC had his bearings. He was surprised that the fire had not been reported by someone nearer to it. He disconnected from his informant and moved into his routine. There were no appliances in the immediate area. He would have to send some from Cloughton, further up the valley. He conferred briefly with his second-in-command, who shook his head. 'Shouldn't think there's anyone in there at this time.'

His fingers were already flying over his computer keys.

'We don't need the mapping system. One ambulance? Two appliances?'

'Should be enough. They'll radio for more if they need them.'

In Cloughton fire station, Red Watch was on duty. All had been quiet during the early evening, but now the alarm was sounding, signalling a commercial fire. Young Jason Brook, their newest recruit, was determined to do himself credit. He knew that he had impressed the SCO training manager during his four weeks in the training classroom. He had enjoyed following the shifts and observing the work as part of Red Watch. It had irked him not to be counted as part of it but he had worked hard and done well in his written and practical assessments. Now he was on active service, though he needed to complete two years' total service to be fully qualified.

This was his second 'real' job. He listened carefully to the details the shift leader was giving them. The fire was at the Bargains Galore warehouse which was owned and run by a character called Gupte and his family. The place was full of salvage goods, taken there to be sorted for resale or 'chucking'. They took their positions in the truck – George driving, Angus beside him to man the radio, Charlie and himself in the back. The place was a couple of miles down the valley. Long before they reached it they could see huge columns of black smoke, blocking out the ribbons of light that gave them their bearings.

Jason reckoned that there would be at least one more appliance sent to a fire this size. They all guessed that the authorities were considering whether this was Cloughton's share of the attentions of the Yorkshire arsonist and he was not surprised to find that the Fire Investigation Unit was already at the scene in the person of Dave Prince. He was prominent in his luminous yellow jacket, his face lit up by the glare from the flames.

Further away, but as near as he was permitted to approach, was a beefy fellow whom Jason recognized as a senior detective from the Cloughton station. He thought it was the same officer who had interviewed his cousin when he had been daft enough to get mixed up with a bloke who was making funny money. This copper had spoken up for Mark and managed to get probation for him.

Jason busied himself with hoses under the instructions of his team leader and strained to hear the conversation of his elders and betters.

'Owner's on his way. Says there's no night

shift. Place should be empty but we're looking.'

'No, don't need keys. Door was rotten.
Lock was kicked out of the soft wood. Young
vandals most likely. Better not lose any of
ours getting the buggers out.'

'Serves 'em right if they've fried 'em-
selves.'

Jason knew that he would be going into
five hundred degrees of heat, though, at
ground level, it would be half that. He
remembered his course instructor's encour-
agement when he'd gone into his very first
fire, lit deliberately for training purposes.
'All you can do is keep your gear on, stay
close to your team and keep your head –
and think on that you can't overpower a
raging fire. You have to out-think it.' He was
glad it was not his job to out-think this one.
That was his team leader's responsibility.
He coughed in the smoke and dropped his
hose for a second to pull his air mask
tighter. He'd got his outer ears singed at his
first fire but he could see why they had to
remain unprotected.

'Ah, here's Rod and Joe.' Several heads
were raised as a second appliance noised its
arrival, then dropped to their various tasks
again.

A radio crackled and began to give information from the owner about the building's
contents as he passed them on. 'No chem-

icals, thank God – at least, none admitted to.'

His hose properly coupled, Jason looked up and saw thick black smoke twisting out of both wings of the long structure. The heart of the fire appeared to be on the first floor. He knew that fire travelled upwards. The whole of Yorkshire knew it now that the telly had told them on the news. He watched for the team of searchers to come out. Once they were sure that no one was in the building they could set up the ladder truck to blast a master stream – a thousand gallons a minute! He had seen it used several times. They had to be careful with it though. That sort of force could push fire back towards trapped victims or cause support walls to collapse.

Here came the two men out of the vandalized door – and a third, down the ladder from a second-floor window which as yet was still a short distance from the flames. One of the pair dashed towards the team leader, the other to the yellow-coated investigator. Jason shivered. Trapped people? Bodies?

News of the fire at Bargains Galore had come to the Mitchells by telephone from PC Smithson whose neighbour was a reporter. Virginia Mitchell had been unsurprised when her husband had abandoned his supper and departed for the scene.

Neither was she disappointed at the loss of his company. The twins were safely in bed and Caitlin on her ten-minute warning. Declan was earnestly busy with his homework and Fran was out playing a chess match, arranged as promised by PC Beardsmore. Virginia had work to do.

She had early discovered that the easiest way to persuade a magazine editor to let her write the piece of her own choice was to convince the woman – and it usually was a woman – that it had been her own idea to commission it. A teacher friend had assured her that it was also the best way of coaxing a headmaster to make a change in the running of his school.

In a semi-official phone call to this particular magazine, Virginia had mentioned her brother's fast-approaching wedding, bewailing her husband's total lack of interest in his own clothes and his refusal to buy a new suit for the occasion. She had prattled on, making her editor laugh. 'I'll manage it somehow. I usually get another of whatever has become disgusting and do a simple substitution job.'

She was maligning Benny unforgivably. He refused to give up a garment just because it had become unfashionable, but his clothes were always. immaculate, which was more than she could say for her own, especially if the twins were around. 'With luck, he won't notice, but, if he does, I agree that the jacket – or whatever – has cleaned and retextured remarkably well.'

By then, the woman had been chuckling and Virginia knew she had almost achieved her object. She hastened on. 'If you pick a neutral enough colour, you can get away with, "What do you mean, new? I'm surprised it hasn't rotted from never seeing the light of day." As long as his wardrobe is full, Benny insists that no purchases are necessary. "I've got fifteen shirts already," he announces, speaking nothing but the truth. You should see his fifteen shirts!' The telephone had emitted hysterical giggles. Virginia had waited and been rewarded.

'Ginny, I've had an idea.' Virginia suppressed her own laughter as the editor explained herself, though the woman's parting shot nearly made her change her mind and refuse the commission. 'Get it to me as soon as you can. It'll be really wacky!' Now, with the deadline for sending the article only twenty-four hours away, she was a couple of hundred words short and thoroughly disenchanted with the silly subject. She would have a ten-minute break to see her two eldest off to bed.

She found Declan stowing away his school books and looking faintly bemused. 'Do you think,' he asked her, 'that it's OK to ask God about your homework?'

Virginia gave the question her serious consideration. 'I can't see anything morally wrong with it. You'd ask me or your father about something you found difficult, wouldn't you?'

'Yes – but everybody else does that. The teachers know that you do it, so it's not cheating.'

'Isn't God available to everybody – more than two parents even?'

'Yes, but I don't go to church or do anything for him.'

Virginia bit her lip. 'I don't think God's like that. Did you ask him?' Declan nodded. 'And did he answer?'

The boy's forehead wrinkled. 'I'm not sure, but I did get an idea to answer the question with.'

Virginia considered. It was half past nine, past his bedtime and she had a piece of commissioned work to finish. Her son seemed curious rather than worried. She sent him upstairs, promising to give his question some thought when she had more time. She returned to her own task, willing the Almighty to give her too an idea with which to fill out her article to two and a half thousand words.

Her spirits sank lower when the door from the hall opened to admit her younger daughter. What weird and wonderful excuse had she dreamed up to justify her reappearance?

Sinead looked triumphant rather than apologetic. 'I've thought of a way to get Daddy a new suit for Uncle Alex's wedding.'

With a great effort, her mother maintained a solemn expression. 'Let's hear it.'

'Declan and Kat and Michael and me can club together with our pocket money.'

Golly! The Almighty had been quick. Sinead was startled to be picked up and waltzed round the room, and more puzzled, when put down, to see her mother in paroxysms of laughter. 'You've solved more than one problem for me. You can have a chocolate biscuit before you go back to bed if you promise to clean your teeth carefully – and quietly!'

When her youngest was safely back in bed, Virginia slid another two hundred word paragraph into her article:

If you're after a drastic change of style, the children may help. Try 'Johnny chose this for your birthday. He saved up his pocket money and, with a bit of help, bought it himself. I know you won't like it, but you'll have to wear it a few times or he'll be upset.' When your partner has been out in the despised garment once the battle is half over.

Of course, when the children do give him presents, you supervise – but gifts of clothes are not always good news. Once, my husband's mother...

Thankfully, Virginia checked through the whole piece and blushed for it. For magazines like this one she hid behind a pen name. She didn't want her friends even to suspect that she read it. She knew that the article would be approved and bought but writing it had made her feel shabby. The fee, though considerable, was not worth knowing that she was pandering to upmarket, down-culture attitudes. The husband that she had anonymously maligned, however he was clad, spent his time doing an always useful, often dangerous job. She would be glad when he was safely back from this particular one.

She felt a momentary panic when the telephone rang and she heard Superintendent Carroll's voice. It was not bad news about Benny. 'Sorry to ring so late ... heard about the fire ... in view of the number of arson incidents ... thought Benny should perhaps...' Virginia let the request peter out before telling him, 'He's way ahead of you. He's been there two hours already.'

The room was warm and she was dozing over her book. The sound of a key opening the front door roused her. She turned to greet her husband but it was Fran who came in. She remembered in time that he was sixteen years old and did not ask him whether he had thanked his opponent for his lift home. She offered to make him coffee and saw from his face that, in the space of thirty-six hours, he had learned that it was expedient to refuse.

They settled together in front of the fire as she asked about his evening with his fellow chess enthusiast. 'Did you beat him?'

Fran grinned and shook his head. 'It was like Declan and me yesterday but the other way round. He beat me twice, then he taught me a few tricks that even Mr Duncan didn't tell us. Only the first defeat went in the match book.' He looked up to gauge her reaction. 'We're supposed to play a return match. Would it be all right if he came here for it? That's what's usual, but I can go there again if–'

'Of course he can come here. What was he like? Did you get on with him? Did his wife give you supper?' He blinked at her. 'Sorry. I seem to be giving you the third degree. I wondered if you were hungry or if you'd been fed.'

Fran nodded. 'We had cake from M&S. He hasn't got a wife.'

Virginia waited, hoping he would continue. Benny had been dubious about letting the nephew for whom they were currently responsible go alone to play his match with a complete stranger, though the man was at least an acquaintance of Bob Beardsmore. Her patience was rewarded. 'I liked him.

He's a lorry driver. His firm used to send him as far as Russia but then he got a bad back and now he only does short trips.'

'What's his name?'

'Roger. Roger Cornish. Where's Uncle Benny?'

'Gone to a fire.'

'Here, in Cloughton?' He had been sprawling in his chair, yawning. Now he sat up, alert again. 'Is it the same person?'

Virginia shook her head. 'How should I know? We don't know yet whether it was deliberately started by anybody – though I'm sure Benny's poking around there because he thinks it might have been.'

'Can I stay up till he comes in?'

Virginia grinned. He looked more excited than her own youngsters would have done. They, of course, were hardened to second-hand disasters. 'I'm in no position to stop you but I don't think it's a good idea. He might stay out there till morning.'

'Where is it?'

'From what I overheard, about ten minutes' drive down the valley. I'm not sure which particular building's gone up. I hope it's not that beautiful old house...' She left the sentence unfinished, realizing that the area was unfamiliar to Fran. Intending to introduce a topic of more interest to him, she began to ask about the family's plans for Australia and his own feelings about the move. How did he feel about leaving his friends and his life in Yorkshire?

He answered politely. Australia was 'a clean, uncrowded country'. His siblings were looking forward to the move and so was he. The little ones were excited. Brisbane was subtropical and they thought life would be one long round of beach parties and bar-becues.

He smiled, worldly-wise. 'There will be less people to the square mile, but, apart from the accent and the suntan, they'll be just like people here. People are all the same.'

'Don't you like people?'

He smiled. 'I like some of them a lot. I like being here with you and Uncle Benny and I like Declan. That doesn't mean,' he went on hurriedly, afraid of offending, 'that I don't like the twins and Kat, but they've been mostly at school or in bed when I've been in, so I don't really know them.'

'Well, I'm glad you like being with us. We like it too. For the children and me, you've brought a new interest to the bleakest part of the year.' Fran looked puzzled. 'The fun of Christmas and New Year are over and it's still too dark and cold to spend much time outdoors–'

'Uncle Benny and I–'

Virginia interrupted in her turn. 'Yes, I know. You have your bike and Benny has his rugby, but five-year-olds can't move very fast and we tend to become tired of sitting with books and jigsaws. Their concentration span is less than a quarter of yours. Benny does his best but the job keeps him fairly frantically busy. You're very popular at the Mitchell house.'

She knew they were not making conversation. She was just filling in awkward silences with words. She stopped speaking and reached for her book. Perhaps taking this as a criticism of his taciturnity, he volunteered, 'Christmas is quite an upsetting season. Bits of it are fun, of course, but I like a normal routine with things running smoothly and everything as usual.'

Virginia's laugh was genuine. 'Spoken like a true Mitchell. I suspect Benny would absolutely agree with you, though he does make an effort for our sakes.' She remembered that her husband and her nephew had spent the afternoon cycling against strong winds in the icy cold. And after that the boy had had to go to – and lose – his chess match. He was probably exhausted. If he wasn't ready for bed she would suggest some television.

Fran agreed with alacrity and leapt up to switch on, tuning in to his preferred channel with a raised eyebrow asking for her approval. 'Is that all right? I haven't heard any news all day.'

Together they listened to the international

headlines which were followed by a summary of local affairs. This included a report on the fire further down the valley and both of them looked out for a glimpse of Mitchell. With the television sound and screen for a background, the boy seemed more relaxed. Perhaps, like her own brother's future wife, he came from a home where the media blared in every room and he was not comfortable speaking into silence.

He turned to her. 'It doesn't look like the beautiful house you were worried about. It's just a tatty warehouse.'

She nodded, her eyes still on the screen. The fire authorities seemed to have offered no concessions and the television cameramen and other reporters had been kept at the same distance from the flames as the local populace who had turned out to enjoy the entertainment. The commentator could tell the viewers little more than they could see on the screen for themselves – a muddle of leaping flames and silhouetted figures moving with practised deliberation to deal with them.

When the programme moved on to the details of a new and revolutionary reading scheme in a local primary school, Fran excused himself. Virginia, after another hour with her book, considered going to bed herself but the sound of the car outside interrupted her preparations.

Mitchell came in, sooty-faced and weary, with a warning for her: 'The super set me to look for a young chap this morning. He's a student, so I thought he was most likely nursing a hangover, or that he'd had a squabble with his Asian girlfriend's family–'

'He's white?'

'If he and his woman are the two people they've just pulled out of that old warehouse, they're past caring about what colour they used to be. I know it sounds callous because, whoever they are, two poor sods have met what's said to be the most painful death there is, but I hope it's somebody else. Otherwise, you're going to be married to a detective sergeant – or even a job seeker – and right at this moment I'm too tired to care which.' He could not leave the subject alone, however, and after a moment went on: 'The two bodies probably are George Varah and his woman, both bumped off by her Asian brothers in their quaint tradition.'

Virginia winced. 'You'll get into more trouble for remarks like that than for neglecting to look for a despised student. You're allowed to rail against students. It's still politically correct to look down on privilege. Anyway, if someone in the Asian family is guilty, why on earth would they have been the ones to involve the police?'

Virginia knew that he was in no mood to be argued with but it was all she could think of to do. 'If you'd put all your forces for the whole day on finding them, you still wouldn't have thought of looking in a ramshackle shed, remote from Cloughton, miles from the boy's college or home–'

'We could have looked harder for the girlfriend.'

'You said Smithson went twice–'

'But I didn't tell him to talk to neighbours and friends or to find out whether the girl had confided anything to anyone. If I'd sent Shakila she'd have come back with their family history right back to the first Queen Elizabeth.'

'She's probably never heard of the first Elizabeth. There is one thing you can do.'

'What's that?'

'Go and climb in the bath. Otherwise you're sleeping in the garden shed!'

## Chapter Three

Mitchell arrived early at the station on Tuesday morning, hoping that the team had recovered their good spirits, as he had himself. If so, they had not spread as far as the desk sergeant, Mark Powers, who regarded him mournfully and rewarded his 'Morning, Magic' with 'This left for you.'

Apart from the superintendent's instructions to set up a search for an irresponsible student, Mitchell's Monday had been devoid of a crisis to set his adrenalin running. After clearing his desk, he had so chafed at the inactivity the afternoon promised that he had taken a half-day's holiday from the considerable number owed to him. He had spent it cycling round and about Cloughton with his nephew, showing him the sights.

Looking now at the superintendent's scribbled note, it seemed that today promised to be more stimulating. He made his painful way up to his office where he found his sergeant at the window, admiring the transformation of the grey roofs outside by the glitter of sun on frost. She came to her usual chair in front of his desk as he lowered himself uncomfortably on to his own. He answered her questioning glance. 'Saddle sore.'

'You've taken up riding!'

'A bike, my ancient one. Thought I'd show Fran around.' He handed her Superintendent Carroll's brief note. She hid a grin as she read it and they settled to their business. 'As you see, the Infirmary seems to have lost an ex-patient, but he's of age and, according to the super, not vulnerable – not now they've patched him up – so he can disappear if he wants to. They discharged him with a follow-up appointment at Jimmy's — he was taken ill here but lives in Leeds. He didn't arrive back there yesterday as arranged. His wife contacted the hospital in Cloughton and they got on to us. Orders from on high read, "No action to be taken unless further developments."'

'What was wrong with him?'

Mitchell shrugged. 'No idea. Apparently we look at the matter again if chummy fails to keep this appointment in Leeds.'

'Where are we with the missing student?'

'Nowhere. Smithson went round twice yesterday to the girlfriend's house but no one was in. The phone's been switched to an answering machine. As far as I'm concerned, the ball's in their court. It seems to me more likely that the new MP is in need of us. It's unlikely that he'd abandon his family, especially if he's not fully fit.'

Jennifer glanced at her watch. 'It seems to me that we know precious little about either man's situation. There might be more from upstairs when you go. Isn't it time for the briefing?'

Mitchell scowled. 'There isn't anything to brief anyone with – as you've just pointed out. The briefing's only happening so that I can tick the box. I shall tell everyone to go on with what they were filling in time with yesterday, which will mean another long breakfast. As soon as I've dismissed you folk

I'm off to the hospital to see what I can find out about this chap they've discharged.'

'But the super said no action until–'

'He didn't tell me I couldn't visit my mother.' He grinned at her as a knock at his door heralded the arrival of DC Clement, Shakila and PC Smithson. The briefing matched its title. Possibly, it was Mitchell's shortest ever.

Quick to admit to his own mistakes, at least to his equals and underlings, he informed them, 'I was responsible for a balls-up yesterday, possibly on a grand scale. I did nothing towards tracking down an MP, just because he was a student and probably nursing a hangover financed by our taxes. I sent a PC to attempt to talk to his girlfriend before skiving off for the afternoon.

'Now, as you'll all have heard, we have two fire deaths and Dr Holland has an inkling that one of the victims may have been Asian. The trusty PC, finding no one in, visited the family a second time. Thank you, Smithson, for your persistence. I shall make much mention of it upstairs. It'll be Brownie points for you and might get me off the hook.'

Smithson acknowledged his honourable mention with a solemn wink. 'Or the PM might let you off.'

'True. And, with any luck, the errant Varah will rise from his drunken stupor and apologize – first to us and then to his frantic lover. We're hoping both PMs will be today.' He read them the superintendent's note and briefly described the fire and his own nocturnal activities. 'So, sweet Fanny Adams yesterday to all systems go today. All of you pray that Varah and his woman didn't make a tryst in this eyesore of a warehouse that I and my nephew cycled blithely past yesterday afternoon.'

He reached for their action sheets. 'I'm looking for Denton, with or without my boss's sanction, so Adrian will be ringing the hospitals including in Leeds. I've only been specifically warned off harassing the actual family. After that, Adrian, get on to the warehouse owner. You'll probably find him shedding crocodile tears over the corpses whilst hoping that his insurance scam comes off. That isn't racism. Gupte strikes me as a man no self-respecting nation would want to claim. The rest of you can read. Take your sheets and do what they say, with the usual licence.'

'And what will you be doing?' This was Shakila, of course. She added a 'Sir' as a precaution against a charge of disrespect, which gained her an answer.

'After visiting my poor, neglected mum, I shall be having a chat with a fire investigator. I wriggled my way into his good books by whistling up a few uniforms to help drag heavy hoses up to the second floor.'

As the team departed on its various commissions, he sat for a minute, remembering.

Promptly at ten thirty, Mitchell went up to Superintendent Carroll's office for their daily telephone link with the surrounding forces. That business completed, he reported his team's lack of progress in the search for George Varah, then waved the now much-crumpled message at his superior officer. 'Can you give me similar details on the other MP? I got your note but it didn't even give me his name.'

The superintendent's lips set in a straight line and Mitchell realized that his tone had been admonitory rather than reproachful. 'The man lives in Leeds and this is a case for the Leeds force – unless or until they get back to us. For what it's worth, the man's name is Simon Denton. I know almost as little about him as you do. He's a bad asthmatic who succumbed to influenza or some similar complaint and had several asthma attacks that they had difficulty controlling.'

'It sounds to me as if we've been premature in considering him not vulnerable.'

'He collected his preventive medication before disappearing.' Carroll's voice had become his angry one, very quiet with all his words enunciated even more precisely than usual.

Mitchell decided to try another tack. 'Do

you think there's a connection between the two disappearances, sir? We might as well consider that sooner as later.'

'Find me one.'

'They're both young and male.'

'You'll have to do better than that. Besides, Denton is only youngish. I believe he has several children.'

'How much more have you not told me?' Mitchell took a deep breath and a hold on his temper. 'They've both disappeared in the same week. They've both gone missing from Cloughton and disappeared from here but neither belongs here.'

Carroll gave Mitchell a hard look. 'What else have you got on?'

'Not much.'

'You're one light on your team.'

'Caroline will be back first thing on Thursday.' There was silence. Mitchell had the sense not to break it.

Finally the superintendent sighed. 'One day, Benny, you won't have an objection to my every directive. When it happens I shall know you're suffering from something terminal.' Still Mitchell waited, though with difficulty, for the superintendent to decide on his compromise. 'You are not to approach the Denton family without my specific permission. You may attempt to trace both men from their last sightings. If another case comes up in the meantime I

81

shall reprioritize.'

Considering this a victory, Mitchell made a polite withdrawal. He lost no time in sending out a recall to his team members. Only one was found in the canteen. Being a keen runner, he was carefully heeding his CI's cholesterol warning.

It was after eight when Mitchell arrived home and he was annoyed that, once again, the twins had had to go to bed without seeing him. He found Virginia seated at the kitchen table, chatting to Fran and leafing through a cycling magazine on the table. His nephew seemed flattered by her interest in his hobby. Some of it may have been genuine, but Mitchell knew that she always seized on publications new to her as a possible source of work.

Virginia looked up, her forehead wrinkled. 'Fran, is this advertisement really saying that seven hundred pounds is a bargain price for just this little part of a racing bike?'

Fran looked over her shoulder to see which little part it was. 'That's not a bad price for new forks. You could pay a lot more.'

'I dread to think what a whole bike costs.'

Fran's tone was defensive. 'Mine wasn't new. We got it on eBay and a mate of Dad's from the club went to look it over for us. I've been saving up for new forks for it but I'm just keeping the money for now. Anything I buy here might not be suitable for the terrain where we're living in Oz. I can't decide now whether to sell my bike here or ask Dad to pay for it to go over there.'

Virginia turned another page and blinked. 'Now I can see why you were worried about the lock on our shed. If your bike is so valuable we'd perhaps better keep it in the porch so that it's covered by the alarm.'

'Good job all six of you didn't want one,' Mitchell put in.

Fran was silent, maybe trying to decide whether he was being accused of being un-fairly favoured. He justified himself. 'Ailish and Maria spend a fortune on clothes. I think I will get new suspension forks. I might be here for a good while and it's great biking country. I'm not sure which to choose though. Magazines and shops and my mates all advise different types. I definitely want over four inches of travel and lockout would be nice to help with climbing. You see, I run HC4 disc brakes and I've got disc-specific Mavic rims...'

Virginia closed the magazine and went into the dining room to clear the supper things. If she had had an afternoon of this riveting topic, Mitchell thought he had better hold the fort for her. At least he could smile and wear an interested expression. He hoped there wouldn't be a quiz at the end. He was used to 'listening' in this fashion when certain of his colleagues went into raptures about the latest IT package. He lived in the twenty-first century, of course, and understood enough about the workings of his computer to find it useful, but machinery of most kinds failed to excite him. He just kept things in proportion, he assured himself. 'What's the pull?' he asked when he could get a word in.

'Of cycling, you mean?' Fran scratched his head as he tried to analyse his pleasure. 'Well, for a start, I can do it. I'm useless at ball games, but I've got stamina. Then, like in any sport, there's the chance to get better at it – and having mates with something good in common. The rivalry's fun, and then there's the little things.'

'For instance?'

'Well, I was riding up a hill on a training run this last summer. It had been raining and the wild rocket and fennel in the grass was being crushed. You could nearly get drunk on the smell of it. I still remember it now.'

Mitchell nodded, understanding at least the boy's enjoyment of the outdoors and the competition. Personally, he preferred contact sports like rugby where everything depended on his physical prowess and there was no equipment to let him down.

'Cyclists don't like lawyers and police,' Fran announced suddenly.

Mitchell was surprised at his change of tone. 'Why not?'

'Because they don't like us. Someone I read about in that magazine–' he pointed to it on the table – 'just moved out from the kerb – with a signal – to stop cars cutting him up. The police said that he was an obstruction to traffic, making the cars cross the white line to overtake. He was fined a hundred pounds with two hundred costs because there was a cycle path on the other side of the road. In the same week, a motorist in Wales killed four cyclists and was only fined a hundred and eighty.'

Mitchell was indignant at the implied criticism. 'The first man should have used the cycle track. Anyway, don't grumble to me. I'm not a traffic cop.' Fran now looked askance at his uncle's change of tone.

Mitchell turned to give his attention to Declan who had come in some moments ago and now stood listening disconsolately. He had nothing to offer that would be relevant to this conversation. His father asked him what he had been doing since school ended. Declan grinned. 'Well, first I finished my homework, then I just sat still while Fran drew me.'

This nephew was full of surprises. Mitchell asked, 'Can I see?'

Without waiting for his cousin's permission, Declan volunteered: 'I'll fetch them all.'

85

So, there were more. Mitchell spread them out on the table and gave them the attention they deserved. The sketches were quite recognizable. They had caught not only his children's features but, somehow, something of their attitudes. Declan's picture showed him, proud, timid, anxious to please, yet assessing the artist who was committing him to a sketching block.

Mitchell shook his head. Perhaps he was reading into Fran's work all that he knew about his elder son. But Michael, gazing up from the next sheet, had also been understood and conveyed, placidly accepting the vagaries of life, but not to be taken advantage of. And there was Kat, lean and hungry, uncomplicated and bossy, the one most like himself. He looked up and saw Fran watching him. Mitchell's admiration of the boy's talent was in his face. He said, merely, 'What's Sinead done to be left out?'

'It's just until I know her better. She never keeps still long enough for me to get a proper look at her. And she's always pretending, so I don't know what she's really like.'

Now Declan had something to bring to the conversation. 'He's going to do Mum as well, and Mum thinks they ought to go in frames on the wall.'

Mitchell nodded his approval. 'Just so long as he doesn't expect me to sit for him.'

Fran laughed and pointed to his own

head. 'You won't have to. It's all in here.'

'So, this is what you've been doing all day.'

Fran shook his head. 'Oh, no. It only takes a few minutes to do one. If I don't get it right straight away I know it's never going to come.'

Mitchell looked again at the pictures and saw that, for the most part, the lines were swift and sure, the image caught and transferred immediately. Declan's picture had been slightly elaborated, to its detriment. 'This one's different.'

'Yes. I tried to put more of him into it because he's the one I've got to know the most. I've spoilt it, though. I'm not good at the fancy bits. Are we going to watch the news?'

'Three of us are. Declan's going to bed – it's well past his time.' Leading them into the sitting room, Mitchell pressed switches till he had the right channel and wondered whether his two missing persons would get a mention. Briefly, they did. So did the suspect whom, on Sunday evening, the North Yorkshire police had picked up for the arson attacks. He had been released without charge.

They switched off after the headlines and Virginia went to fetch a coffee tray. Left alone with his uncle, Fran volunteered: 'I went to see Gran again this afternoon.'

'How was she today?'

'I thought she'd be a bit scared. That's why I went, to cheer her up and pass the time. She was getting all her test results today.'

Mitchell said with compunction, 'They phoned them through. You must have been either out or upstairs. We should have let you know. Sorry.'

Fran shrugged. 'That's OK. She enjoyed telling me herself.'

Mitchell reflected that he didn't know Sean's children as well as he would have liked. They were so many and so close together! When the two families visited it was difficult to learn much about a particular child with up to ten of them running around. He and Ginny considered Sean and Moira to be neglectful parents and their children to be out of control. He was glad of the opportunity now to extend his acquaintance with at least one, and was liking Fran increasingly. He was about to commend the boy's concern for his grandmother, but Fran spoke first.

'You know those missing men – on the news? Are you having anything to do with looking for them?' Mitchell nodded. 'Well, I've met one of them.'

Mitchell turned to him sharply. 'Go on.'

'On Sunday, when I went to see Gran, she and this man, Mr Denton, were talking to each other in that TV-sitting-room place.' His eyes went back to the magazine that he had brought into the front room.

Mitchell repeated, 'Go on.'

'What about?'

'Anything you can tell me about him.'

'He made to leave when he saw Gran had a visitor. She said to him not to go and she introduced us. He comes from Leeds. He's got three children. His wife's pregnant. He was hoping to be discharged the next day. Gran was sending her good wishes for the baby, saying she was sure it'd be fine. I wondered if there was a problem with it. There was something said about him looking for somebody. I'm not sure about that. They were discussing it when I first went in. I waited for a minute in the doorway, didn't want to interrupt but then Gran saw me and waved me in. Then we chatted in general about boring stuff.'

'Did you get a good look at him?'

Fran grinned. 'Enough to draw him, you mean? Yes, I think so. Do you want me to do it now?'

'It would be very useful.'

Fran departed to fetch paper and a handful of pencils. He sat, quite unselfconsciously, at the table and stared at the blank sheet with deep concentration. Then, selecting a soft pencil, he made several firm strokes. He used considerable pressure so that one sweep across the paper ripped it slightly.

Fran scowled, changed the pencil for one

even blacker and softer and deftly added shading. After a minute or two, he surveyed the finished work with an undefinable expression before handing the sheet to his uncle. 'Why,' he asked, 'don't you just ask his wife for a photograph?'

Mitchell shrugged. 'For some reason known only to himself, my boss doesn't think that's a good idea.'

## Chapter Four

Despite his good intentions, Mitchell had not been able to free himself to visit his mother the previous day. He therefore entered the Cloughton Royal Hospital on Wednesday morning with mixed feelings. Uppermost in his conscious mind was a deep thankfulness that no pernicious wasting disease was to end his mother's life in the immediate future. Not far below that was guilt for spending his Monday afternoon cycling through the winter countryside when he should perhaps have been here in the bleak and sterile ward that had been his mother's refuge for some weeks now. He had heard the doctors' good news by then and he should have found time to rejoice with everyone.

He wondered how anxious his mother had

been for herself. He didn't think she had been afraid to die. God, whom he and his brothers and sisters had spent their childhood dodging, was his mother's friend. Ginny had reported a great improvement in her general appearance after the medical verdict had been announced, though her relaxed expression might be the result of the care and rest that she had enjoyed in the ward. He approached her bed, sat on it and surveyed her. She sat, content, in her armchair. That frill of wrinkled flesh around a set mouth had disappeared and her old enthusiasm for life was apparent in her face.

It did not suit his purpose to find that she already had a visitor. Father Xavier, more scrupulous than himself about the ban on using beds as seating, was struggling with a stacking chair which refused to be separated from its fellows. Mitchell settled the old man, returned to his own seat and endured the traditional greeting, teasing and joke telling. '...Well, Benedict, what have you to say to that?'

A change of subject seemed to be called for. 'You'll be pleased to hear that Declan intends to attend church with Fran for the duration of his visit.'

'And why can he only come with his cousin's protection?'

'Ginny doesn't think it's for protection. Declan doesn't think it's fair to ask for God's help with his homework without offering something in return. The length of Fran's stay sets a time limit to the deal – debt paid.' Niamh Mitchell laughed.

Her priest nodded sagely. 'The Almighty is not proud. He accepts all our approaches.'

'Declan has a few objections to God.'

'He's not alone in that, but I'd be interested to know the nature of his complaints.'

Mitchell grinned. 'He says the Paternoster sets an example of bad manners. "Give us this day... Forgive us... Lead us not... Deliver us..." Not a sign of a please or a thank you.'

'It's in the tone of voice, Benedict. In any case, God reads hearts, not lips.' Turning to Niamh, he added, 'The boy's his father's true son. He believes that attack is the best method of defence. We shall see, though. We shall see.'

To Mitchell's relief on several fronts, the old man rose to leave. The visit to his mother had been slotted in before the Wednesday morning Mass in the hospital chapel. Niamh chose to enjoy more of her son's company rather than attend the service. Mitchell, in spite of a genuine concern for and sympathy with his mother, wondered how soon he could begin on his barrage of questions about Simon Denton.

As he deliberated she regarded him impatiently. 'I'm waiting.'

'I can see how much better you are without asking—'

'Don't waste time, Benny! It's the middle of a working morning. There's a man missing. I've met and chatted to him. You're a policeman. Just get on with it.'

He grinned shamefacedly and pulled a folded piece of paper out of his pocket. 'Is this Simon Denton?'

She studied the drawing for a moment, then handed it back. 'This is Fran's work.' It was a statement.

'You knew Fran could draw?' She ignored this redundant question. 'Has Fran met Simon somewhere else or is this what he remembers from Sunday afternoon?'

'Just that.'

'It's uncanny. Neither Sean nor Moira can draw, though it's no more so, I suppose, than Declan being very musical when none of the rest of us does any music at all. Has there been talk in the ward about Simon? How did it become common knowledge that he was missing?'

'Dorian – the nurse – told us. He'd been asked questions by the Senior Clinical Management, whoever they might be. The Denton family had been ringing round to ask what had happened to him.' Mitchell fished for a notebook as his mother went on, 'Look, you're pressed for time, and it's clear in my head. Tell me what you know already and I'll fill in where I can.'

Mitchell shook his head. 'You're assuming that this is a full official enquiry. Unfortunately...' He wasted several minutes of the time he was pressed for in explaining the situation and maligning his superintendent.

Once she had hushed him, his mother was succinct. 'He's an ordinary, pleasant chap. He was in Cloughton because he was searching for his parents. He was adopted at six weeks and has been told that his birth mother is from round here.'

'How old is he?'

Niamh shrugged. 'Mid-thirties, I'd guess.'

'So, why wait all that time and start looking now?'

'Because his wife's pregnant. The two of them want to know all they can about what the child will inherit, especially in the way of any congenital disease.'

'A worrier then?'

'Yes, I'd say so, but not paranoid. It's just all the pre-natal scans and tests you're given now. When we had our six, we didn't know there was anything much to worry about. You can get the rest from Dorian – Nurse Shaw. He'll know the medical details and probably a lot more. The two of them had become quite friendly. Oh! You might just find that Cavill knows him. He sings.'

'Denton does?'

'No. Only Dorian Shaw. Sorry to get your

hopes up.'

Knowing that his mother would understand, Mitchell took his leave and her advice. In the small office to which he'd been directed, he waited for the nurse to finish his attentions to a patient and wondered how far he dared give the impression that his enquiries had been sanctioned by his elders and betters. Shaw proved to be obliging and made Mitchell's task easy by asking merely, 'What do you want to know?'

The man would have as little time to spare as himself. Mitchell asked for details of Denton's discharge from the hospital and observed Shaw as he answered. The office contained two upright chairs and a small table, so that the nurse sat opposite to him. Shaw was tall and thin, with a narrow face and receding hair, yet he had a youthful air. He looked at Mitchell as though he were interested in what he was hearing and he made direct eye contact when he spoke. In spite of the lean face, the lips were full and twitched now and then. Mitchell had the impression that, on more suitable occasions, he might be amusing company.

Shaw counted on his fingers as he described the hospital's discharge procedure. 'The doctor did his round on Monday morning at about ten o'clock. He said Simon was fit to travel to Leeds. He prescribed the discharge medication – more antibiotics and steroids. I sent the order form down to the lab and had the stuff sent up to the ward. We sent a letter to Simon's GP in Leeds. It probably won't have arrived yet. It described how we came to be treating him and what we've done since he came to us. He had an uncontrollable asthma attack in the street and a passer-by rang for an ambulance. We found an infection that caused it and treated it. He had X-rays, antibiotics and extra steroids to control his bronchial inflammation. He already had enough of his usual inhalers.'

'Any chance of a copy of that letter?' Mitchell dared not make his request less tentative.

'We make four carbon copies of the letters. Obviously the GP gets his, then one for the patient, the top copy goes in the patient's file and the last – usually the one you can't read – is for the hospital pharmacy. I'll photocopy that one for you and if you can't read it I'll translate.'

Mitchell wondered whether to ask for copies of Denton's case notes but decided not. He might be refused and, in any case, no one he was allowed to question would understand them. They wouldn't run away.

Shaw was looking at his watch. 'Look, I've got more to tell you but there are people out there needing me.'

This was immediately verified. They had left the door ajar. Through the gap, they saw an elderly woman, clearly distressed, struggling along with the support of a Zimmer frame. 'But, Your Majesty, I'd do anything rather than offend you...' The wail was piteous.

Shaw was already out of the door, soothing his patient, assuring her that the Queen was equally distressed by the misunderstanding and that all could be set right. He seemed to convince her and she reluctantly allowed a probationer nurse to escort her back to her cubicle. Shaw returned to Mitchell and scribbled on a post-it note which he handed over. 'That's my address. I'll be back there by four with luck. Simon should have met me last night but didn't turn up. I did see him leaving here as I went off shift yesterday morning. I saw him get a lift in a lorry. It's no use asking. I didn't make a note of the registration and I don't remember much about it. I was watching Simon – and the traffic, of course. I suppose you know the young man who keeps coming to see your mother this week?'

'He's my nephew.'

'Well, he was passing on his bike so he's your man.'

Mitchell rang his home even before he left the hospital car park. Virginia answered. 'All right. You're going to be late. Don't worry. I didn't expect anything else at this stage of the game.'

'Actually, I wanted to speak to Fran.'

'Oh... He seemed a bit out of sorts this morning.'

'Enough to see a doctor?'

'No, I'm sure he's not ill. I think he's a bit fed up about losing those chess matches. He seems to feel quite humiliated. Perhaps it's in his genes. You and Declan are both poor losers. Anyway, Fran's out on his bike. He should be in better spirits after another dose of fresh air. I'll get him to ring you as soon as he comes in.' She hung up, obviously having a programme of her own that did not include family interruptions.

Mitchell sat for a moment longer, considering her accusation. Was he a bad loser?

DC Adrian Clement had soon established to his own satisfaction – and, he hoped, to his superiors' – that neither of the missing men had been treated in any hospital in either Cloughton or Leeds since each of them had disappeared. Now, he decided, he needed some physical action. The address he had been given for the owner of the burned warehouse was only a mile and a half away. He would walk – carefully though – on the icy pavements that sparkled in the powerless sunshine.

His prejudices had suggested that Mr

98

Gupte would live in a run-down terraced house in an exclusively Asian area. The modern semi-detached house was a surprise. The property, with the exception of the garden, was as well kept as the adjoining one, its curtains clean and its paintwork fresh.

There was no one at home. He had been unable to make an appointment as a young man at BT had informed him that 12 Cliff Gardens was one of the few Cloughton properties with no telephone connection. Presumably the fire investigators and his own colleagues would prevent the man being on his ruined business premises this morning. Where now?

Fate answered his question in the person of a lady of uncertain age in the house next door. Her authoritative gesture through the window indicated that she wished to speak to him. He walked back along the overgrown path of number 12 and stood looking over her neatly trimmed hedge. Her door opened promptly. 'It's DC Clement, isn't it?'

Clement tried frantically to remember where he might have come across her before. Failing, he acknowledged his own name, adding, 'I wonder if you could help me.'

'If I can. But, actually, I was about to ask you for help.'

Clement surveyed her. Her manner was crisp, her attire of the twinset and tweed variety. Pearls, he decided, would be at the ready for when the occasion required them. He spoke frankly. 'Your problem doesn't seem to be life-threatening. Is it as important as sorting out last night's fire?'

She came down the garden steps towards him, smiling. 'I wasn't going to ask you to find my cat.' Her cat was surveying their shivering forms from the window sill of a warm room. It looked far too comfortable and sensible to lose itself. 'I think what I wanted to ask is germane to your investigation.'

Clement grinned at her. 'I bet you were a teacher.'

Her smile disappeared. 'Don't alienate me by overestimating my age. I still am a teacher. Look, our business is urgent and it's freezing out here. Come in.' She led him into a sitting room at the back of the house which overlooked a neat garden and a sweep of hillside, covered in dead heather, rising to an uncertain horizon where remnants of snow mingled with white sky.

Waving him into an easy chair and seating herself, she offered him no refreshment. 'I know nothing about the fire, beyond that everyone is telling me that it happened. All I know about Mubarak Gupte is what his wife, Salma, has told me and what I've heard through the wall. Salma has become my friend and I look after her as far as I can.

'She's older than her husband and I'm worried about her.' The woman was an academic and had prepared her story carefully. 'The account gossip gives is that he came from Pakistan five or six years ago for an arranged marriage with a young relation. The girl had the sense and courage to refuse him and he was likely to be deported when his temporary visa ran out. He had become friendly in the meantime with Salma's brother Nasser. Salma's family were becoming embarrassed by her advancing years and her single state.'

She paused as the door opened and the cat entered to inspect her visitor. It advanced to within a foot of him, stared at him solemnly, sniffed at his shoes, then turned tail, crossed to its owner and sprang lightly on to her lap.

Clement asked, 'Has he rejected me or is that a confirmation that I'm no threat to you?' She shrugged and he nodded to her to continue.

'A deal was struck. Nasser had had a flourishing antiques business but he had TB. He was treated here but not before the disease had damaged his lungs and made him a respiratory cripple. The business was going down. If Mubarak would marry Salma he could become Nasser's partner and run the shop. It didn't work out well for any of them.'

Clement wondered how much, if any, of

101

this was what Mitchell wanted to know. The CI gave all his officers blanket permission to let their interviewees tell all however irrelevant the all seemed to be, but this woman was not someone he had been sent to see. He suddenly realized that he didn't even know her name.

Her tale was not over. 'Salma thought she would never become pregnant. Mubarak treated her slightly better when she did. Before that, I used to hear screams every evening but she would never admit to being ill used and her face was never marked. As I said, we became friends. She studies in my house when her husband is in that shack he called a warehouse – just GCSEs till she's ready for more, plus English conversation and reading together. She spoke good English when she lived with her family but Mubarak only lets her speak Urdu and it's all he speaks to her.'

Clement managed to break in. 'Why aren't you at your school today?'

She laughed. 'Salma's is the only teaching I do now. I was teasing you, but warning you as well. Ladies only want their ages exaggerated when they're over eighty and boasting of having been strong enough to outlast their peers.'

She resumed her tale. 'Last night was quiet at first but then a crowd of Mubarak's friends arrived and there was a lot of angry shouting. Then, Salma didn't come over this morning and, when I called there, no one was in – at least there was no response. I thought Mubarak might be with the fire people or your colleagues.'

Clement shook his head. 'Not us. They've just sent me.'

'They won't be letting him salvage his stuff yet, presumably – though I'm not sure that that would be in his plan.'

Clement took her hint and made a note to enquire into Gupte's insurance arrangements. 'So, what did you want from me?'

'To know what's happened to Salma.'

'Presumably she's assisting her husband, even if he doesn't deserve it.'

'I doubt it. I've told you. He thinks her place is the house, keeping it spotless. She isn't allowed to do gardening, not because she's pregnant but because she might get emancipated ideas from talking to the neighbours. I never risk speaking to her if he's at home. One day I hope to persuade her to break away, but my interference in any other way would spell disaster for her.'

Clement closed his notebook and slipped it back in his pocket. 'We'll try to refer her to an organization that will help but, for now, it seems to me that she's too docile and useful to him for him to harm her seriously – though it depends how you define harm, I suppose.'

She said, quietly, 'I'm especially concerned for her at the moment. Two days ago they found out that the baby is a girl.'

Early on Wednesday afternoon, copies of the *Cloughton Clarion* were delivered to the newspaper kiosk in the main thoroughfare in and out of the bus station.

FIRE THAT CAUSED TWO DEATHS IS ARSON screamed the billboards and the headlines. Dorian Shaw, wishing, now that the promised snow had not fallen, that he had risked riding the Kawasaki to work, bought a copy to while away the twenty minutes he had to wait for his bus. At least the coffee bar was open. He found a corner table and began to read for himself the news that he had been hearing second-hand from his patients. The headline's enormous block capitals left room for only a brief piece below.

Police are now certain that the fire that burned down Mubarak Gupte's warehouse at Cragvale on Monday night was deliberately started. The fire (full report with pictures, see pages 2 and 3) began in the early evening and was reported to the fire station by Craig Heppenstall, 19, a student at Manchester University and spending his Christmas vacation...

Dorian skipped the rest of the paragraph, smiling at the description of the lad 'putting the animals to bed'. Made him sound like Mr Noah. After a tribute to the efficient fire service, the account continued.

The bodies of a man and a woman, found on the first floor of the warehouse, have yet to be identified. The jury is still out on whether the Cloughton fire was started by the man responsible for 14 other fires throughout Yorkshire during the last seven months.

Dorian thought the metaphor was ill chosen. Not a few of the *Clarion's* readers would assume from the mention of a jury that the case was already being tried. Obeying the further reminder, Dorian turned to the two-page spread to learn more. He was expecting a blazing inferno in pictures that had been computer-enhanced. There were three, but their perspective was long and the fire appeared a tame affair compared with the picture painted in the melodramatic phrases below. The police and fire authorities seemed to have divulged very little and the reporter had been hard pressed to fill the space allotted to him. Even the owner of the ruined warehouse had let him down. 'Mr Gupte, whose wife is missing and may prove to be the woman who died in the fire, was too distressed to speak to our reporter.'

He had apparently been too distressed to be photographed too.

The reporter had had to make do with the comments of two spectators who were only too pleased to appear. Mrs Gladys Baxter, a child-faced woman, stared from a picture that took up an eighth of the page, round-eyed, as though still mesmerized by the flames. 'I trembled for my house,' she had declared, although the address was given and Dorian knew that it was two miles from any danger. Another smaller picture showed Mrs Janet Cotterill, Mrs Baxter's sister and churchwarden at St James & St John. She sat indoors, the cross round her neck and the large Bible on the table prominent, and assured readers, 'I prayed for police and firemen all the time the danger lasted.'

A glance at his watch sent Dorian scurrying for his bus, where he sat downstairs and read the *Clarion's* PROFILE OF AN ARSONIST. There was no byline, and no credentials were given for the description that followed. Dorian tired of it and turned to the inside back page, hoping to find that Greystones was no longer on the market. He was not in the mood for more arguments about it today.

The arsonist profile was being read with closer interest by DC Shakila Nazir.

'Our reporter has been discussing recent

events in Cloughton with a forensic psychologist who takes a special interest in fire investigation, Dr Anthony Morton.' There followed a photograph of the great man which, Shakila knew, had been taken from the cover of the book which had been her bedtime reading for some weeks. She doubted very much that he had abandoned his university commitments and rushed over to Cloughton to be interviewed by the local press – particularly as the local police knew nothing about such a visitation.

'Only a small proportion of arson is thought to be motivated by serious psychological problems ... the major motive is for insurance fraud ... vandals and thrill seekers ... extortion ... to conceal crimes...' This first paragraph ended with the encouraging thought: 'An increasing number of fires are thought to be arising from domestic disputes.'

Shakila grinned. That narrowed the police's job down nicely. She read what followed with some puzzlement. It seemed that Dr Morton believed these miscreants were mainly under eighteen and only over thirty-five if they had a revenge or profit motive. There was a ninety per cent chance that they were male and three-quarters of them were white. There was an overriding probability that they were lower working class with an IQ in the region of 80. Absent

and abusive fathers and emotionally dis-
turbed mothers came into the reckoning,
along with learning difficulties. The list of
helpful clues concluded: 'Almost all of them
have arrest records.'

Shakila folded the paper and put it away.
She had assumed, as she began to read, that
the reporter had found a copy of Dr
Morton's book and stolen sentences from it.
So far as she could remember, however, none
of the opinions expressed here had come
from the volume through which she was
struggling by the light of her bedside lamp.

Mitchell's stomach was rumbling as he
made his way to Dr Holland's lab. A visit to
the hospital, the morning call with the
superintendent and a session with a fire
investigator had left scant time for lunch,
and the corned beef sandwich that the
canteen had sent up to his office was just a
memory, though not a fond one.

He had chosen PC Beardsmore to accompany him to the post-mortem. The lad had
disgraced himself, at least in his own eyes, at
his first ordeal. He needed to regain his
confidence and this dissection might be
easier than the last. The smell was different
with burned bodies. There would be less
liquid and smoke would veil the body
odours that remained.

The young PC was waiting for him in the

sheltering porch of the mortuary, his expression a mixture of apprehension and determination. The powerful muscular frame and shaved head could appear threatening. The light blue eyes were alert and penetrating, but they had a benign expression and Mitchell had heard the man described as 'the sort of copper people tell things to'. Mitchell had high hopes of him. Beardsmore saw him approach and grinned, his mouth so wide it almost split his face in half.

They found Dr Holland in the small office that adjoined the lab and learned that he had chosen to attend to his female victim first. 'You'd better see if some Asian family is one lady short.'

Mitchell glared at him. 'We've got one already, and there's some question about the whereabouts of another.'

Holland beamed. 'Excellent! In that case, they absolutely must let us play with DNA.' He waved an arm in the direction of the chilled cabinet across the room. 'Our gentleman friend in there will have to wait till this evening, I'm afraid. I'm due in court when I've finished with the lady. We've got a villain who'll slip through the net without my input but I won't let him if I can help it.' He bent his gaze through his bottle-bottomed lenses to his current customer once more.

Mitchell concentrated on the pathologist's

face rather than his hands. It was watchful and intelligent and he knew the man was well thought of throughout the Yorkshire forces despite his eccentricities. His delight was in discomfiting his audience, offering them, alternately, upsetting and highly technical details and ridiculous – and probably apocryphal – anecdotes. Beardsmore was whispering and Mitchell leaned towards him to hear. 'How can he see the body when, from our side, we can't see his eyes through his lenses? You can't do an operation looking down the wrong end of a telescope.' The pathologist peered at them over the maligned spectacles and Beardsmore blushed.

Mitchell knew that his PC was merely trying to distract himself from the procedure in front of him, but he glared at the lad to silence him.

Dr Holland, his eyes down again and his hands busy, began the entertainment. 'Actually, autopsy means self-examination, though two thousand years of lobbying haven't altered it to necropsy.' When this met with no response, he went on, 'The first known application of medical knowledge to the investigation of death was in 44 BC. Antistius, a Roman physician, was sent for to examine Julius Caesar's body. He announced that he knew which of the would-be emperor's twenty-three stab wounds had proved fatal. The Romans gave us "forensic", you know. It means stuff to be brought before the Forum.'

The pathologist's hands were occupied with removing shreds of unburned clothing from the shelter of joints and bent limbs. The material looked silky and the scraps were chiefly of orange and turquoise fabric. Was this woman George Varah's girlfriend? And the man? Mitchell refused to allow himself to speculate further about them until more information was available. He watched Dr Holland's minute examination of the external body, realizing that his task was not easy with the corpse's legs and arms so stiffly bent. The hands were merely claws which Holland opened gently as far as he could without breaking the bones.

At the same time he continued his crusade to educate the Cloughton police force. 'There are six degrees of burn injuries, but we haven't got the full range here.' He pointed to odd areas, under the arms and where the stomach had been pressed against the second victim. The skin there was inflamed and swollen and had shed scales from its surface. 'These are just first degree, but here on the upper arms and the back of the thighs we've got second degree with blisters. That's lucky.'

'For you, maybe.'

Ignoring his assistant's mutter, Holland carefully inserted the needle end of a syringe into several of the blisters and drew out small quantities of fluid. 'We shall test this for proteins that will tell us if the lady was alive when the blisters formed.'

Mitchell looked more closely at the still form, pointing gingerly at marks on the calves and thighs. 'Has she had a beating?'

'Possibly, but some severe burns can cause body tissues to rupture in a way very similar to how they would after a battering from fists or a blunt instrument. Analysis will show us whether there's been bleeding as the result of wounds.' Mitchell regretted his question and turned to judge the effect of the answer on his young colleague.

Beardsmore was bearing up well and asked, 'How?'

'If the splitting of tissues was caused by heat the blood will already have congealed. Personally, I don't think this lady burned to death.'

'Smoke suffocation, then,' Beardsmore announced smugly.

Mitchell was surprised when the pathologist merely nodded and continued his ministrations to his dead patient. After some time, his stream of information continued. 'The Corps of Vigiles, the Roman fire fighters, operated in Britain during the occupation. When their organization and the legions disappeared from here, fire fighting was left to well-disposed citizens. They defended us against fire to the best of their ability, but in a disorganized fashion, for the next twelve centuries.'

Suddenly, Beardsmore grinned broadly and took Holland on. 'An organized fire brigade and fire insurance offices started after the Great Fire in 1666. The insurance people only dealt with the fires of people insured with them though. It was the 1820s before we had professional municipal brigades.' Dr Holland stopped work and gazed at Beardsmore, then resumed his attempts at the difficult task of taking out his victim's tongue, neck tissues, chest contents and abdominal organs in a piece.

When he had gathered his forces once more, he began another story. 'There was a PI in Japan – a sort of Asian Sherlock Holmes – a man called Fukuda. He could predict outbreaks of arson simply by studying the evening newspaper and noticing when low pressure was forecast. He knew this affected people with sinus problems – they couldn't breathe. Some sufferers relieved their problems by starting fires because the image of the roaring flames somehow removed their sense of suffocation, caused their noses to clear. Some people set dozens of fires in dustbins. Others liked one spectacular blaze.' Mitchell was listening in spite of himself.

'One schoolboy who thought the weather had made him do badly in exams set fire to his school. Fukuda interviewed a boy who had been selected for questioning because of his sniffles. He asked him not, "Did you set fire to the school?" but "How long did the image of the fire remain in your brain?" and the lad said, "For more than two weeks," his eyes shining at the memory.'

Mitchell waited to see if his PC would find a reply to this. When nothing was offered, he remarked, deadpan, 'Remember that, Beardsmore, if we ever get a suspect.'

As the two officers drove back to the station, Mitchell asked, 'Where does he get it all? He must spend every spare moment reading. Whatever the topic, he's got an outrageous story to fit it.'

Beardsmore pulled up at the traffic lights and sniffed derisively. 'You're too easily impressed, sir. I bet he just gets up early, types the subject of the day's job into Google and tells us all about whatever comes on to the screen.' Mitchell grinned and decided that Beardsmore's second PM had cured him of the trauma of the first.

Shakila had not been surprised to find that her action sheet sent her to interview George Varah's girlfriend. She had not expected, considering the low priority the CI had put on finding Varah, to be accompanied by her sergeant. The two officers had driven out of Cloughton, a couple of miles down the valley, and then up a ferocious ascent. There they found Throstle Heights tucked away behind the tall shrubs that grew wild on the slope below it.

Number 2 was the middle house of a terrace of three, no different from its neighbours except for a bright orange door. Jennifer knocked on it to no avail and the cottages on either side seemed deserted.

The two officers walked round the little terrace via the left-hand dwelling and here found signs of occupation in all three houses. They immediately understood the occupants' preference for the other side of the row. Each house had a long garden, stretching away upwards towards the horizon. All three were well tended and in summer would be a riot of colour. Shakila thought that they were equally attractive now. Number 2's plot had several birches at the bottom, some shining silver in the chilly sunlight and a couple festooned in ivy. Smaller trees in the border made interesting branch patterns against the fence and the sky.

'You only notice interesting shapes when the colours aren't there to distract you,' she remarked as they walked along a wide flagged path that separated the cottages from their gardens. Jennifer looked puzzled, shrugged and made an assault with her fist on number 2's back door.

This immediately produced an attractive, dark-skinned girl in a sari. When the two officers had displayed their warrants and the girl had confirmed that she was Reeta Mistry, she beamed at them. 'You've tracked George down at last.' There was no trace of any accent but the local one.

Jennifer stood back and let her DC take charge. Shakila asked, 'What does he look like?'

The girl was quick to assess the implications of the question. 'You've got a body, haven't you? You'd have asked for a photograph if–'

Shakila held up her hand. 'Slow down! We've got a female body. We thought it could have been yours. Look, can we come in?'

The girl apologized for her lack of hospitality. She led them through a narrow hall into a small sitting room with panoramic views down into the valley and across to the upward sweep on the other side. The three women stood paying their respects to it for a moment before settling to their business.

'Why should a body you've found bring you here – even if it is dark-skinned?'

Shakila grinned. 'Because, to be honest, we weren't sure that your family's tolerant remarks about your friendship with Mr Varah were sincere.'

Reeta considered this for a moment. 'I'd be angry if a white person had said that.'

'That's probably why my boss sent me. So, your father's genuinely happy to have an English son-in-law?'

The girl laughed. 'He'd be a hypocrite if he wasn't. My mother's Scottish. Her hair's dark – as dark as mine – but she has blue eyes and a very fair skin.'

'Then I owe all of you an apology.'

'Accepted.' Reeta added, with a flash of spirit, 'You people need to slow down too. George and I aren't even engaged. We only met two months ago.'

'I apologize again, but we do actually have a deceased male, as you'll hear on the news before very long. Our pathologist though thinks that he's a bit older than George – unless he's a mature student. Is he?'

Reeta laughed again. 'He thinks he is but he's only twenty-one.'

'You don't seem very concerned about him. Do you know where he is?'

'No, but I think I know what his problems are. He's too fond of his beer and his folk are less tolerant than mine. They don't fancy little wogs as grandchildren, so they're doing what they can to nip our friendship in the bud and–'

She was interrupted by a tap on the window. A tall blue-eyed man with designer stubble on his head as well as his chin was peering through. Reeta appeared delighted and waved permission for him to come in.

Shakila raised her eyebrows. 'Mr Varah, escaped from his family's clutches?'

Reeta shook her head. 'He might have, but this is my brother Jamil.'

The arsonist, in his red anorak, was changing his routine this afternoon in two different ways. He had found a new area of the county to operate in and that meant carrying out his activities at a new time of day. He had had to risk daylight this time. He needed to be back in the lorry by three thirty. The roads were icy, the rush-hour traffic would be building up and it had to be back in Jim's yard for reloading by half five. He would need at least fifteen minutes to get back to where he had left it, but he still had a little time left.

He was sitting in the fork of a tree, several hundred yards from where he knew the ugly flats were blazing. He'd have a better view farther up but only this first division of the branches promised to bear his weight. He felt quite safe from notice here. The gloom of the afternoon made an artificial dusk and he could only see his watch as luminous figures and hands. He adjusted the focus slightly on the magnificent pair of binoculars he had borrowed without permission. Without them he would have seen none of the detail of the conflagration he had started. A pair like these ought to be the next thing he saved up for.

The flats were a bit too close to civilization for him to watch from nearby. He wouldn't have long to wait now. The cloud of smoke above the building was tinged pink, making it visible even from here. That meant there would by now be a good blaze below it. He waited breathlessly for the flames to appear.

Flames were like a drug – not that he had ever taken any. He had a better way to get his fix. This time, he was missing the exciting, tentative beginning of the fire. That excited him as much as all the other stages. The first tiny flames looked so pretty and innocent, and yet they had all that power to unleash. Then they stopped being pretty and became beautiful. He was finding a different thrill out of knowing how the fire was progressing behind the white concrete walls that in this light were dull grey. He could see the first flickering now. Licking was just the right word for what flames did. He supposed all familiar sayings became common because they were just right. Once it started, a fire wasn't simply a thing any longer. It turned into a living creature with power of its own.

The arsonist drew in his breath sharply as a ball of flame seemed to leap from one source of fuel to another – as though it had smelt it out to devour it. He could only smell the smoke very faintly from here. That was a pity. He loved the smoke catching in the back of his throat, reminding him that it could choke and burn just as well as the flames.

The fire had a good hold now. In the light of it, he could see that the building was beginning to give way. A huge chunk of hot concrete dropped from the top storey to the ground in front. He watched, transfixed, not thinking any more, and felt a thrill of joy as the whole front of the building collapsed in one piece, revealing the inferno behind in all its nakedness. He suddenly realized he was wetting his pants.

This was further away than he had ever watched one of his own fires. Would it give him an orgasm at this distance? He thought not. If it were going to happen, it would have happened already. When he was a thirteen-year-old boy, he had been smoking, experimentally, one day in a hay barn with his friend Colin and Col's two cousins. One of them had tossed a butt into the hay and the barn caught fire. The other three had run away, but he had felt compelled to stay and watch the police and firemen arrive and set to work. This was quite normal, at least for him, but the sexual sensations from the sight of the flames were new to him. He had read about the blaze the next day and felt the same excitement, the same stirrings.

Another time, he had lit a fire in a wood, mostly conifers, and he had watched one pine after another being consumed, the flames fanned by a sharp east wind. Fantastic! And so his strange career had escalated.

He willed the fire service not to arrive at his present fire until those flats had been dealt what they deserved. Were the firemen afraid of fire? Of course they were. He was afraid of it himself. That was an essential part of his fascination – its potential for destruction. Sometimes, he was afraid of his own potential for destruction, the violence hidden under his calm, patient-seeming surface.

He shook this thought away. He was becoming morbid, and, anyway, it was time to go. The euphoria was disappearing as he passed, through the almost-dark, back to the lorry. He climbed in, feeling his clothes moving, wet and cold against his skin. As the cab heated up, the smell of urine became the smell of shame – shame not for lighting the fire, but for the way his body had reacted to it.

Every fire brought him a sense of relief, the possibility of a new start. It worked off his resentment against people who put him down because they had no time for him, failed to understand him. He always felt, as he struck his match, that the fire it started could solve any problem because it caused the total destruction of all that was wrong. But all that soon floated away, and then the depression hung over him again.

DC Adrian Clement had been settled in the station canteen for just fifteen minutes to enjoy his late and well-deserved lunch, when his cell phone rang. 'Sylvia Townsley,' was all the crisp voice said to him. He immediately pictured the Guptes' neighbour with her silver sausage-roll curls and expensive dentures.

He made an equally terse reply: 'DC Clement.'

'I thought you would like to know that Mubarak Gupte has returned home.'

'With his band of men?'

'No. Nor with Salma. Just himself.'

Clement thanked her, sighed, burned his tongue and throat as he swilled down the coffee he had intended to enjoy and set off once more to Cliff Gardens.

He was not welcome there. Mr Gupte scowled at the warrant he presented and refused to look at Clement, let alone ask him in. He answered the DC's questions in his own fashion and in a sing-song voice. The accent was almost Welsh, but the English was fluent.

'What the hell has it got to do with you folk? I've been up all bloody night with damn-fool questions from the fire people–'

'I should have thought you'd be grateful to them.'

'Not the nosy pair who were hassling me. If they'd gone and done something useful they'd have had the bloody fire out quicker.'

Clement's face was solemn. 'Mmm. Don't suppose that occurred to them.' He enquired about warehouse security.

Gupte shook his head impatiently. 'No need for any. Nothing there's valuable in itself. It'd take a bloody great truck to get a usable haul. There'd be no profit for a petty thief.'

'I thought you dealt in antiques.'

'Well, my bloody antiques aren't as old as other people's. Mine's a specialized market.'

'Is that so?'

'Cheeky young brat! Don't try to be clever. I'm not ashamed to be a junk dealer. It's a case of always knowing who wants what somebody else doesn't – and that's a special talent.'

'I expect it is, only Mrs Townsley said–'

'*Miss* Townsley,' Gupte pointed out spitefully. 'You don't think anybody would marry that old bitch?'

'I don't see why not. Someone agreed to marry you. By the way, where is your wife?'

'If it's any of your business, she's bloody disappeared, hasn't she?'

Clement's expression became sympathetic. 'Oh dear. Well, I can understand you've been taken up with more important matters. You haven't had the chance to tell us about that yet. Never mind, Mr Gupte, we won't hold that against you. We shall look for her and, I promise you, we shall find her.'

Seeing no point in a further exchange of insults, Clement decided to withdraw and replan. It would be sensible to consult HOLMES about Gupte, check his insurance arrangements and see what the other neighbours said about his marriage before challenging him again. He was unsure about whether the man was deliberately keeping silent about the two people who had died on his premises or whether the fire investigators had withheld that information for reasons of their own.

He didn't suppose Mitchell would be pleased with what he had achieved. What did he care? There was nothing left on his action sheet and, in any case, Shakila would have the whole affair sorted out by tomorrow morning. He was going for a run and, after the debriefing, he was off to the pub.

Mitchell had decided to send his sergeant to hear what Nurse Shaw had to tell them. Then, intrigued by being offered information that had not been sought, he had made his small acquaintance with the man his excuse for accompanying her.

In the hospital that morning, Shaw had

seemed quite at ease. Now, in his own home, his chatter was nervous. He apologized for his casual dress. Mitchell wondered what was wrong with the thick white cotton sweat-shirt. It had braid over the shoulders and down the sleeves, black with red on either side, perhaps the uniform of some sports club. It was shabby and rather baggy but perfectly clean.

They were offered tea and Mitchell, who never drank it, accepted. Shaw was apologetic about the plain white crockery that he was laying out on the kitchen table. 'We bought it in the sale when the Green Dragon hotel closed down. Becca's parents disapprove of it.' Waiting for the kettle to boil, he looked round the room, seeming to see it with his visitors' eyes. His survey took in the creel above them on which a long row of men's socks were drying. 'I have really sweaty feet, I'm afraid, especially on the ward. I have masses of socks. I need to change them several times a day.'

Mitchell, who had not noticed them, continued his own appraisal of his surroundings. Two of the three shelves of an old and attractive dresser held domestic equipment. The centre one was filled with nursing text-books and a paperback set of the writings of the major philosophers, some of whose names he failed to recognize. He wondered which of the two read them.

The tea, when it arrived, was strong and he saw that Jennifer at least was glad of it. He decided that they would learn more if he managed to put the man at his ease. With this in mind, he asked, 'Has your patient made up her quarrel with the Queen?'

'Oh, they're the best of friends again. Her Majesty sent a photograph of herself and Philip with a handwritten message across the corner. Fortunately, Margie didn't recognize my writing.'

Ignoring his sergeant's puzzled expression, Mitchell nodded approvingly. 'Your ward is lucky to have you.'

Shaw smiled. 'She's rather a special patient. She's my godmother – but I do care about all of them. Your mother has been delightful company. My mother is seventy-eight. She chose Margie as my godmother because she's eight years younger. She had more chance of living long enough to keep me on the straight and narrow if my mother should fall under a bus.'

'Was that likely?'

'She never spoke about her demise in any other terms. No feeble fading for her – and no bus driver brave enough!' The man raised his eyebrows each time he spoke and held his head on one side, reminding Mitchell of a friendly robin. Possibly he had a slight facial deformity as, when he smiled, one side of his mouth turned up far more than the other.

It was time to get down to business and, if possible, to get rid of the remainder of his tea. He took a breath with which to stem the flow of inconsequential chatter. Shaw, possibly used to reading body language in the course of his work, tried to justify his verbal rambling. 'Margie is relevant to what I was going to tell you. I'm not sure if you know, but, Simon Denton was adopted as a baby. His wife is pregnant now and...'

Mitchell assured him that his wife and nephew had explained Denton's presence in Cloughton. 'How can Margie help?'

'It's what I know about her that could be relevant. She's never married, but, when she was younger, she had a son. She wasn't actually all that young – well into her thirties. Apparently everyone was astonished and the baby boy was discreetly disposed of by the family. My mother told me that he'd been given to rich young parents who would provide him with a better life – a more respectable one, I suppose she meant. I don't know how Margie felt about it. I was only a child then and I haven't thought about the whole business for years.

'When I was just a kid, though, for a long time I examined every lad of the right age that I met, trying to find Margie's features in all their faces.'

'And now you're doing it again? It's a long

shot, isn't it?'

Shaw wheeled round to face Jennifer, his nervousness gone. 'I'm a nurse now. I do have various kinds of evidence, though I admit that none of it is conclusive.' He seemed to be reviewing it now as he poked the tip of his tongue into his cheek, making it bulge. 'Simon's second name is David, the name that Margie gave her baby for the few weeks that she kept him. Yes, I know how common it is...'

'And you can see Margie's features in Simon's face?'

Shaw gave Jennifer a hard stare which produced a rueful grin and an apology. 'They aren't in the least alike physically – but the baby was operated on for a heart defect, even before adoption. It was entirely successful, so I was told, and he was expected to live a perfectly normal life. Simon has a long-standing scar which might be the result of such a procedure – though it might have a lot of other causes.'

'Did you ask him about it?'

Shaw turned back to Mitchell. 'No. I'd agonized about whether it was right to speak to him about this child and I only decided when I knew he was being discharged and that I wouldn't have another opportunity. I couldn't let him go without mentioning the possibility.'

'Any other evidence?'

'Simon seemed very drawn to Margie, sorry for her. He'd take her back to her bed and sit with her when her wanderings round the ward interrupted our routines. I'm not reading too much into that fact. He is a kind man and made himself useful, and Margie needed company. What might be significant is that, when they talked, I heard her sometimes address him as Davy.'

'You mean you thought she recognized him?'

'Hardly. What I wondered was whether Davy was the name of the baby's father and the reason for Margie giving the child that name. If I'm right and Simon resembles his father, that might be who Margie thought he was.'

Mitchell saw that Jennifer was scribbling and turned back to his host. To his horror, he saw that his cup, which he had managed to tip discreetly over a plant whilst Shaw talked to his sergeant, was being refilled. He let the rest of the story continue without questions. 'In the end, I decided I ought to show Simon some old photographs and documents that belong to my mother. I didn't tell her why I wanted them. I invited Simon to come round here on Monday afternoon after I'd done the second half of my split shift. He rang here after I'd left. He asked if I'd meet him in the Woolpack at about nine because something had come up.'

'You've still got the message on your answering machine?'

He shook his head. 'No. Becca, my partner answered him after I'd left.'

Mitchell sighed. 'Then we'll have to come back when she's in, unless...' He glanced at his watch. It was well after five. 'Will she be on her way home now?'

Becca, it seemed, was going 'out with the girls' when she left work at six. Shaw gave details of her company and its location and they left with scant ceremony to catch her before she left.

'What did you make of that?' Mitchell demanded as they returned to Jennifer's car.

She refused to be drawn. 'Nice hands,' was all she offered.

With her work hopefully finished for the day, Shakila remembered her empty refrigerator and vegetable rack. She therefore drove completely round a roundabout to make for the car park of the late-opening Tesco in the town centre. Tired, and, for her, somewhat depressed, she abandoned all her good resolutions, quickly filling her trolley with any foods that took her fancy. She waited less than patiently at the checkout and set about humping heavy bags from the trolley into the restricted space behind the back seat of her elderly Renault 4.

About to climb into the car, she remembered the birthday card in her handbag. A glance at her watch showed her that she had missed the last collection from the box outside the supermarket. She sighed. Her niece hit double figures tomorrow so it was a special birthday. She would have to walk to the GPO and post Amala's card there. She would leave the car because the quickest way was through the snicket past the market and across the pedestrian precinct. Her stomach told her it was hours since lunch. She dipped into the nearest carrier bag, pulled out a sizeable chocolate bar and slipped it into her pocket.

In the precinct, she came across Fran Mitchell, dutifully heeding the ban on cycling there and wheeling his machine. His luminous green cycling shorts and garish jacket made him noticeable and instantly recognizable and she had waved to him automatically. Reluctantly, she went over to speak to him. They stood with the cycle between them as she asked after the progress of the Australian visas. He said there had been very little, then volunteered that his sister had rung from the flat where she had been billeted on Mitchell's sister Siobhan. 'She says she hates it there. She wants to know if I'll swap with her.'

'Will you?'

Fran shook his head. 'No fear! I know when I'm well off.'

'So, where have you been today?'

He grimaced. 'I wanted to get to Settle but I only made it to Skipton.' He added hurriedly, 'I could easily do the distance but there was a strong headwind all the way there that slowed me down.'

'Better than all the way back when you're tired.'

'I suppose so. Anyway, it had dropped by then.' He lifted a paper bag out of his saddlebag. It had the name and logo of a Skipton confectioner. Fran opened the top to display chocolate teddy bears. 'I got these for the twins. I suppose I should have bought something for Dec and Kat as well.'

Shakila reached into her pocket and produced her own chocolate bar. She leaned over the bicycle and wedged it in beside the boy's offering. 'They can share that.' She moved away again quickly. After a day's hard cycling his body odour was unpleasant.

He thanked her, then said, 'I'm getting cold and stiffening up. Do you mind if I move on?'

She let him go. She had done her good deed for the day but it had not made her feel very happy. Her stomach growled. She posted the card and was hurrying back towards the snicket when Patrick Seddon sidled out of it, giving her a sheepish smile that seemed intended to allay suspicion. When she stopped in front of him, he was transfixed, the smile still in place but meaningless.

She refused to return it, merely demanding to know whether he had met his friends as usual at Gupte's warehouse on Monday evening.

He relaxed enough to nod. So, progress. When she had interviewed him at the station he had denied knowing the name of the building. 'Did you keep obbo without arousing their suspicions as I told you?' He nodded again. 'I suppose you know the place went up in flames on Monday night?'

A further nod. Time for an open-ended question. 'And what do you and your pals know about that?'

The boy's face turned so white that she thought he might faint. Shakila scolded herself for not thinking this out before. There were several old warehouses in the same area, adapted barns and shacks that had been used to hold wool as it waited to be packed on to the backs of horses. The animals had made a track up the valley side and down into the market in town that was still used by hikers now. A shot in the dark had found its target. How mobile were these boys?

She asked the cringing youth, who admitted that they had 'an old banger'. Had she found the Yorkshire arsonist – or arsonists – all on her own? She felt a sudden, enormous relief.

When she had eventually seen him on Tuesday morning, she had told Mitchell that Seddon's friends got their weekly supplies on Monday nights, that Seddon was their lookout, and that, not being able to find her CI in the building, she had given the boy instructions to continue with their usual arrangement. He was to keep in touch with her. Mitchell had feared that Seddon would warn his friends. Shakila knew Seddon was more afraid that his friends would find out that he had ever spoken to the filth.

She had spent too long thinking things out, giving the lad time to work out an answer. 'We met a lot earlier than that – not long after dark. I went back home to set the table for Mum, ready for when Dad got home from work.'

'What time was that?'

''Bout half seven.'

'And your mates?'

He had no idea what they'd done. They'd sent him away. It was no fun to question him – no contest – though he did make an attempt to save face. 'They knew me mum'd ask questions if I dared be late back for me tea. She'd want to know what'd kept me.'

Shakila realized that, though these youths might well have been responsible for their local fire, it would be more likely because of a dropped cigarette end than because of a master plan to terrorize major properties throughout the county. She attempted again to get Seddon to identify his friends. On Tuesday he had purported to know only two of the six names. She had discovered their addresses and enquired at all the likely schools. One had left his reputation behind him at his comprehensive. The other, surprisingly, was a sixth former at one of the town's two grammar schools, studying for three A-levels. Seddon volunteered now that the other four were 'a bit older'.

After arranging to see him at the station the following day – in the afternoon since no school or job of work prevented him – she let him go. He heaved a deep sigh. 'If I'd left them bloody CDs alone I wouldn't be 'aving any o' this. You wouldn't even have heard of me.'

Shakila wandered back to her car feeling no happier than her victim.

In the opulent foyer of Burton's Financial Services sat an obliging receptionist. She summoned their employee, Becca Lambert, at DC Taylor's request. Jennifer had formed a mental picture of her quarry, based to some extent on the besotted expression on the face of Dorian Shaw whenever he mentioned her. She was surprised when the receptionist indicated with a smile and a nod towards the woman descending the stairs, that here Miss Lambert was.

For a moment, Jennifer felt that she recognized her but she could recall no occasion when they might have met. Not a beauty, she decided. The woman obviously considered that the surplus weight she carried was no bar to wearing fashionable and rather brief clothing. She almost got away with it. The casual sweater showed a tantalizing but not indecent amount of cleavage. The hair was good, thick and holding its shape because it was expertly cut. The skin, she saw as the woman came closer, was open-pored but blemish-free. The mouth was small with two large square incisors which rested over the lower lip.

Where was her attraction then? Perhaps in her self-confident manner which promised assertiveness and made her someone with whom you would not take too many liberties. Dorian Shaw was a little above middle height but Jennifer thought that this woman would be the taller of the two. She was well muscled and walked with a spring in her step even at the end of a working day.

Jennifer shook her hand. 'You look like a games player.' This appeared not to be the greeting that Becca expected. Jennifer smiled, pleased that she too had administered a small surprise.

'Well, some track and field. I throw a mean javelin.'

Light dawned in Jennifer's head. 'For Yorkshire? I remember you – in the *Clarion*, in the summer. There was a picture, with your mother looking very proud and you looking very embarrassed.'

Becca acknowledged this with a facial movement that was half grin and half grimace. 'She's pleased if I win but she'd really prefer me to do something a bit more lady-like, a little gentle – and successful – tennis, for instance.' Jennifer smiled. She had been wondering about the sweater's neckline in January, but the girl's revved-up metabolism was obviously keeping her warm.

Becca looked up, her forehead wrinkled. 'Is something wrong? Have I done something I shouldn't? Or – oh! Is it about Dorian's missing patient?'

Jennifer nodded. 'Is there somewhere we can talk? It probably won't take long. I know you're going "off with the girls", I think Mr Shaw said.'

The reply to this was a sly grin. 'Well, there might be some girls, I suppose. We're meeting in the Drum and Monkey, but not till seven.' Jennifer made no comment. The low-cut jumper was further explained. 'What I usually do till then is lay a good foundation for a few drinks.'

'And you still throw a javelin for the county?'

'I only said a few.'

At the thought of food, Jennifer realized that she was extremely hungry. She realized too that there was more to be discovered about the situation between this woman and Dorian Shaw. 'I'm starving. Suppose we talk and eat together till then? Pizzas over the road?'

The place had hardly begun its evening shift and several tables in conveniently private alcoves were still free. Jennifer was having difficulty in keeping her tone friendly. After the short interview with him, she had summed up Dorian Shaw as a wimp. She thought again of the pathetic row of frequently changed socks and the sweaty feet that he had been sad enough to mention. Still, she resented Becca's assumption that she would acquiesce in this deceitful meeting with other men. Dorian seemed good-hearted and deserved better. She made an effort.

'I usually try to spend this bit of the evening with my kids but they're at the cinema with my mother-in-law tonight.' She waited for a similarly trivial confidence. When it was not forthcoming, she asked, 'What's your relationship with Dorian Shaw?'

'Is that what you came to ask?'

If she apologized, Jennifer knew that the easy atmosphere would be lost. 'You don't have to answer if it's awkward.'

Becca seemed not to have been offended.

'It's only awkward because I don't know the answer. We're living together for the moment. I think he'd tell you that that's permanent and that we'll eventually get married. I'm not sure that that's what I have in mind.'

Because she was genuinely curious, Jennifer pursued the subject further. 'How did you meet?'

'Dorian fixed it.'

'Fixed it?'

Becca cast up her eyes. 'He tried to chat me up in the street a couple of times when he first moved into his flat. I had one further down the road, opposite the school playing fields. He annoyed me at first and I snubbed him.'

'So, how did he fix things?'

She laughed. 'You won't believe this. He put a couple of books into a parcel and sent it to himself at my address. He must have thought there was a faint chance that I wouldn't see through it – Newlands Court and Newlands Buildings. His number's 12 and mine was 21. I thought it was quite sweet and at least it was a bit more original than his usual chat-up lines. I took it round. It seemed a bit churlish to hand it back to the postman when he'd taken so much trouble. So...' She held out her hands, inviting Jennifer to imagine the outcome and almost knocking their pizzas out of the hovering waiter's hands.

Order restored, she continued. 'He opened

some wine and asked me out. I'd just had a huge barney with my mother and needed to moan about her to someone ... so, we just drifted to where we are now.'

'And you still aren't sure about the parcel?'

'Oh, I am. The words were written in block capitals but he'd crossed the 7 in the postcode like he always does and written a Continental figure 1 with a long tail.'

'Did you tell him you knew?'

She shook her head. 'No. He'd have been embarrassed.'

Jennifer altered her assessment of her companion from spiteful to merely spoiled and insensitive and said, 'I'd better ask what I was sent to ask you. You took a phone call from Simon Denton on Monday afternoon.' Becca nodded. 'Would you give me the exact words as far as you remember them?'

She screwed up her eyes and mouth as a small child does when trying to please adults with his mental efforts. 'He said sorry to mess Dorian about when he'd already given up time to help him. He said he had to speak to someone else on the same subject. This person–'

'Did he give a name?'

Becca shook her head. 'He just said he would come to the Woolpack and would Dorian meet him there.'

'This person – he or she?'

'A man. Simon promised he wouldn't keep Dorian long because he had to drive home again to Leeds and snow was promised. I hadn't heard we were having snow, and we didn't. I didn't know what he was talking about – I assume it was about the adoption business.'

'You knew about that? Dorian had told you?'

'Not then but he explained afterwards.'

'Any particular reason?'

'That he didn't tell me at first, you mean? You'll have to ask him. We only met in passing this week. Sometimes the shifts he has to work are really unreasonable.'

'And then you went back to work. So, when did you give this message to Dorian?'

'I rang him at the nurses' station in his ward as soon as I'd given him time to get there. It was probably about three o'clock. I didn't go back to work though. I started a migraine and rang in sick.'

'But you went out in the evening.'

'Yes. If you treat it in time, migraine doesn't last long. Is all this going to help you find this Simon?'

Jennifer shrugged. 'I've no idea, but the more you know about a whole situation, the more chance you have of finding the bits of information you need. That's a text from my boss's bible. Did you go to bed?'

'No. I sat around, waiting for my pills to

work, then I went next door to check on the cat.' She anticipated Jennifer's interruption. 'They're away next door so I'm feeding it. It's pregnant so I don't want the kittens born outside – they'd freeze to death. I love cats but we can't have one. You can't coop it up in a flat, unless you live on the ground floor...'

Jennifer allotted Becca another point in her favour but brought her back to the subject. 'What time did Simon say he'd be in the pub?'

'About nine.'

'And he said he was going to drive back to Leeds? That pub's on the Leeds road, isn't it?'

'I don't know. I always use the ones in town where there's more going on.'

Jennifer put down her knife and fork and looked at her watch. 'It's time I went. You don't know what Simon drives, I suppose? Never mind. Enjoy your evening. Oh, by the way, don't be so dismissive of tennis. It's kept me fit for a good many years – or maybe that was the water skiing. Thanks for your time.' Becca was still blinking as Jennifer disappeared through the door.

DC Caroline Jackson was making preparations for her return to work to a background of music that did not appeal to her. Her husband was aware that she was tolerating it

142

as part of the lot that fell to a musician's wife and that she was shutting it out by concentrating on the contents of the bag she always took with her on duty.

He heard her sigh, though, as he rose at the end of the first track on his compact disc and began to play it again from the beginning. He smiled to himself as he saw her relief when the doorbell rang. Now she could go to let in Declan Mitchell who was arriving for his piano lesson. Whilst they greeted one another and the boy hung his coat in the hall, Cavill read through the notes that he had made on Béla Bartók's piano sonata.

'The sonata shares, with the suite and the first concerto, an approach to writing for the piano that is essentially percussive.' That was reasonably OK. 'Ostinatos abound and tightly packed tone clusters take on a purely colouristic function...' Would that grab his readers? He thought not. '...the thematic content is appropriately shortbreathed; there is no room for grand rhetorical statements as the constant insistence of the rhythmic pulse presses the music ever onward.'

Cavill sighed. It was all much too precious.

Declan came into the music room and stood listening, his nose wrinkling. 'That music sounds as if it's in a hurry.' It did. That was exactly what Cavill had been trying to say. 'There isn't much tune, is there? It's just a rhythm – you could play it on a drum even.'

'Do you like it?'

Declan considered. 'I'm not sure. Can you play it?'

Cavill grinned. 'I hope so. I've got to play three of Bartok's pieces in a concert in London in three weeks.'

'Where did Bartok come from?'

'Hungary.' He indicated his notes. 'I'm trying to write something about the pieces to put in the programme.'

Declan nodded solemnly, thought for a moment, then asked, 'Why? Will that make the audience like them any better?'

Cavill laughed, relaxed and put his papers away. 'Declan, you're a breath of fresh air. I'm trying to help the audience to understand the music. You've just shown me why what I'm writing fails to do that.'

Not sure how he had achieved this useful purpose, the boy changed the subject. 'Mr Jackson, do I have to learn the piano?'

Cavill was startled. 'I suppose not – but I thought you enjoyed your music.'

'I do, but I like flutes and clarinets better than pianos.'

'They aren't any easier to play well. You'd have to do just as much practice.'

Declan sought the technical terms he thought his teacher required, then gave up and explained himself in his own. 'I know, but I like echoing music better than plinky-plonky or scraping music.'

Cavill bit his lip. 'That sounds like a good reason for learning to play a woodwind instrument. I'll have a word with your parents. Now, shall we see how much plinking and plonking you've done on this week's piece?'

Caroline picked up her belongings and left the two of them to their lesson. Cavill listened critically to his pupil's rendering of a collection of chromatic scales and a slightly simplified version of part of a Chopin nocturne. He enjoyed teaching the boy and felt that Declan too enjoyed his lessons and found pleasure in playing. He had good musician's hands, the fingers long, strong and broad-tipped for an eleven-year-old, a big advantage to a pianist. He had played the Chopin fluently and sensitively, as far as the simple little tune allowed.

When the hour was up, Caroline returned, offering to take over Cavill's task of driving the boy home. Gratefully, he accepted. While she was out, he would translate his technobabble on Bartok into a commentary that Declan and his family might understand. Caroline's agenda, once the boy was safely returned to his family, was to find out what she would be facing when she went back to work the next day.

Sprawled in an easy chair by the fire, Virginia Mitchell came to the end of the chapter she was reading. Returning reluctantly to the real world in her own sitting room, she closed her book and became aware of Fran's voice coming from the entrance hall. He had come in half an hour or so ago from his day's cycling. After politely sticking his head round her door to announce his return he had disappeared to shower and change. Now, he was apparently speaking by telephone to his parents. She rose to close the door and give him some privacy but halted before she reached it.

'...Uncle Benny's the same as always – but he's getting quite fat. He's very tidy, which is a good job because Auntie Ginny scatters her belongings all over the house.' If he noticed the sound of the door closing now, he would realize he had been overheard and be embarrassed. She sat down again, unable to stop listening because she was trying not to. 'I've met some really spooky people. There's a man I play chess with who's a friend of PC Beardsmore. Oh, and a weird lady who's in Grandma's ward at the hospital. She thinks the Queen is her friend and she's told Grandma that Prince Edward is her lost son. She says you only have to look at him. I don't think she realizes that Charles and the others are in their fifties somewhere... My bike? It's in the shed. Yes, it's a good shed and a posh lock. Any news of the visa yet?... No, it's good here. I don't mind how long I stay, but they might. Declan and Michael are having to share a bedroom. I think Dec was hoping to be in with me. I'm glad he isn't. He throws his stuff around as well.'

Virginia wished her son too might be eavesdropping on this salutary conversation. Since he seemed to be taking Fran as a role model it would be useful to know that he was condemned by him in this respect. She glanced at her watch. She had things to do and couldn't stay here any longer. She called, raising her voice: 'Is that you, Fran? However long have I been asleep?' She hoped that, by turning her face-saver into a question, she had avoided actually telling a lie.

A long run and a good meal had done much to reconcile Clement to both his work and his colleagues. Nevertheless, he completed the plan he had made earlier and, at eight o'clock, was in his local pub behind a tankard of best bitter. He was not especially gregarious and had always preferred the company of just a couple of friends to being one of a large crowd. He had avoided the group round the fire, therefore, and seated himself in a quiet corner near a man whose face he half recognized. Pleasantries were exchanged and then both men drank in a companionable silence.

The conversation on the other side of the saloon bar had turned to the recent fire. The nine days' wonder was, after all, only on its second day, Clement supposed. The talk roused his companion from his reverie and revealed him to be one of the fire fighters. He addressed his remarks to Clement in an undertone, patently not wishing to be set upon by the gossip-mongers. 'They don't know the half of it. Burning to death must be the most agonizing way to go. I once went in and found a woman in tatters, lying on the ground. Her hair and eyelids were burnt off and her skin was dripping from her body like melted wax. She was alive, but begging to be killed to take the pain away. I was carrying my pickaxe and, just for a second, I considered doing it – but I couldn't. Was I a coward or what?'

The man had closed his eyes and failed to see Clement's sympathetic shake of the head. 'A body doesn't stand a chance against the appetite of a fire. It's just more fuel for the flames. We had some police help for this last job.'

Clement raised an eyebrow. 'Is that right? They do have their uses then.'

'They were bloody brilliant. We couldn't use the ladder wagon.' He waved a hand at Clement's enquiring expression. 'Too technical to explain, but we had to drag and stretch the hose up two lots of stairs. Some-one went to smash windows for ventilation and cooling because our low air bells were all going, giving us the five-minute warning. We radioed for fresh crew. They didn't come because we'd had two more calls to smaller fires.

'Then a fat bloke in a duffle got his phone out.' Clement hid a smile. 'Four uniformed PCs arrived out of nowhere. We lent them what protection we had and they got stuck in, dragging and winding the hoses – muscles like ropes. The fat bloke was some sort of boss man but he mucked in with the rest. We wouldn't let 'em any further than the top landing.' The man took a long draught from his glass hoping to wash away his memories. Clement saw that he needed this outlet for the fears he had to repress every active work-ing day and was happy to listen as he dis-posed of his own modest half-pint.

'When we'd breeched the corridor door, it was like going into the flames of hell. They were blocking the view of everything.'

'But you'd got your water supply in place by then.'

The man sniffed derisively. 'Didn't help us personally. You water flames? Steam fills the place. Your mask gets fogged over and you try not to get boiled alive.'

As he described his release from the situation, the man relaxed. 'When we came out a' Monday night, our masks were half melted, moulded to our faces. Everything you looked at seemed to have dark edges. You felt as if the veins in your head were bursting and your legs wouldn't hold you – and the bloody air tasted so sweet – you could understand why fancy talkers say it's like wine.'

Wonderingly, Clement asked, 'Why do you do it?'

He received the stock answer. 'Somebody has to.' Then, with a shrug and a grin, 'And because there's a streak in me that just loves living on the edge. I don't take back a word about the horror of it – but it's just so bloody exciting.'

Clement saw on his face an expression he had often seen on both Mitchell's and Shakila's. He envied them. He wished he could feel so involved and driven. He pulled out his wallet and pushed his warrant across the table. 'I appreciate your compliments to our chaps. I'll make sure they're passed on.'

Arrived at the Mitchells' house, Caroline gave only a brief answer to their polite enquiries about her holiday before asking for an update on the matters she would be dealing with the next day.

Mitchell obliged with a quick summary of most of the open files, thanking the gods because almost all his team had the same

150

positive attitude to their work as Caroline. Perhaps Caroline was a shade too keen, he decided when she refused his home brew in favour of his offer of coffee.

Sprawled in a comfortable armchair in his little study, she leafed through the top file of a pile on his desk. 'So,' she asked, as he came back with his tray, 'your missing student has not been roasted in a tatty warehouse fire. Where and when did he turn up?'

'A phone call from his mother just as I was leaving the shop.'

'What had happened to him?'

Mitchell sniffed disgustedly. 'Depends who you believe. Went on the bender of his life according to his friends. Had his virtuous drinks spiked according to his doting parents. The parents at least gave a sober account but his friends gave an unbiased one. Either way, his mates took him home and when he hadn't come round thirty-six hours later they got worried. It had taken them more than half that time to become compos mentis themselves. They took him to hospital and dumped him there in a corridor. They say they left a slip of paper with his name and address but no one found it.'

'What about his girl?'

'Ask Shakila. She went there. Apparently it's not the first time he's got legless and this last time is the end of the affair as far as she's concerned.'

Caroline grinned. 'Great. Now all we need is for your Leeds friend to turn up and then I can have a calm day tomorrow to break me in again. Tell me about the fire. I only know what the TV news has told everybody.'

'OK. You know almost as much as we do and there's a bit more in the file about what the fire investigator told me earlier today–'

'You've written it up already?'

'If I weren't such an honest man, I'd say yes.'

'You mean, if you thought I'd believe you, you would.'

'He kindly gave me a sheaf of notes which Shakila has taken home for bedtime reading – under pain of death if she doesn't return them tomorrow morning.'

'Was there a forced entry?'

'There was only a noddy lock on the door.'

'Alarms intercepted?'

'You're joking! Gupte hasn't heard of alarms. Go and look at the place.'

'I don't suppose they'll let me.'

'They do think it's arson. They looked for a long fuse, a charred trail of twisted paper or rags. They found debris that might have been that, but they also found places un-affected by the fire that had been sprinkled with petrol. Some distance away there was a reeking garden spray.'

'The Yorkshire arsonist then?'

Mitchell shrugged. 'I'm not sure. In any particular place, an insurance scam or vandalism or spite against someone seems more likely than a deranged pyromaniac, even when there's one about.'

'And the bodies?'

'Dr Holland has some scraps of information about the Asian victim. I was going to send Jennifer to the second PM but she gave me a quick call to say that Dr Holland was involved in a traffic accident on his way back from court. Nothing too disastrous – cuts and a sprained ankle – but the X-rays and so on didn't leave enough evening to do the job properly. Anyway, I don't suppose he'd have been at his most efficient after all that.'

Caroline held out her cup for a refill. 'It always amazes me that a blazing inferno can be put out by what appears to be just a dribble of water through a thin hosepipe.'

'It doesn't take much to put out a fire in an enclosed space. Water expands into steam that's seventeen hundred times the volume.'

Caroline grinned. 'You sound quite the expert – but only because you've been talking to one.'

'Yes, but I read all his notes and I've learnt them by heart as I've just proved. What else does it take to make me an expert?'

Virginia appeared at the door, a copy of that day's *Clarion* in her hand. 'Is this private? I'm tired of my own company.' Mitchell slid out of his comfortable chair and offered it, perching himself on a stool. 'I thought you'd like to see how interested the local media are in all that you're doing.'

Mitchell spread the relevant pages on his desk so that Caroline could read over his shoulder. Suddenly, he laughed.

'What's funny?'

'This reporter who's filled nearly a page with pictures of a Mrs Baxter and Mrs Baxter's sister and their inane remarks.'

'What about him?'

'He's called Wayne Baxter.'

Virginia smiled. 'You've got an honourable mention yourself.' She pointed. 'He says you're playing your cards close to your chest. I suppose that means you wouldn't answer his questions.'

'That should get me a dishonourable mention. Anyway, I never played cards in my life. Why waste precious evenings holding a fistful of bits of cardboard and wondering which ones to put on the table? Nearly as daft as pushing bits of imitation ivory across a chessboard, but don't tell Fran I said that – or Beardsmore either.'

Virginia picked up the newspaper and began to refold it. 'The *Clarion* won't be very pleased that there's been another fire today. By the time the next issue's out, the news will be a week old.'

Mitchell was startled. 'What! When? Where?'

'Just north of the Derbyshire border and about mid-afternoon. It must have been set in daylight this time.'

Virginia settled herself into the proffered chair to listen as the two officers returned to their interrupted discussion.

'Is it possible,' Caroline asked, 'that the Cloughton fire setter was hoping to dispose of the warehouse owner?'

'Anything's possible. There's a report in the file from one of the uniforms. He interviewed someone who worked for Gupte and who said he was a slob and mean with it. He only makes a profit because his workforce isn't officially here. Oh, and Gupte claims that his wife is missing.'

'Proves she's a sensible woman.'

'Possibly, but Clement thinks, and I agree, that she's vulnerable. If she isn't lying on a slab in the morgue, then I think we've got to look for her too.'

'If he wasn't very expert, the other body you've got might be the arsonist himself.'

The two officers blinked at Virginia's interruption. As they considered her suggestion, Fran appeared, clad in his dressing gown. 'Auntie Ginny said you wanted me.'

'That's right. You might be able to help me again. It might be worth a pint of my home brew. Have a good ride today?'

'Sort of. Didn't get to Settle because of the wind. I turned round in Skipton. Got the twins some chocolate teddy bears from my favourite sweet shop there.'

Caroline got up to go. 'I'll leave you to your cross-examination, Fran. Cavill will think I've left him. I'll see you in the morning, sir.'

Virginia went with her to the front door and Fran, feeling very important, answered questions, first about the man whose portrait he had drawn and then about the lorry which had transported him apparently to oblivion.

## Chapter Five

On Thursday morning, Clement surprised Mitchell by being the first to arrive in his office. Though rarely late, the DC was seldom before time since he had usually run from home and needed to shower, change his clothes and devour a second breakfast before presenting himself.

Mitchell raised an eyebrow and hazarded a reason for this break from custom. 'You've got a theory that's too harebrained to parade in front of everyone else without getting my backing first?'

Clement gave a wan grin and shook his

head. 'I did wonder if the fire was a suicide bid by Gupte's wife–'

'We don't know yet whether it's her body.'

'True. Anyway, I've abandoned that idea.' He gave his CI a flavour of the confidences he had received from the fireman the night before.

Mitchell nodded. 'It's more likely, if she did start the fire, that it was her revenge on her husband and that she failed to make her escape.'

Clement sighed. 'I suppose so. I'll stop having theories and go back to the only thing I'm good at – chatting up old ladies.'

'You are good at it.' Mitchell saw that more was needed. 'There are lonely single people around every situation we have to deal with. They find their reason for living through involving themselves in other people's lives. Often, but not always, they're women. They know a lot of what we need to know. They're usually considered a nuisance and are used to being sidelined. They find you sympathetic and without them we couldn't do our job so easily. Stay with Salma Gupte's friend. She might crack the case for us.'

Clement's mouth turned down at the corners. 'Sir, I know all that – but it's all I'm ever commended for. I feel...'

Mitchell was used to thinking on his feet. Clement would do a more efficient job if he was allowed to unburden himself. Since his young wife had died giving birth to their first son, he had been subject to mild fits of depression. Such things were not supposed to happen in the twenty-first century. The efficient Sergeant Taylor equated depression with fecklessness and made her feelings plain. Her arrival was imminent and relations between her and Clement would deteriorate further if she interrupted his soul-baring.

The team needed Clement. Shakila and Mitchell himself took risks, acted on impulse. His troubled DC, together with Caroline, balanced the group. Thank all the gods he was getting her back this morning.

He took a deep breath. 'Look, Adrian, having Shakila and myself out on a limb is about all the tree will bear. We provide the dramatics. You and Caroline inject a dose of sanity – and sensitivity – into the team. It works because, between us, we've got it all.'

Mitchell saw that Clement had been expecting a pep talk rather than an affirmation, and followed up his advantage. 'I can't give you a personality transplant and I don't want to. I know, because they've said so, that Caroline rates you – and Shakila does too. Jennifer doesn't. If I tried to tell you otherwise, you wouldn't believe me. But, do you like her? When I send two officers out together, I expect them to spark each other off, get the best out of each other

– and the job done. When you and Jennifer are a pair, you're fed up, looking for a put-down from her. She's looking for resentment and wound-licking from you. Only the two of you can put things right.'

'Yes, but have you said all this to her?'

Mitchell's tone was sharp. 'That's my business and hers.'

'So, you think it's mostly my fault? You think–'

Mitchell put up a hand to stem the stream of self-pity. 'Adrian, I've taken Jennifer to task about a great many things, but not this situation because she's never come whinging to me about it. When she wants to discuss it with me then I'll give her the benefit of my opinion. Think about this. When Joanne was alive, did you respect one another?'

'Of course we did.'

'So, you don't really want a change of your basic nature?'

'I wouldn't if I got some respect for what I do.'

'Do you respect what you do?'

'What, being good with old ladies?'

Mitchell the counsellor departed. Mitchell the hothead came in. The door opened and his sergeant presented herself as he exploded. 'Bloody hellfire, Adrian! Are you a DC or a parrot?' Clement walked over to the window and gazed out unseeing. Jennifer sat down and began turning the pages of her notebook. After some moments, Clement took the chair furthest from hers.

The excitement of the Mitchell children when, after breakfast, Fran handed over his present of chocolate, was something akin to Christmas morning. Sweets were an occasional treat and Virginia had insisted that cereal and orange juice should be safely consumed before the gifts were offered. Fran seemed pleased to have given so much pleasure.

Usually anxious to make every experience a learning experience, Virginia suggested, 'I think we should find out where this chocolate came from before we eat it.' The children's faces were resigned, but, seeing Fran's expression, their mother hastily sent the older two in search of the atlas. She turned back to her nephew. 'What's wrong?'

Fran was definitely upset. 'Where do you think it came from? It's from Hickory's chocolate shop in Skipton. It says so on the bag. Look! I'd have saved the receipt if I'd known you'd–'

Virginia was appalled. He thought she had accused him of stealing. She hastened to placate him. 'Of course it does.' He was still thrusting the torn remains of the green and white paper bag at her. 'Michael can only read that with help and even Declan has only a vague idea where Skipton is.' She had intended to find Africa and point out to the twins that cocoa wouldn't grow in the UK. It seemed better to stay with Skipton for now. 'I want them to find it on the map.'

Fran remained scarlet-faced as Declan and Caitlin returned, triumphantly, bearing the huge volume between them. 'Sorry, kids. I didn't mean to land you with a geography lesson.' His tone was insolent.

Virginia gave him a hard stare. 'Francis, I actually meant to make a little ceremony of your kind gift as well as trying to teach these youngsters something new. I'm not quite sure what interpretation you put on my remarks but I think your reaction to them inappropriate.' Her tone, as well as her use of the boy's full name, indicated her annoyance.

Fran recovered himself and apologized all round, then set himself to helping Michael with letters. 'What does Skipton begin with?' he asked. The twins hissed at him. 'Now, what comes next?' He repeated the name with emphasis on the second letter.

Sinead demanded, 'Is it curly C or kicking K?' Together they spelt out the whole name and Virginia arranged papers over the map until only a small section was left showing. Even so, it took the twins a whole minute to find the town whilst Declan and Caitlin sighed impatiently.

However, all was sweetness and light in every sense when the chocolate was eventually unwrapped. Virginia decided she had been hard on Fran. He had left behind his school, his friends and his family and, until now, had behaved impeccably. This morning was only a glitch and nothing compared with what her sister-in-law, Siobhan, was enduring from Fran's sister Mairead. Even so, she had enough work looking after four children without a fractious and maybe disorientated nephew. She willed the other Mitchell family's visas to arrive swiftly so that the reunited family could embark on their adventure on the other side of the world.

Watching a post-mortem was not Mitchell's favourite form of entertainment, though the two corpses in this case had troubled him less than usual. Yesterday's had been so unlike a person that he had not been able to identify with it. Nor had he felt his customary indignation on behalf of the victim whose life had been stolen. That body had not lain here on Dr Holland's table with a face, a shape, garments and adornments that revealed a personality. What the pathologist had been dealing with had been a biological specimen, a physical conundrum, and he had been welcome to it.

This morning's remains seemed more likely to give them some help. The body had been protected by its fellow victim's lying on top of it. Even part of the face was left. Mitchell scrutinized it, trying to recognize any feature from his nephew's drawing. 'Human bodies,' Dr Holland informed everyone, apropos of not very much, 'are extremely resistant to complete destruction by fire.'

Mitchell supposed this was true. He was not sure that he would have picked yesterday's corpse out of the hot debris and recognized it as the remains of a person, yet they had already used the snippets of information that the pathologist had thrown to them as he worked. When the results came from the samples sent to the lab at Wetherby they would learn still more.

His hands busy with routine incisions and removals, Dr Holland began another of his familiar lecturettes. 'The word "coroner" comes from one that means keeper of the crown.'

The stolid holder of that office present in the lab today roused himself from his apparent lethargy to ask, 'How do you know?'

Mitchell glared at the man. 'Don't encourage him!'

The pathologist had his answer ready. 'A Kentish manuscript. "September Articles". 1149. In those days, coroners were always on the lookout for signs of suicide–'

'Why?' Mitchell asked, in spite of himself.

Dr Holland went on cutting as he raised his eyes. 'It was a crime against both God and the King. The punishment was to forfeit the estates of the offender/victim – a handy source of royal income. It meant destitution, of course, for the corpse's relations, but there was a rich reward if the coroner could please the King by finding evidence.'

The pathologist seemed to have found a great deal of evidence of his own. Rows of wide-necked bottles along a side table now contained blood, spinal fluid and tissue from brain, liver and kidneys. Holland had abandoned the anecdotal method of instruction and delivered a direct fact. 'Burn injuries in the living produce leucocytes to surround a wound, so we get hyperaemia and blisters... Hello!!'

His audience, who had been ignoring him, sprang to attention again at his change of tone. 'Remember what I said yesterday about blisters? Burns in death show no signs of vital reaction. They're hard and yellowish. If there are blisters, there's little or no fluid in them. I think there's just a minute amount here.' He stuck a syringe into an evil-looking yellow crust of skin. 'If there's enough to test, I suspect there'll be no positive protein reaction. It's my guess that chummy here didn't die by fire.'

After Dr Holland's pronouncement at the second postmortem, Mitchell had wished heartily that he had not agreed to Fran's tour of police headquarters at the end of that morning. He decided, however, to keep his promise. As this case, or possibly these cases, gathered momentum, there would be increasingly less time for such frivolities.

The boy had approved of his uncle's office as Mitchell had known he would. Another area of the station that had fascinated him was the custody suite with its charge room and cells. Fran had made some telling comparisons. 'It's a bit like the waiting area in A&E at the hospital,' and later, 'It's about as comfortable as a station waiting room. It's OK to be here if you've done what you're accused of but a bit rough for those who haven't.'

Mitchell supposed the area was a bit short on comfort and luxury. 'Don't worry,' he'd assured Fran. 'The place has a hard purpose and not many folk get here who don't deserve it. Lots of them are regulars.' He had the impression that the lad had not enjoyed this brush with harsh reality and that he regretted his impulse to ask to be brought here. He had better take him to the canteen to cancel out some of his bleak impressions. It was brash and noisy there but it was also cheerful and the food was impressive.

Uncle and nephew waited at the service counter, each eyeing the other's tray with satisfaction. They both understood that the loaded plates on one helped to justify those on the other. Fran noticed that a lively-looking plainclothes constable he recognized had joined the queue behind them. As they moved away from the counter, she spoke. 'Hi, Fran!'

Fran grinned and jerked his head towards his tray. 'Sorry I can't shake hands. Come and join us though.'

Mitchell eyed her curiously but politely seconded the invitation and soon his DC and his nephew were deep in conversation, leaving him to eat and listen in peace. Fran described his tour of the station. 'I didn't think the breathalyser would be a great grey cabinet that comes up to my chest. Uncle Benny let me be tested on it but I'd had no alcohol.' He cast a reproachful glance for this omission in Mitchell's direction.

'What else did you do?'

'I saw the cells. I didn't think they were too bad – better than I was expecting. That was until I sat on the bunk and the door was locked for a minute. Then it gave me the creeps. I saw one that hadn't been cleaned since they let the last person out. That was disgusting!'

Shakila grinned at Mitchell. 'He's obviously led a very sheltered life.'

Fran was determined to be on his best behaviour. 'It's a nasty building to have to work in but it must be very satisfying to be helping people all day.'

Shakila was not impressed by the nice manners. 'Huh! People call us for everything. If the toilet overflows they call us instead of a plumber. Once, a woman rang the desk sergeant and asked him how to baste a turkey. A few months ago I was chasing a thirteen-year-old and his mate. They'd stolen a car, holding its owner up with a replica gun, and drove it at eighty miles an hour – the car, not the gun – both on the motorway and off. When I eventually cornered the lad, hauled him out and searched him, he said, "Hey, what about my rights?" This job gives you a pretty jaundiced view of people. Everyone we deal with is either in trouble or making it!'

Shakila's grin belied her words and Fran laughed. They were all silent for some moments, the two officers eating with the speed and concentration of those who knew that a meal might have to be abandoned at any time.

Her plate empty, Shakila took up her social responsibilities once more, enquiring how Fran intended to spend his afternoon.

'I was hoping someone would invite me to speed around with them in a squad car, but...' He looked hopefully from one to the other officer. His uncle continued to chew stolidly. 'Oh well, I suppose I'll do a gentle loosening-up ride. I did sixty miles yesterday, so it'll just be a slow five or six today.'

167

'Got your eye on the Tour de France then?'

Fran nodded solemnly. 'Oh, yes.'

Her own remark had been flippant, but Shakila could see that the boy was perfectly serious. 'What's the longest ride you've ever done in a day?'

'About a hundred miles, but it was mostly flat, round the Vale of York.'

Shakila was obviously impressed and asked him if he had tried the new sports centre on the Bradford road out of Cloughton. 'It probably wasn't open last time you visited. How long is it since you were here last?'

Fran wrinkled his forehead, thinking. 'Months ago, in the autumn sometime. Might have been October half-term.'

Mitchell laid down his knife and fork. 'It was last September. I remember because you helped with the twins' birthday party.'

'Oh, yes.' He turned back to Shakila. 'Do you do sports?'

She shook her head. 'I try to keep fit, run the odd couple of miles with Caroline, but I'm not in your league or Clement's.'

Mitchell looked at his watch, then his nephew. 'Time that gentle training got started – or rather, it's time Shakila and I were back at work.' Shakila obediently rose and left them. Mitchell watched her go, his expression thoughtful.

Mitchell had called his team together for the unconventional hour of four in the afternoon, hoping that, by then, he would have received something in writing from Dr Holland. As he waited for them, he telephoned his wife.

'I'm intending to be pretty late tonight. Does that cause any problems?'

She thought not, '...except that this chap Cornish, who's coming to play his return match with Fran, will have to drink coffee made by me.'

'Fran can make it. It's his visitor.'

She laughed. 'OK then. Bye.' She knew better than to keep him chatting when there were two unidentified bodies lying in the lab.

'Don't ring off! This Cornish is a lorry driver, isn't he? We're interested in lorry drivers. I'm also quite anxious to meet a stranger who's knocking around with Fran whilst the lad's in our care, so I'll be home for at least part of the evening. It'll be work, though. I won't stay to be sociable.'

'Huh! There's nothing to stop you making coffee whilst you chat to a visitor. It'll put him off his guard.'

Mitchell replaced the receiver as a tap on the door preceded the arrival of the full complement of his team at once. They settled quickly, all facing him.

He knew what they were waiting for and held out empty hands. 'I haven't got it yet but he's on his way now. As usual he's going to give us a translation with additional thoughts – hopefully some of them relevant! So, in the meantime, where are we?'

Caroline, ever to the point, offered, 'We've two missing persons and two bodies in the morgue.'

'Gut instinct says to match them up but it worries me. I can't think of any reason why they should have been lying there together.'

Mitchell nodded his agreement with this remark from Jennifer and asked, 'Anyone have a suggestion – however unlikely?'

They looked at each other, everyone's gaze finally resting on Shakila as the most likely source of a wild idea. She had nothing to offer and Mitchell suspected that her thoughts were elsewhere. 'So what next?' he asked. After another silence, he answered himself. 'We follow Denton from leaving the hospital and getting into a lorry on Monday and see if the trail leads us to Gupte's warehouse.'

'Are we looking for Denton with the super's permission now?'

'Presumably someone from the Leeds force has seen his wife.'

Having spoken together, Clement and Jennifer each gestured to the other to continue.

Mitchell answered them both. 'Leeds have got all the details Louise Denton could give. They've also spoken to his adoptive parents. If Dr Holland confirms that Denton is our man, then Cloughton is the place where he was last seen and also where he was found, which definitely makes him our pigeon. Of course we shall liaise with Leeds – and have the good manners to let them know when we're on their patch. Let's look at the few things that we do know.' Now, hopefully, the team would be more forthcoming.

Clement led the way. 'He took a lift in a lorry only two minutes after leaving hospital. We've a witness to that. Dorian Shaw was going off duty and driving behind the lorry.'

'We've two witnesses. My nephew Francis was cycling in the same direction and overtook the lorry at the relevant time. He said he only glanced at it because he was coming up to an awkward junction. I suppose I should be pleased about that. He didn't see Shaw. He'd only met him in the hospital ward and wouldn't recognize his car. He did recognize Denton because he'd chatted to him when he visited my mother. He had the impression that the lift had been planned – that Denton had been expecting the lorry to be there.'

Jennifer added, 'The nurse knew him fairly well. He said Denton was a good-natured chap, chatted to patients who, like himself, had no visitors.'

'That was odd...' Clement realized he had interrupted the sergeant and glanced at her. She waved him on. 'Leeds isn't far. Why didn't his wife come over?'

'If Dr Holland brings us the news we're hoping for we can go and ask her tomorrow.'

Jennifer asked, 'What about the last phone call that Denton is supposed to have made to Dorian Shaw's woman?'

Mitchell was interested. 'Supposed to have made? Don't we believe her?'

'I'm neutral for now.'

'What's he supposed to have said?'

Mitchell allowed the question since Caroline had asked it. She could hardly have memorized the whole file in one day. 'It changed the arrangements for meeting Shaw to nine o'clock in the Woolpack. He said something had come up but didn't explain what.'

'No mention of a lorry driver?' Mitchell shook his head. 'And subject of proposed meeting to be found in the file, I suppose.'

Mitchell beamed at Caroline. 'You can take it home and keep it under your pillow, which reminds me – Shakila, have you returned the great thoughts of Dr Morton?' Shakila started and seemed to bring her mind back from a great distance. She let Mitchell's question repeat itself in her mind before reaching into her bag. 'I've got it here if anybody's needing it.'

To give her time to gather her thoughts, Caroline asked, 'Who's Dr Morton?'

Shakila hurriedly pulled out the sheets. 'He's a psychologist who's a fire investigator.' She offered the papers. 'Do you want to take this?' Caroline shook her head. Shakila looked round, saw that no one objected and pushed the sheaf away in her bag again. She had contributed nothing to the discussion until directly addressed. Mitchell gave her a hard stare. She was saved from his scrutiny by the arrival of Dr Holland.

Mitchell was well aware that the pathologist considered him a boor and that he was offended when both his official news and the entertainment that accompanied it were received with no show of enthusiasm. He could see that the man was overjoyed to find that, on this occasion, he had an audience of five. He perched on the corner of Mitchell's desk and beamed at them, his thick lenses refracting the light from Mitchell's desk lamp.

Perversely, Dr Holland had no entertainment for them. Pushing the file he had brought in with him across the desk towards the CI, he announced, 'In spite of the unpromising appearance of our two victims, each of them was able to tell me a story. Our lady was not burned to death. She died from a combination of smoke suffocation and carbon monoxide poisoning, both of which take effect quite quickly. Blood tests will confirm my opinion, but soot in the windpipe and lungs are sufficient evidence for now.

'Because she was lying face down, diagonally across the man's body, the middle area below her stomach was relatively undamaged. I believe, though, again, I need confirmation from Wetherby, that, very recently, this lady miscarried a reasonably advanced pregnancy, after which she received, I believe, no medical treatment.' He paused for breath.

Mitchell was groaning inwardly over the pathologist's convoluted sentences. It suddenly struck him that Beardsmore was right. The man had the aural equivalent of a photographic memory. He read – perhaps aloud – information and anecdotes from the computer screen and reproduced them at will at moments he thought appropriate – though, appropriate for what only Holland knew. Now, he was merely reciting to them the carefully balanced sentences of the main parts of his report.

Quickly, Mitchell took the opportunity that he was offered. 'Thank you, sir. Your last point is more useful at this moment than you realize. It means that we can probably identify the lady today.'

Reluctant to lose his audience, the pathologist hastened on. 'As I've already indicated to your CI, I believe that our gentleman probably did not arrive at the warehouse under his own steam. The nature of his blistering and the clean condition of his windpipe and lungs mean that he was dead before the fire touched him.'

Mitchell smiled grimly as his team reacted with surprise. The evidence of the blisters had been contained in a memo he had sent round to all of them as soon as he returned from the post-mortem.

Dr Holland was continuing. 'There were few specific features to identify the body. We didn't need the marked superciliary arches to indicate a male skull when our lady corpse had obligingly protected half of the penis. Most of the facial soft tissues were gone, leaving lots of charred ligaments. All the teeth are present and seem to show no abnormality except four small posterior cavities where fillings have been destroyed.'

'Is that too common to be any use for identification?' Mitchell asked, mainly to break the monotony of the pathologist's voice.

'Afraid so. Before proceeding to the stage of facial reconstruction–' now he had everyone's interest – 'I intend to call on Dr Keith Terry who has a special interest in dental forensics. Indeed, I have already done so. It has meant overtime for me since he required removal of the ligamental tags restricting the movement of the TM joints.' Mitchell's glare round his team both forbade a mocking groan of sympathy for the pathologist's extra work and defied anyone to hold up the tedious recital with questions about the nature of TM joints. 'I have sent the radio-graphics and photographs he requires and I have stressed the urgency.'

Here, Dr Holland's peroration came to an abrupt end. Perhaps he had remembered that more corpses awaited him. Leaving behind the copy of his report that he had brought for the file, he made his farewells and departed.

Jennifer and Caroline rose to follow him but Mitchell indicated that they should remain. 'We were interrupted and there's a bit more from me. Thanks to some thorough work from Adrian,' he told them, 'I think we can now assume that we've found Salma Gupte. I know you were all sloping off to finish your day having tea in the canteen. Sorry about that.' He handed action sheets to Caroline and Shakila who went off together.

'Adrian, go and find Gupte's GP and get everything you can from him. Let's see how many counts we can get that callous bastard of a husband on.' Clement, still blushing from his commendation, followed his col-leagues.

Jennifer regarded him enquiringly. 'No job for me?'

'Yes. Find out what the hell's eating Shakila.'

When Jennifer left, Mitchell went in search of Beardsmore. He found him eventually waiting at the bus stop opposite the station, on his way home, and offered him a lift in exchange for information on his chess-playing friend. Beardsmore accepted eagerly. 'I do have a car but it has a mind of its own. This morning it decided it wasn't coming to work with me. I don't know what I can tell you that you won't have put in the file already.'

'What you told me about Roger Cornish I didn't put on file. At the time it was just a personal matter. It may still be.' Beardsmore was fastening his seat belt. Guiltily, Mitchell did the same.

'I can't remember what I've already told you. I don't know any ill of him. I've played against him quite a few times – your lad will have to be good to beat him.'

Mitchell nodded. 'Yes, Fran's already lost twice.'

'Well, he's a bit of a loner. I suppose you have to like your own company. It's all you have when you're driving a lorry.' Beardsmore scratched his shiny head and tried to give Mitchell better value for his lift. 'He has a bit of a fetish about the soundness of his house. That might be because he's away a lot. I was there one match night when he had a spectacular row with his neighbour. The chap was putting concrete planters out to cheer the place up a bit because the doors open straight on to the street. Meaning it as a friendly gesture, he had put a couple under Roger's window sill. Roger went berserk because he said it was too near his vent brick.' Beardsmore scratched his head, trying to work out what sort of information Mitchell was looking for and why.

Mitchell asked, 'Do you know any of his friends?'

'He doesn't socialize much, but that doesn't make him a criminal. There was a big do for a fortieth – someone at the chess club the other week. There was food, booze and a mini-tournament. I would have thought he'd enjoy it but he wouldn't go...'

By the time they had reached Beardsmore's house Mitchell had become extremely dubious about Cornish's presence in his house when he was absent himself. As the young PC was about to open the passenger door, Mitchell turned to him. 'Bob, before you come in tomorrow, can you find some way of checking where Cornish went in his lorry on Wednesday?'

Beardsmore grinned. 'I wonder whether asking him might do the trick? Or do I have to be more discreet?'

'Make it a personal question then – don't let him think he's helping with enquiries ... and, if you could just keep an eye open when you have time...'

'Spare time? With the workload you give us?'

'You usually finish early enough to hang round the station making sure you don't miss anything. You're getting like Shakila.'

'I shall take that as a compliment.'

'I think I meant it as one. Actually, Bob, this is a favour I'm asking. I don't want it aired at any briefings.'

Beardsmore beamed. What Mitchell had thought might put him off had been the best card to play.

As Mitchell drove home, he told himself he was being ridiculous. What had he got against the man? Was he linking him unjustly with the driver who had spirited Simon Denton away? Out of the scores – possibly hundreds – of professional drivers in the Cloughton area, why should Cornish have been the one to pick Denton up? In any case, they had nothing yet to prove that Denton didn't climb out of the lorry after a few miles and go about his business. They knew far too little about far too few people in this case.

Fran Mitchell had lost his chess match

again, but was rather more sanguine about it than last time. Tonight his hopes had not been dashed because he had not expected to win – and he had lost by a much narrower margin. Cornish had spent another hour patiently replaying the game, pointing out all the threats to his pieces that the boy had failed to see and all the opportunities he had not taken.

Mitchell had arrived home soon after Cornish appeared and surprised Virginia by staying for supper. As Mitchell had directed, she had told Fran to set up the board in the dining room and she had left the hatch casually open so that a listening brief could be kept. She had absolutely forbidden any peering through.

When Fran brought his opponent into the sitting room to be introduced to his uncle, Mitchell was surprised. He had been expecting someone older and asked himself why. The man was frankly fat, not beefy but flabby. He had two quite separate chins, the lower spreading to the width of his face and the upper sitting like a plum on top of it. Nevertheless, the skin was totally unlined and Cornish was probably no older than late twenties.

In the sitting room, Fran was regaling his aunt with the story of his match. Mitchell took Cornish into the kitchen where the man overflowed a chair, his huge shoulders hunched and making a hollow to rest his head. He had made himself uglier by close-cropping his hair. Longer, it would have balanced his round face better. His manner was friendly enough, Mitchell supposed, and he might have been reasonably good-looking without all the weight. He had nice eyes and a pleasant expression – but then, so had Ted Bundy.

As the two men swapped stories about Cornish's chess and his own rugby, Mitchell kept asking himself whether his own continued presence here tonight meant he was losing his sense of proportion. Had he lost the plot? Where was the harm in this acquaintance of Beardsmore's? It was no use. He could not argue himself out of his anxiety.

The man talked easily but his mannerisms were nervous. He rested his hands over his huge thighs. If they had been less wide, Mitchell thought, he would have grasped them. The hands slid together, palms facing, and Cornish hid them between his knees. Most of the time, he kept his eyes on these hand movements. But then, many grossly overweight people felt unsure of themselves and of the reception they would be given. Casual clothes would have flattered the man more. The smart crisp shirt and conservative tie threw into relief his undisciplined body.

He must stop staring at the poor man. It was no wonder that he was twitchy. Turning away to stir the coffee, Mitchell invited, 'Tell me how you got into long distance lorry driving.'

It proved a long story. Like a lot of reserved and lonely people, once started Cornish could not stop talking. He had left school without qualifications. He hated being indoors. He liked driving. Then, his father had left him a little money and he had used it to qualify to drive a heavy goods vehicle. 'It wasn't an instant success, though.'

Pointing a podgy finger, he explained his problems. 'It was Catch 22. I had no experience, so no one would employ me, so how was I to get experience?'

Mitchell, carefully pouring water on coffee grounds, had nothing useful to suggest and simply asked, 'How did you?'

'Went on the knocker, but no dice.' He shook his head. 'Then I answered an agency newspaper ad. Rang them, then I went to see them. I offered them everything, days, nights, last-minute jobs and so on. So I got taken on. The gaffer, as everyone called him, was a bit casual. Told me not to tell anybody I was sent to that I was new. Said, "Don't hit anything as you leave though." He stopped, waiting for some appreciation of this jest. Mitchell did his best and managed a grin.

'One day, he asked me if I wanted to go on

the Continent. He needed a single man. Wives and girlfriends don't like it. That was a good time, a great life.'

He hauled his bulk to one side to allow Mitchell to reach for the sugar. Virginia had forgotten it since he allowed no one in the household to sully his coffee with it.

The movement made Cornish breathless as he continued his tale. 'I had to stop the long haul stuff, though. My back got bad and I couldn't do nine hours' driving in a day any more.'

'Was your boss understanding?'

Cornish sniffed. 'What do you think? I had a bit put by at that time though and some contacts – so I bought a truck of my own. I'm my own boss now so I can book myself up when my back's OK and go easy when it's bad. It's not such good money but there's nothing to spend it on. Reading and TV and chess don't cost much and that's what I mostly do.'

The coffee was now perfectly brewed, and Mitchell accepted when Cornish offered to carry it through. They joined Fran, who was still describing the new tricks he had learned to his aunt, and Virginia, who was trying not to look completely mystified.

Cornish said, quite apologetically, 'I'm afraid this coffee's too strong for me.' Virginia addressed the complaint by adding more milk and a further two spoonfuls of sugar.

Happy again, Cornish caught sight of Fran's pictures on the wall, mounted now in the frames they deserved. 'Are those your kids? Who drew them?'

When Fran claimed the pictures, Cornish whistled and deemed them worth the effort of hauling himself out of his armchair for a closer look.

Mitchell rose too. 'Hang on a minute.' He left the room but was back in a few moments with a duplicated copy of Fran's drawing of Simon Denton. He handed it to Cornish. 'Fran did this one too. The man's a friend of yours, isn't he?'

Cornish took the sheet and studied it. 'That what he says, is it?' He shrugged massive shoulders. 'Can't say as that I remember him from anywhere.' Mitchell had watched carefully, and had to admit that there had been no visible flash of recognition in Cornish's face. Fran took the sheet and returned it to his uncle, looking resentful.

When Cornish got up to leave, a little while later, Mitchell requested a lift. 'Don't go out of your way. Just drop me off at yours. I only want to be in Crellin Street, just round the corner.' He felt thankful that he knew his patch so well. Virginia's face remained deadpan. Mitchell knew that she would not call his bluff but he had a feeling that he would be pushing his luck if he asked her to fetch him back home. He wondered what he was hoping for. To see how the man drove and what it betrayed? To examine the house that the man guarded so carefully? Fran would surely have mentioned it if the lorry driver he saw had been Cornish – if, of course, he had seen the driver clearly and not just the lorry.

When he eventually arrived home, his house was in darkness. Ginny must really be annoyed then. She'd not only failed to collect him but hadn't even waited up for his return.

The following morning, Virginia seemed determined that the subject of Cornish should not arise again. She talked valiantly to the children as the family followed their usual routine at the start of the day. Mitchell came into the kitchen, absentmindedly picked up a sliver of bacon and put it in his mouth.

With no introduction to the subject, he began: 'He's single and always alone. I don't like it.'

This was met with stony silence. He reached out and stole another, bigger piece of bacon. Virginia slapped his hand, then turned back to the cooker.

Mitchell sighed. 'He had a job that he liked, that kept him in touch with other people. Three years ago, it went wrong because of health problems. Now, he's probably still paying off for the truck, not earning much, holding a grudge against his former employer – and only the TV and chess for consolation. Just the sort of chap we should all be following up–'

'Benny!!'

Caitlin appeared at the door. 'Are you cross with Daddy?'

Virginia began carrying food to the table. 'Not seriously. I just don't agree with everything he says.'

'You tell us we should discuss things reasonably when…' She caught her father's eye and subsided.

Mitchell sat down at the table and called the other children to join him. 'Well, the matches are played now. That should be the end of it.'

## Chapter Six

Mitchell's spirits rose the moment he stepped out of his front door on Friday morning. The cold stung his face, but the pale sunshine shone through the branches of the birches in the front garden. He looked up and saw that they were decorated with a rook's nest from the previous year, three torn plastic carrier bags and a magpie. Normally the bags would have annoyed him, but on this invigorating early morning they were part of the cheerful bustle of the day's beginning.

Thin lichen, spreading on the trees that grew along the street, had turned them as green as in summer, though they made winter patterns against the pale sky. If time had permitted, he would have walked to work. He guided his new Vectra to join the first of the journey's queues, at the junction where his road met the main route into town. His sanguine mood continued. As he lifted his gaze to the green and brown humps of moorland rising ahead above the morning chaos, he made a vow only to leave Cloughton if he was offered the chance to work in the Lake District – and perhaps not even then.

The motorist behind him roused him from this resolution and he turned his mind to his driving and his day's work. He knew it was going to be a day for being patient, letting the evidence they needed come to them, and he knew he had not the temperament for it.

He found Beardsmore hovering in the corridor outside his office. Without a greeting, he asked, 'Where was he then?'

Beardsmore shook his head. 'You didn't want a direct question. The best I could do was to arrange a quick drink with him at lunchtime. His back's bad today, so he's not driving.'

Ashamed of his abruptness, Mitchell grinned at his willing PC. 'Good man. Phone me when you know.' But he unlocked his office, grim-faced. He supposed a back might well not be in prime condition after its owner had set and escaped from a major fire. Then he admonished himself once again for his victimization of this unfortunate man and made preparations for the morning briefing.

He prayed that the first arrival would not be an aggrieved Clement and the prayer was half answered. Clement did arrive first but he seemed well satisfied with his task of taking the law's revenge on Mubarak Gupte. 'I don't think he is pulling an insurance scam,' he announced, settling himself in the chair that was usually Jennifer's. 'In two days of phone calls, I haven't found a company that he's dealt with. The neighbours support Sylvia Townsley's account of how he treated his wife but, as you might expect, no one wanted to get involved. They still don't. HOLMES hasn't found us anything. His crimes are nasty but private and his family obviously cover up for him. I think he was genuinely surprised that there were people in the warehouse when it was fired. Not that he cared. He said that if they were trespassing and pilfering then they deserved to be fried. He thought they wouldn't have taken anything because you need outlets and contacts for stuff like his. It's clever work apparently. We'd better remember that. He thinks either of the victims might well have caused all the damage with a fag end.'

'Well, we don't agree with him – unless one of them helped things along with accelerants applied with a spray can intended for weedkiller. Anyway, Denton was already dead – or at least he was when the fire got to him, though there's no proof that he wasn't killed after he'd started it. Not that I think he did. So, what about Gupte's wife?'

'Is the female body her?'

'Not officially yet, but I'd say so.'

'He doesn't think so.' Clement hastily scrambled out of his chair as Jennifer came in and took his more usual one. 'Gupte is a brute but I don't think he killed her.'

'Why not?' Mitchell held his breath. Jennifer's tone had been sharp.

Clement, however, was sure of his ground. 'Well, you'd think, if he'd done it, he'd pretend to be upset, play the grieving husband. What he is doing is storming around in a rage because he's been deprived of his servant-housekeeper. He thinks she's just part of his property.'

'What about the immigrants who're working for him?'

Clement looked pleased with himself. 'I've found two of them. One won't open his mouth at all. He probably speaks no English. The other won't shut up. He wants to do a deal. He'll tell all in exchange for work papers and permission to stay.' He handed Mitchell his report to stem the flow of questions.

Jennifer asked, 'Could our friend in the morgue be another of them?'

Mitchell shook his head. 'Dr Holland thought there was evidence that he was probably British and quite prosperous.'

'If the workers have been living in that shack they might be sleeping rough now.'

'They'll have frozen to death then. It's been bitter until today.' Mitchell turned back to Clement. 'Did you see Salma Gupte's GP?'

'Yes. He was horrified at the condition of her body, knew exactly what was going on and couldn't persuade her to admit it. He thinks it's quite possible Gupte's kicked her around again, probably with the deliberate intention of aborting his daughter. Proving it is something else. He says count on him for any evidence he has to give. He asked me if I'd let him know as soon as we had our ID. I didn't promise.'

'But said you'd do your best, no doubt.

Where are Shakila and Caroline? It's five minutes after time.'

'But it's a first offence.' Mitchell smiled. Clement could be relied on to defend Caroline and here came his distracting question. 'Do you think Gupte's subtle enough to continue his furious search for his wife if he's killed her?'

'I don't know about subtle. He's certainly sly enough. Don't forget he made the *Clarion* reporter think he was too distressed to talk to him.'

'True, but he didn't say what it was that was distressing him.'

The door opened and Shakila and Caroline crept in. Caroline said apologetically, 'We lost track of the time. Shakila was telling me a bit about a book on the psychology of arsonists that she's been reading and how she thinks it applies to our situation here. Sorry.'

Jennifer's sharp glance and tightened mouth told Mitchell that she resented Caroline's having been the recipient of the confidences from Shakila that she herself had been asked to obtain. He thanked providence that Shakila had not chosen to share her ideas with Clement. Now was not the time to enquire further into them.

He nodded his acceptance of Caroline's apology and briskly allotted the tasks for the morning. 'Dr Holland has obviously made the urgency of our situation clear to Wetherby. They're working on his samples now and have promised us at least a progress report for tomorrow.'

Action sheets were distributed. 'Jennifer, back to Dorian Shaw. Anything you can get, but especially details of Simon Denton's car or his alternative transport arrangements. Caroline, to his landlady in Cloughton. Report back to me personally, please.'

Caroline looked surprised that anything particularly important might be expected from this source. Mitchell's expression persuaded her to keep back her question.

Mitchell had cleared a satisfactory amount of paperwork by ten o'clock, the time for the daily link-up with the other local forces. He was ready to agree to any plan that the superintendent might have for the rest of his day. He would be marking time until they had the promised lab report and the investigation proper could at last begin. This tolerance of orders from above was soon put to the test. The Leeds force had invited Dr Morton, whose book had been quoted in this week's *Cloughton Clarion,* to address representatives from all the Yorkshire forces that afternoon.

'Misquoted,' Mitchell put in, 'according to DC Nazir who keeps Dr Morton's book under her pillow.'

'Whatever.' Superintendent Carroll waved a hand. 'He's lecturing in Leeds on the psychology of serial arson and its relevance to our Yorkshire perpetrator in particular. I think you and I should go.'

Mitchell thought that Shakila should go too. It would be an opportunity for him to find out what was dampening her usual keen interest in the rest of their enquiries. Besides, she seemed genuinely interested in the fire raiser. He opened his mouth to plead for her inclusion in the visit to Leeds.

Superintendent Carroll cut in to prevent the objections to his proposal that he was expecting. 'I've spent the last five years humouring you, Benny. Now I have a yen to nail this bugger, preferably for his work on our patch. Just humour me for a change. And, if she's not vital to this afternoon's work in Cloughton, bring young Nazir along. It'll keep her out of worse mischief.'

Mitchell smiled and graciously accepted the invitation for both of them. The smile returned when, in the intervals of filling in the rest of his hated forms, he recalled his ready agreement to the programme laid out for him and the shocked expression it had produced on his superintendent's face.

Shakila, when, in the early afternoon, she found herself wedged between her CI and a stranger in uniform, was extremely pleased

193

with her lot. The crown and pip on her neighbour's arm told her that he was a chief superintendent but he didn't intimidate her. They had all come to listen rather than to talk. What she had dreaded was being placed between Mitchell and Carroll. She would have been quite at ease conversing with either of them. Her embarrassment would have been because her physical presence between them would have inhibited their mutual whispered exchanges.

For some reason, she had expected a lecture hall, but the assembled company found themselves sitting round a vast table in a sort of conference room in the Leeds station. From the wall opposite, a row of faces stared at her, the first adorned with mutton chop whiskers and the last and most recent one reminding her of a test cricketer whose name temporarily escaped her. She supposed that the faces all belonged to past chief constables, but the print beneath the pictures was too far away and in some cases too faded to be read.

As she waited for something to happen, she wondered why she had been brought along here. She suspected that Mitchell had manoeuvred her inclusion in the party from Cloughton and that his motive was to discover what theory was obsessing and distracting her. She was annoyed with herself for letting it affect her general demeanour.

Was she obsessed with it? And, more importantly, was her preoccupation justified? She had made a fool of herself once already in the eyes of both these senior officers. Until she was certain about what she suspected, she determined to keep as low a profile as possible. She was not sure that anything she heard this afternoon would help her.

The current Leeds chief constable, not yet immortalized on the wall, entered the room accompanied by his guest. Shakila surveyed him with interest. This was the man whose ideas and opinions she had been imbibing for several weeks. It was uncanny to see him in the flesh. She decided that the photograph on his book jacket did him no favours.

'Well bred' was the phrase that entered her mind as she watched him. The man had regular features, small eyes, neat brows and a straight nose. His mouth was well shaped, with thin lips and regular teeth. He was in his late forties, Shakila guessed, with taut skin for his age. The hair was slightly receding but still thick and fine with a neat side parting.

The man nodded and smiled modestly in reply to the chief constable's fulsome welcome and introduction and began to speak. Mitchell, Carroll and Shakila found themselves addressed, although, not knowing their faces, Dr Morton did not embarrass them by looking in their direction.

'The attendees from Cloughton, if they read their local paper, will be under a misapprehension that I should like to correct before I speak to you all. The list of characteristics of fire setters attributed to me in the *Clarion* was certainly, in one sense, taken from my book. I was, however, in that passage, quoting from someone else's document, with which I proceeded to take issue.' Shakila was glad to have that puzzle solved. She wondered how many other of these guardians of the law had read the man's book in its entirety.

The voice was quiet but clear. The face had promised an Oxbridge accent but his North Midlands, disciplined-by-culture one suited it just as well. He spoke briskly with an air of controlled authority. However, he wore a red shirt, open-necked with no tie. Shakila awarded him points for his unassuming attire and settled down to listen.

Dr Morton was getting this collection of police and fire officers on his side. 'Yours is practical work and mine is theoretical. I'm well aware that investigators sent to the scene by the fire services don't use stereo-typical profiles like mine to bag arsonists. They analyse the physical evidence they find on the site. Their tools have become very sophisticated. They can use DNA to fingerprint trees or track stolen timber and they apply metallurgical principles to establish the melting point of power lines.

'Without getting so technical, there are, of course, simple tactics that are useful. I am told that good leads often come from the local A&E where our perpetrators have gone to be treated. Finding them in this physical manner is a challenge, very similar to the one you face in a chess match, where the way to win is to anticipate your opponent's next move. Of course, our version of the game is played for much higher stakes.' Shakila felt Mitchell sit up straighter and knew what he was thinking.

Having established what he was not, Dr Morton proceeded to explain the nature of his studies and writing. Shakila felt her CI's concentration lessen. After another half-hour, their mentor granted them a break and they heard the welcome clinking of coffee cups being wheeled in. Dr Morton public-spiritedly joined the queue at the trolley, waving away the chief constable's services as waiter. Shakila gathered her papers and her courage and pushed gently through the crowd until she was directly behind him. When he turned to smile at her, she began immediately on the three questions she was burning to ask.

From somewhere behind her she heard Superintendent Carroll's voice. 'Is there no end to that girl's cheek?'

Dorian Shaw and Becca Lambert were nearer to a quarrel than they had ever been. It was his day off, the weather was mild for the middle of January and the sun was bright. Against his better judgement, Dorian had allowed Becca to persuade him to visit Greystones. He had expected that they would walk in the grounds of the former mill owner's beautiful house, admiring the restrained lines of its frontage and enjoying its extensive gardens, which, now that the house was up for sale, were being treated almost as public property.

The excesses of the late Victorians made people write off the whole period, together with its art and its architecture, he decided. They should come here and see this. Even in the depths of winter, surrounded only by smooth lawns and seen through a lacework of bare branches, the place was gracious and welcoming. The stone was a warm grey. Grey wasn't always a cold colour.

Arriving at the front door, he found, to his great annoyance, a red Fiesta. Out of it a brash young estate agent climbed. The man was evidently expecting them. Dorian was tempted to turn round and walk away but didn't dare.

He had too little confidence in the strength of their relationship to step too far out of the role that Becca had created for him. For a few minutes, he had followed her and the agent in a red haze of fury.

Soon, however, the place had seduced him and he allowed its tranquillity to cool his mood. He came away with a soothing impression of spacious rooms with high ceilings. A clear memory of the magnificent window over the staircase with its dozen huge squares of rose, white and blue leaded panels had not been spoiled by seeing it again in reality. They had sat for a moment on the velvet-cushioned window seat under the huge crystal chandelier, lit, not by candles, but by the afternoon sun.

They had driven home without speaking. He knew that Becca realized how angry she had made him when she went to put the car in the garage without breaking the silence. Then she could keep it up no longer. She perched on the arm of his chair and ruffled his hair. 'I knew you'd fall in love with it when you saw it.'

He tried not to sound sulky. 'I never denied that it's a wonderful place. I've been in it before. It was lent to a friend of mine, a year or two ago, to exhibit his paintings in. They deserved the house as a setting. He sold nearly all of them.'

'Well then?'

'What?'

'You agree it's perfect. What are we

waiting for?'

'I'm waiting for some tea. I'm starving.'

'What would be a fair offer?'

'Egg and chips and plenty of them.' She glared at him and he shook his head sadly. 'The difference between us, Becca, is that I can love something without needing to possess it. Not that I have the money to buy it even if I wanted to – as I keep trying to make you understand.'

'That's just a quibble. It's willed to you. Margie won't live for ever – probably not for much longer. She's only half living now.'

'That's all you know. At least she doesn't exhaust herself chasing after impossible dreams. I don't think, even when Margie dies, that the money will be mine...'

The hair ruffling stopped. 'But of course it will. Even if your crazy imaginings about this Simon and Margie's baby had come to anything the man's dead now. And the money would be safe in property. What else would you do with it all? I can't imagine you doing clever things on the stock market with it. You'd only have people gathering round, scrounging from you if you kept it in the bank–'

Suddenly, Dorian had had enough. He shook her arm off his shoulder, got up and went towards the door. 'They don't worry me. With you around, they wouldn't get a look in!'

A resounding slam from somewhere inside the flat drowned Jennifer's knock. She tried again and the door was jerked open by a red-faced and dishevelled Dorian Shaw. He stepped outside and the sun shone on them both from the window on the landing.

He glared at Jennifer and then grinned. 'I suppose you've gathered that you arrived at an inconvenient moment. I'll talk to you if we go outside. There's a bench round the side of the block that's quite sheltered.'

Jennifer followed him silently down the two flights of stone steps and they sat, one at each end of the bench. It was out of the wind but also out of the sun and struck cold through Jennifer's thin trousers. She had not contemplated an outdoor interview. Taking out her notebook, she began it briskly. 'There's only one specific question I've been sent to ask. It's about Simon's car. Miss Lambert said he intended to drive to Leeds after he had talked to you on Monday night, so he must have had one in Cloughton...'

Dorian shook his head. 'I suppose he must, but I never saw it and I don't remember him ever mentioning it. Presumably he arrived from Leeds in it so his landlady here might know. Why aren't you asking his wife?'

'Technical reasons.' She could hardly tell him that the superintendent was still hoping that Simon Denton had arrived in Leeds on Monday and that the force there would have the trouble and expense of investigating his disappearance. 'We haven't proved yet that Simon is the male victim of the warehouse fire here.'

'I hope he isn't, but, in any case, I can't help.'

Jennifer thanked him, got up to go, then sat down again. 'Can I put a question I wasn't sent to ask?'

He eyed her warily. 'I don't promise to answer it.'

'Why are you so anxious to know if Simon is – or was – Margie's son? It's too late for her to do anything about it now. She probably wouldn't recognize or remember him. Simon's wife is already pregnant, so anything they wanted to avoid genetically is inevitable. Aren't you likely to upset everyone for nothing?'

'Margie's medical records would still be of interest to Simon. If he's dead, his wife might wish to see them. From what I've seen of them, there's nothing transmissible or nasty there. I think Margie's strokes are more a result of her lifestyle than in her genes. But, there's the money you see...'

It was almost half past five when the three Cloughton officers arrived back from their trip to Leeds. Shakila was given permission by the superintendent himself to spend the half-hour before Mitchell's debriefing in the canteen. She offered suitable thanks but, as soon as he had disappeared in the direction of the stairs, she grabbed coffee in a plastic cup from the machine in the corridor and hurried to the computer room. Extracting a disc from her briefcase, she carefully inserted it.

She dared not keep her document in the machine and kept the disc always with her. She felt anxious as she settled to work. Had she said too much to Caroline this morning? Not that Caroline would repeat what she had been told, but Shakila knew that – in fact, hoped that – she could still be wrong and she coveted Caroline's good opinion almost as much as her chief inspector's.

Half an hour should be enough time to record Dr Morton's replies to her questions whilst they were still fresh in her mind. Dealing with the physical evidence first, she typed quickly. 'Pyromaniac often needs to urinate or empty bowels when he sees flames. He may feel guilty because of this – and his sexual reactions – though not about setting or enjoying fires. This may lead him to wonder about confession, or at least leaving a clue. On the other hand it may lead to escalation of fire-raising activities in a desperate attempt to gain relief.' Dr Morton had compared this to the temporary relief of a businessman who goes jogging to recover from stress.

Shakila sipped from the plastic cup and regretted having given up her fix of strong canteen coffee. Now for the question of background. 'Lack of supervision in a dysfunctional family may provide children with a greater opportunity to experiment with fire. Lack of parental attention gives rise to a pressing need for approval of others and assurance that they are "doing good" in their own eyes. As they become adult they want to punish a society they hate. They need acceptance because of their achievements but success doesn't satisfy. They always need more.'

Finally, she had asked if arsonists generally told the truth. 'They are often pathological liars. They sense what people want to hear and provide it. Lying is manipulation, but they come to believe what they are telling. Will say anything for praise and reward.'

As the door opened, Shakila hurriedly saved what she had typed. She was stowing the disc safely away in her case when Clement came into the room.

Immediately after Friday evening's debriefing, Mitchell drove home. Virginia, startled at seeing the car stop outside so early, left the four children and Fran round the supper table and went out to meet him.

Before she could ask a question, he demanded, 'Has Cornish any more matches to play against Fran?'

Virginia shook her head. 'Not matches. They're going to play some friendly games. Apparently Mr Cornish thinks that's the best way to learn.' A slight emphasis on the man's title warned Mitchell that his own reference to him had been disparaging and that she meant to continue her defence of him against his vendetta. 'Fran's going round tonight–'

The warning was lost. 'No he isn't!'

He waited for an explosion, but Virginia spoke with calm reason. 'Benny, it's freezing out here now the sun's gone. We'll finish this in the kitchen.' He followed her meekly into the house and sat at the kitchen table. The sound of the children's chatter reminded him that they were only across the hall and he rose to shut the door.

Virginia began making him a sandwich as she pointed out, 'You can't have it both ways. You scoff at professional psychologists and psychiatrists and then come out with all this nonsense about TV and chess pointing to frustration and criminality. Mr Cornish reads a lot. He asked me the other night, when he saw all our books around, if I'd ever tried George Eliot. He's just finished *Middlemarch* and enjoyed it. It's a marathon read, I can tell you.'

'There you are. That's something else he does that cuts him off from normal people.'

'It doesn't do that to me.'

Mitchell decided it would be best to leave that statement unqualified. Instead, he said quietly, 'When I heard about the Rotherham fire, I asked Beardsmore to find out where Cornish was driving his lorry to on Wednesday.'

Virginia was aghast, sweet reason abandoned. 'So, the poor man hasn't only spirited your hospital patient away. He's also been lighting fires all over the county, not to speak of outwitting chess opponents, reading nineteenth-century novels and driving lorry-loads of goods all over the UK. What a man!'

Mitchell sighed. 'Ginny, Beardsmore told me that he drove to Nottingham on Wednesday morning to drop off a load and stopped in Sheffield in the early afternoon to pick up another and bring it back here.'

He watched her study a mental map. 'OK. That's pretty near Rotherham. If he had any fire-setting tendencies, he could have managed the time and the place – but you haven't any tangible reason to think he might do anything of the kind. The other day you besought Beardsmore to find you some evidence that his behaviour was in any way abnormal and all he could come up with was an objection to having plants outside his house. His worries could have been well founded. The containers might well have blocked his air bricks and if he was away on a long trip the plants would all die.'

She paused, then added in a changed tone, 'I've just remembered something. I overheard Fran ringing home the other night. I shouldn't have been listening. I heard that you were getting fat and that I'm shamelessly untidy – but he told his folks that he'd met some spooky people. His mother obviously asked for instances and he mentioned Margie at the hospital, the Queen's friend, and – well, Cornish.'

This small concession made Mitchell patient again. 'I can see why you think this is a pig-headed crusade against a possibly, even a probably innocent man, but I'm afraid for Fran. For the moment you and I are just as responsible for him as for our four. In a way, even more so. He's older which means our protection can't be so hands-on as with the younger ones and so we need to be even more vigilant.

'If I leave this situation to develop, the lad could be spending time with the person responsible for Simon Denton's disappearance or who might have set a series of fires, one of which destroyed a local warehouse and led to two deaths. He might be just a nice, good-hearted chess player, anxious to encourage youngsters to take the game up seriously – or, he might be planning, when we get on his tail, to take Fran hostage as something to bargain with. I'm not saying that's more likely. I'm just saying we mustn't risk it happening.'

Suddenly, Virginia capitulated. 'Right. But, what am I to tell him? Presumably not what you've just said.'

Mitchell grinned. 'I have to get back. I'm sure you'll think of something.'

It was sometime around midnight on Friday when Mitchell reached over the arm of his study chair for his briefcase and rummaged in it. In the fond hope of having a few minutes of peace and quiet, when the rest of his family had retired for the night, he had brought home the folder containing the PM report that Dr Holland had left on his desk late that evening. He had skimmed the first page at once. Now he would study it and go to bed when he couldn't stay awake any longer.

The pile of sheets was slightly thicker than usual and began in the pathologist's inimitable style. Mitchell concentrated, looking for the main facts. As he reached the fourth sheet, both the expression and the handwriting changed. He read on, finding the simpler style easier to follow.

'There is little of dental significance at first sight' – the last three words were heavily underlined – 'except that the overall appearance must have been a full even smile. There is no sign of gum disease or calculus, probably because of thorough oral hygiene and regular visits to a dental hygienist.'

Was this, Mitchell wondered, a preliminary and very prompt report from Dr Keith Terry, the man Dr Holland had appealed to for help? The man must have set about his task immediately and spent the intervening twenty-four hours on it.

And had the pathologist intended to leave it with the police? Mitchell would have thought he might prefer to give his own summary of the expert's conclusions with irrelevant anecdotes for good measure.

'...balanced occlusion and four beautifully sculpted ceramic fillings. These are radiolucent and so are not cavities or lost fillings as my colleague thought.'

Mitchell chuckled to himself. This was the first PM report that he had ever enjoyed reading. 'All teeth are *not* present in the upper set (sorry, Ray).' So, for a second time, Dr Terry had taken issue with Dr Holland's conclusions. Now Mitchell was quite sure that this document had been left in the folder by mistake.

'Two premolars are missing, most likely for orthodontic purposes.' Did that mean purely cosmetic? Mitchell asked himself. 'Two wisdom teeth are not yet erupted. They are seen on the posterior trap.'

Mitchell thought that sounded painful. He was losing the thread of the reasoning now, amid all the technicalities, though one further sentence, of some importance, he did follow. An upper incisor was missing and had been replaced by an implant with a perfectly matching crown. 'High quality work indeed', in Dr Terry's opinion. This apparently could only be identified by X-ray, so there was no bracketed reproach to Dr Holland for missing it.

The final sheet ended with a summary. Their corpse had had a very clean, well-cared-for mouth. Some facial trauma had led to the loss of a front tooth. The extractions for cosmetic reasons happened before the front tooth was lost.

Mitchell went off to bed feeling considerably more cheerful. Tomorrow they would have some specific questions to ask of various people which would lead to a speedy identification of their second body. He would keep the second report to himself and not humiliate Dr Holland in front of the team, but he would enjoy handing back the sheet he had not been intended to see.

# Chapter Seven

At the Saturday morning briefing, the team sat to attention as one man and Mitchell had no need to call for order when it was time to begin. He knew the reason for this was the pathologist's folder that lay on the desk in front of him. He indicated it with a wry smile. 'The contents of this package are quite interesting. However, they don't bring us quite to the final step in what feels like the longest-ever ID process.

'What we're most interested in, of course, are the conclusions of Dr Holland's forensic dentist friend. Some of you will read and understand more of what he says than I did. That's not a criticism of his very clear style but a confession of my ignorance of any aspect of his business. It finishes, though, with a description of the owner of the mouth he has examined which seems to fit Simon Denton very well.'

Mitchell paused, hearing his last remarks again in his head. He sounded like poncy Carroll. Sitting on this side of the desk must do it to you. Picking up the folder, he came round to the front of it and perched on the corner, then continued. 'The victim had good teeth, cleverly mended in a clean mouth. The repair work on these teeth was unusual. That much I did understand. If we had to tout this information round all the surgeries in West Yorkshire, we'd still be at it in the summer.

'The good news is that the details went to Leeds first thing this morning to be shown to the Denton family's dentist. With luck, we could get a yes or a no before the day's out. I propose we stop pussy-footing round the folk upstairs right now and start looking at who benefits by Simon Denton's death.'

'But we've no information to look at. We haven't been allowed–' Shakila again, of course.

Mitchell raised a hand to silence her. 'All right. I'll change that to looking for those people. We won't push our luck. The confirmation either way won't be long and I won't send anyone to Leeds till we've got it. Now, what great thoughts have we got on yesterday's developments?'

Jennifer raised a hand. 'I've found the money in the case.'

'Splendid. Did you confiscate it?'

Jennifer ignored him. 'Do we all know about mad Margie, the Queen's friend?'

Mitchell glanced round his team. 'If anyone doesn't they'd be wise to keep quiet.'

'She's worth a cool one and a half million.' There was an impressed silence before Jennifer went on, 'Dorian Shaw is her godson and heir.'

'So why,' Caroline demanded, 'isn't she in some expensive nursing home?'

'Because he's guarding his assets?' Clement suggested.

Jennifer shook her head. 'Not on the face of things. I'm not sure how much of what he told me I believe. He says Margie was a bit of a good-time girl with a heart of gold. Thirty-odd years ago, one careless slip produced a son.'

Mitchell said, 'This bit is already in the file, Jen. Move on to the money. Did the rich adoptive parents pay for the baby?'

'That I can't tell you but it would hardly be the sort of money we're talking about. Margie had an eccentric old neighbour whose relatives were putting her into residential care. Everything was to be of the best. They were loaded and weren't shutting her up in the local council place. Margie had done shopping for her and for a while had kept a general eye on her. The old woman, crippled with arthritis and with heart trouble, was nevertheless of an independent turn of mind. The two old dears, Margie and her friend, decided to make a public and shaming fuss about overriding the invalid's wishes. The upshot was that a modern bungalow was bought and the two oldies, one of them hale and hearty, were moved into it. Margie looked after her friend on a salary from the rich relations.'

'Is this story going anywhere?' Mitchell sighed. Sometimes Clement deserved all he got from his sergeant.

Jennifer ignored him and glanced at her CI. 'Do I go on?' At a nod, she added, 'The rich family came to a sticky end in a road accident, all three of them together, and Margie's friend was the only living relative. You can guess the rest.'

Mitchell thanked her and mentally included Clement. Without his question the story might have been even more protracted.

'So, Margie, being of the same mind, chooses a state hospital where she can be nursed by her godson,' Caroline finished for her. 'Are we to assume,' she added, 'that Margie too is without relatives? Is that why her godson will obligingly take care of the money?'

Jennifer answered with just a nod. Mitchell examined her face. Surely Jennifer of all people was not sulking. He was relieved when she went on, 'Dorian is afraid that the girl, Becca, stays with him for the money.'

'He shouldn't have told her about it then.'

Caroline was puzzled. 'Joking apart, Jen, you've given a lot of time to all this, both telling it now and listening to it in the first place. Can you see some significance in it that I'm missing?'

Jennifer grinned. 'There's usually considerable significance in huge sums of money. I can think of several ways that it might come into this story. Dorian must know that we'll check it all out so it must be substantially true. If his theory about Simon Denton being Margie's son is right, it'll be a central theme. If Simon is – or was – the son, then Dorian thinks the money should go to him or his baby.'

Mitchell looked bemused. 'You mean the nurse was helping someone to relieve him of over a million quid?'

'So he told me yesterday.'

'What's he like, besides being totally crazy?'

'Is it crazy to be honest?'

'Did he know about Denton's car?'

At the introduction of this new subject the hubbub of questions died. Jennifer shook her head. 'No, but he thought the Cloughton landlady might.'

They all looked at Caroline, who disappointed them. 'She says she saw it on the day Simon arrived. She thinks it might be blue.'

'That's it?'

'That's it!'

Mitchell asked, turning to Jennifer, 'Anything else?'

'Yes. He insisted on talking to me outside and I thought I'd freeze to the bench we were sitting on.'

'Why on earth?'

'Because he'd just had a major row with his woman. Perhaps she'd agreed with you about his attitude to his inheritance. He didn't say that. It's just my clever deduction, based on a lot of door slamming, his red face and the fact that he spilled all this information to me in one go, as if he wanted to burn his boats, tell someone official about it so that things were taken out of his hands.'

'Right. Do you think it would be useful to talk to them together, see what we can gather from how they spark each other?'

Jennifer considered. 'It could be, but please not me. One dose of the Lambert female was enough.'

'I thought our primary brief was to identify the two bodies in the Cloughton fire and follow up how they got there. Are we interested in this dreary pair, however rich one of them is?'

Caroline, Mitchell thought, could always be trusted to bring them all back to what really mattered. He grinned at her. 'That's our chief problem. We've all got different priorities, and, as always, we've several investigations going on simultaneously which might or might not be connected. The super's ambition yesterday afternoon was to deduce who the Yorkshire arsonist is, using evidence from his activities in Cloughton. That's why Shakila and I had to waste it kicking our heels in Leeds. Still, at least the coffee was up to standard. Anything that we ought to pass on, Shakila?'

'Well, he described some interesting cases.'

'Did he? For example?'

'The young man who was dating a respectable girl whilst burning her relatives' property – and, in his spare time, decorating the house of her aged aunt. And he was doing brilliantly in his university course as well. It made me think again about the kind of person we should be looking for.'

'But we aren't the people who are looking, are we? This man, if it is a man, will be trapped by some team of fire officers or police who have time to look at all the sites of the fires throughout the county.'

'I think he'll eventually be caught by one particular team – or even one particular officer – having a massive stroke of luck.'

Mitchell raised his voice over the free-for-all that was developing. 'Let's move on to Gupte, shall we? I've consulted my elders and betters about what we can get him for. Their answer? Not much.'

Caroline, who had overheard part of this exchange, grinned as she replayed it in her head.

*'For manslaughter of his baby daughter?'This*

217

*had been Mitchell, hopefully.*

*The superintendent, monosyllabic and crushing: 'Don't think so.'*

*'For murder of his wife by fire?'*

*'You can have a go but you won't prove it.'*

*Mitchell again, losing his hold on his temper: 'What's the matter? Do you like this bastard? What about the army of illegal immigrants, working and living in his shack for just enough food to keep them alive?'*

*'I think we can get him on that one.'*

Caroline had heard footsteps towards the door and hurried on her way. Now she snapped her attention back to the present and realized that the distribution of action sheets, the inevitable closing ceremony of a morning briefing, was under way.

She took her own and saw that she had been allotted the task that Jennifer had rejected. If Jennifer had talked to both Dorian and Becca separately, it seemed to Caroline that she would also be the best person to spot the little ways they had deceived each other when they were challenged together. She couldn't believe that the switch to herself as catalyst was just Mitchell's submission to Jennifer's whim.

Mitchell had written a reminder to her that Dorian Shaw was a musician, a pianist and singer. Perhaps a visit on that ticket was supposed to put the couple off their guard. Did the piano playing refer just to the hymns that she had been told he accompanied at services in the hospital chapel? She hoped not. If Jennifer had exhausted what the man was prepared to say about his missing patient, she could maybe offer to play duets with him. What would the CI have to say about that?

The man was certainly not in Cavill's church choir and she was not sure about the Cloughton Choral Society. She might ring Cavan Cully and ask if Shaw was known to him. The name did ring a musical bell, though. There were plenty of Shaws but not many Dorians. Suddenly, she remembered. He had sung tenor in the chorus when the local amateur operatic society had put on its notorious production of *Carmen*. He was very good. She recalled now a rehearsal which she had accompanied and at which the professional who was singing Don José had been late. The director had asked him to fill in for the celebrated absentee and he had made a fine job of '*Carmen, io t'amo, t'adoro*' in the last scene, though his acting had been bad enough to arouse unkind giggles.

Feeling a little more enthusiasm for her task than when she had first read the sheet, she got out her cell phone to track her quarry down.

As the members of his team left his office,

Mitchell had touched Shakila's arm. When she was the only officer remaining, he closed the door. He hoped that he was not going to regret instigating this conversation, but the matter had already gone unresolved for far too long. Jennifer had failed to gain Shakila's confidence. If he was right in thinking that Caroline had succeeded, she was obviously not about to share her knowledge. Time for a direct approach.

He waved the DC to his sergeant's chair and regarded her as she perched on the edge of it. She seemed uncomfortable in every sense but she still looked him in the face. He plunged into what he had to say, anxious to get it over. 'Shakila, work has always come first with you, in this building at least. Jokes about your becoming our first black, female chief constable are half serious. All that seems to have changed. Are you not well?'

'I'm fine, sir.' She was still watching him.

'Are you worried about something then?'

Now she looked down. 'Yes, sir.'

'Do you want to talk about it?'

'No, sir. Thank you.'

Should he go on? He knew he would. 'Is there anything I can do to help?'

'I don't think so, sir. Not at the moment, at least.'

'Fair enough.' She took this as her dismissal. He let her get as far as the door, then stopped her. 'Shakila, find someone who can help. Doctors or church ministers are unlikely to betray confidences – not that I know about your...' He ground to a halt.

'I'm not a Muslim any more, sir, but our Imam is just as trustworthy as a Christian priest.' She closed the door quietly.

Mitchell sighed. He had learned nothing, failed to help and had succeeded only in offending her.

Caroline's call had made Dorian Shaw very uneasy, particularly its demand for Becca to be present at the interview. She would be annoyed at being denied her usual Saturday lie-in and these days she was not at her best first thing in the morning. She wouldn't be on her guard.

He wished that that phrase had not come into his mind. Why should he want her to be guarded? The police were looking for an arsonist who had inadvertently become a killer, not a dabbler in a few recreational drugs to release the tension caused by a stressful job and a pushy mother. Mrs Lambert made the impossible demand that her daughter should be brilliant in almost every field. 'All I am, as far as she is concerned, is bragging fodder,' Becca had declared after the woman's last critical visit.

The cause for criticism this time had been Becca's job, in which she was actually making good progress. In three months, she had graduated from general office filing to become PA to one of the directors. Some of Becca's suggestions had been incorporated into the man's routine, not ground-breaking, but leading to greater efficiency and his approbation. Her mother's response had been to ask when she was going to stop marking time and sort out a career for herself.

Dorian had tried to comfort her after her mother had departed. 'You already have a career. Mr Ainsley couldn't function now without you and he knows it. Why else would he pay you over the odds for what your job description shows you're worth?'

She had snarled at him, 'It's still not enough for all I do,' and disappeared into the bedroom. His heart had sunk as he heard the key turn in the door. He hadn't dared challenge her about the drugs. He had never even told her that he knew about them. She surely realized that, as a nurse, he recognized the signs. She must know too that it could be no one but himself who regularly searched the bedroom and quietly removed any illegal substances. He'd been surprised that she hadn't found somewhere else to keep them. Then he had worked out that it was worth losing some of her hoard from time to time in order to have a place where it wouldn't matter much if they were discovered.

He sighed now and gave her another call.

There was no response beyond a twang of springs and a thump. He hoped this meant that she had climbed out of bed. Why should he care? he asked himself. Had he not, in some ways, been happier before she moved in? He walked over to the rack and selected a CD, one of his favourites which he knew would annoy her.

One of Bartok's arrangements of old Hungarian folk-songs was good music to wait to. Each section was less than a minute long, so that, when whatever you were waiting for arrived, you could interrupt without insulting it. One day, he would get hold of the sheet music and try playing them himself. The fifth one was a scherzo which he especially liked. He hoped that DC Jackson would not come until it was finished.

She didn't, but the increased volume brought Becca out of the bedroom to complain. She still wore her nightdress, roughly tucked into jogging bottoms. She had thrust her arms into the jacket sleeves but not zipped it. Her hair was unbrushed and her face stormy.

For the hundredth time, he asked himself whether the excuses he made for her were justified. It was certainly true that her mother had both spoiled her and expected too much of her. Should she not have recovered from that by now and grown up? Maybe she would have done if she had not resorted to drugs as a prop, so that now she was in double trouble. The doorbell rang.

Dorian looked up at her. 'Would you like to see our lady friend in?'

Becca scowled. 'I'd rather see her off.' She went out into the hall, returned with their visitor and sat down again without introducing her.

The DC's greeting was unexpected. 'Hello, Dorian. Nice to see you again.' He seemed to panic for a moment but then recognized her. 'Cavill's playing a Bartok concert in Paris next month. Can we have it off though? I'm very tired of hearing him practise it and to talk through it would be disrespectful.'

Becca made her first animated movement of the day to remove the disc. Dorian pulled a chair forward for Caroline, then sat waiting for her to begin her agenda. The weather on his second day off was as bright as the one before had been, but with a keen wind which had reddened the DC's cheeks, making the scars across them gleam silver-white. He could see that she was oblivious of them now and at ease with herself and was glad for her.

Becca had come to sit on the sofa next to him. He watched her making an assessment of Caroline and trying to work out when and in what capacity the two had met. Caroline cut through the surmises of them both and began on a meticulous re-examination of their every movement on the previous Monday.

To Dorian's relief, she seemed to discover no major discrepancy between their individual stories, nor between what they had said before and what they were saying now. His relief was short-lived as the ordeal continued with thorough enquiries into the seemingly unimportant fine detail of their activities. Caroline took the name and address of the friend that Becca had visited last Monday evening and asked how she had travelled and where she had parked. Becca was asked the name of her GP and what he had prescribed for her migraine.

Turning back to Dorian, she had demanded details of the route he had taken on his motorcycle trip to the Woolpack and a description of the man whom he had beaten at darts. He was able to oblige with the man's name and suggested that she should try the landlord for his address. Not until he was feeling thoroughly frightened and Becca appeared to be on the verge of hysteria did Caroline give up. She left, thanking them with a smile that caused her scars to form a new pattern.

As he closed the front door after seeing her out, Becca got up and made for the bedroom, speaking to him over her shoulder. 'I'm going to finish my lie-in.'

Thankfully, he let her go and sank into an armchair. Where was he going to go from here?

Shakila, having completed both tasks on her Saturday morning sheet, and with a good hour to spare, had invited Patrick Seddon to visit the station again. It was an invitation he dared not refuse and he was beginning to believe that to have taken his punishment for the ill-gotten compact discs he had been selling would have been a better plan than suffering this unmerciful harassment by DC Nazir.

On this occasion, however, she met him with a friendly smile and even offered him a Coke. 'I think we're quits now,' she told him. 'This time you're really only being asked if you will help with our enquiries. Your slate's clean.'

'I'm going to keep it clean. I never want another week like this one. I'm not going to join their gang even if they ask me. I'm not going to do obbo for 'em either.'

Shakila nodded. 'Good thinking. What I want to know about now is the warehouse last Monday.'

'What about it?'

Shakila grinned. 'That's the trouble. I don't know and that's where you could help us. When you met there last Monday, was there anything at all you noticed that was different from the other weeks? Did you see anything odd, hear anything, smell anything?'

'Like smoke, you mean? I told you, it was too early. There weren't no fire to smell, no flames to see, no nothing. Our lot didn't do it.'

'No, but someone did and they could have been hanging around waiting for you to go. Maybe someone had been around earlier and left what they needed, ready for it to be used when it got dark.'

The boy shook his head. 'Nothing like that, except a fat cow in a tracksuit, telling us to clear off home.' Shakila held her breath. 'Came up to me on obbo and the other two young lads were just behind me. When she saw the men – them as I don't know the names of – she cleared off 'erself. The older 'uns pretended they wanted rid of her but I wondered if she was buying, and her and them were just acting like.'

'What did she do next?'

'Went back to her car.'

'What was the car like? Colour?'

'There weren't no light except them orange street lamps – but I'd say it were light not dark. Could've been pale blue or green. Not white or it would have just looked pale orange.'

'Size?'

'Biggish. Bigger 'n my dad's.'

'You didn't see any of the registration?'

The boy pulled hideous faces as he tried to dredge from his memory something to please her. Eventually he shook his head.

Shakila changed tack. 'What kind of track-suit was it?'

'Eh? Oh, dark colour. Had a hood. I couldn't see that at first when I come up to the building. She pulled it over her hair when she saw us coming.'

'What did the gang do?'

'Me and my mates went home. I think the men went inside the warehouse. They were banging at the door and shoving it.'

'And where was the girl when you left? Still in the car?'

He nodded. 'Yeah, just sitting there.'

Shakila considered for a moment, glanced at her watch and decided this was suffi-ciently important to risk being late for the CI's one thirty call. 'If I gave you a lift, could you show me where she parked?'

He nodded vigorously and trotted beside her to the car park. The rusty Renault 4 seemed to be a great disappointment to him. Shakila smiled. Perhaps he had been expecting a squad car with the siren swit-ched on. He climbed in without comment.

The muddy patch Seddon pointed out to her a few minutes later gave her second thoughts about the point of their trip. It was criss-crossed with the tracks of several cars, none of them very sharp. Treading gingerly, she looked around, stirring the grass growing around the mud with a stick broken off a dying shrub. She was about to give up and take Seddon home when something caught her eye, small and dirty white – two slightly disintegrating tablets. She picked them up by sliding a coin beneath them and dropped them into the small plastic container she always kept in her handbag.

She was encouraged to search further but she found nothing else and after not much longer she led Seddon back to her Renault. 'Could you,' she asked him, 'recognize that girl if you saw her again?'

He thought about it then nodded. 'It were dark mind, but I reckon I might.'

For the price of driving on the hobbies run, Virginia Mitchell earned herself a child-free morning on most winter Saturdays. The twins attended a kids' film club in the local church hall and Kat played netball for her junior school team. Declan, not to be outdone, had volunteered for his school's second team in Cloughton's under-twelve soccer league. His parents knew that their elder son's various talents did not include any form of sport. They suspected that this team consisted of all those willing and enthusiastic no-hopers who should nevertheless be encouraged. It was a cheerful party.

Fran had asked if his aunt would extend her drive into the town centre and drop him by the bus station. She thought he might be meeting some young woman whose company demanded something smarter than racing bike gear. She was anxious to oblige him, being grateful that he had accepted their ban on visiting Roger Cornish's house the previous evening with little fuss and very few questions. He had merely insisted that the cancellation and apologies should be made by a telephone call from himself.

She had dropped off her own children at their various destinations and was approaching a lay-by conveniently close to where he wanted to be when Fran, suddenly and abruptly, ordered, 'Follow that lorry.' Without stopping to think, Virginia found that she had resignalled and obeyed.

The case moved on on Saturday morning faster than even Mitchell, the personification of impatience, had hoped for. Summoned at ten for what Carroll referred to as the ring-round, Mitchell found him beaming broadly.

Like a small boy holding on to a secret for as long as possible, the superintendent waved a sheet of paper but kept it in his hand. He remarked to Mitchell merely, 'You'll like this.'

Mitchell too could be maddening. He sat where the great man indicated, answered,

'That's nice,' and began an unnecessary search in his bag for a pen. Carroll tired of the game and began to read. "From Derek Clayton (letters) to Superintendent John Carroll. In 1983 a patient of mine had orthodontic treatment in the form of the removal (by me) of two premolars to retract and straighten the upper front teeth. An accident in which a cricket ball damaged the front of his face in 1995 led to crowns as illustrated below. Later (2001) the upper right lateral incisor was extracted and replaced by a titanium implant and another matching crown. This latter feature is only recognizable on X-ray. The boxed plaster casts sent by Dr Holland last night match this patient's jaw exactly. I have informed the pathologist but thought I should save your time by communicating directly. I am pleased to tell you that your Mr X is Simon David Denton etc., etc." It goes on and on but it's all stuff that will be more use to the lawyers when we've nailed our villain than to us now.'

Mitchell looked up straight-faced, his pen now in his hand and said, 'Interesting.' Then he rather spoiled his apparent calm with a war whoop. He sat as politely and patiently as possible whilst the telephoned details of cases that were troubling Leeds, Huddersfield and Bradford were explained and discussed.

He escaped at the first opportunity, but,

having arrived back in his office, wondered what his hurry was. He had no team to work with and no officers likely to appear until one o'clock. Shakila was up the valley with her teenage delinquent. Caroline was with Shaw and his moll. Clement was with Sylvia Townsley, attempting to obtain evidence to convict Mubarak Gupte. What should he do now? The question was about to be answered by his wife.

He picked up the phone on its first ring. Since she rang him at work only in the direst emergency, he was surprised to hear her voice. 'Nothing's wrong. I'm at Jameson's garage on Crellin Street.'

Alarm bells began ringing again. 'That's only round the corner from Cornish's place.'

'It may well be. Shut up and listen.' He was surprised again. She usually made her point with precise and icy politeness if she wanted to put him down. She must be excited. 'Fran's recognized the lorry that picked Simon Denton up on Monday.' Mitchell kept back his questions, knowing she would tell her tale clearly and concisely if he left her alone. 'He'll give you the details himself. Something to do with a sticker on the back, and, of course, he recognized the general appearance of the vehicle as soon as he saw it again. We were behind it in town and followed it until it stopped, which fortunately was soon. Both Mr Jameson and his Monday driver are prepared to come to the station. Quite reasonably they intend to ring the main desk from here first to check that you want to see them. After all, they don't know me from Adam – well, from Eve, anyway. You should get the call in a minute.

'By the way, Fran hopes you want him there too. He says, after drawing you an Identikit picture of your victim and then finding the vehicle that spirited him away, the offer of a permanent job wouldn't be too much to expect. Anyway, I'll get off the line and pick Fran up when you've finished with him. Cheers.' Mitchell would have preferred the lorry driver to be unaccompanied. He could see no way in which an excited nephew and the inquisitive employer of his witness would aid the investigation.

A knock at the door was too early to be the eagerly awaited man. It was Shakila, looking harassed and deflated. 'I've taken Seddon home. Anything else before the briefing?'

Salvation! He sent her down to meet Fran and to show him round the computer room, bringing up on the screens such material as it would do no harm for him to see. His nephew should be well pleased with this privilege, and Shakila too seemed more enthusiastic for her task than he had expected. She was becoming quite computer-obsessed.

For Mr Jameson, Mitchell decided on fulsome thanks for the loan of his employee and entertainment in the canteen by an adequately young and personable female officer. He noticed through the window a blue Escort arriving in the car park. Splendid. Caroline would do nicely. He rang her cell phone and watched through the pane as she took it from her pocket. She appeared less pleased with her instructions than Shakila had. He grinned to himself, then took a small pair of scissors from the tray on the desk and set about a couple of ivy plants that had been trailing artistically from the window sill.

The next knock heralded his witness, ushered in, surprisingly, by the desk sergeant who departed wordlessly, leaving his protégé standing in the middle of the office.

'Doesn't say much, yon PC,' the man remarked.

Mitchell offered his hand. 'No, just odd words. We're going to promote him when he manages a whole sentence. Do sit down.'

The man made himself comfortable. 'Is his name really Magic?'

'No, it's Mark Powers and the humour in this joint is pretty infantile. You'd better tell me what your name is.'

'Hunter-Brown. Bit upper crust for a garage hand but don't blame me. I didn't pick it.'

'I know the feeling. My first name's Benedict, but you'd better not try using it. By the way, my wife doesn't make a habit of press-ganging witnesses for me.'

Mr Hunter-Brown grinned. 'I know. The boy explained how it happened. About Monday – it's all very simple. Mr Denton had a bit of an accident a couple of weeks back, getting through his landlady's gateway to park his car in her drive the first day he was here. Wasn't used to the narrow entrance, you see. I suppose he thought his lady wife wouldn't like the dent in his front wing. Got us to hammer it out and respray it. Then he got taken to hospital.

'We didn't know that. We wondered why he didn't collect. We even wondered if he'd told us a load of lies and the car was stolen after he'd done a job with it and that he'd buggered off. Then word came and we were glad we'd waited a bit before making a fuss.'

'Hadn't you got a phone number for him?'

'His landlady didn't know where he was when we rang there. She was all for chasing him up as well. And his mobile was off because the hospital said it had to be. Anyway, after he got a bit better, he rang to explain and it was arranged that he'd let us know when he wanted the car back. Mr Jameson offered for me to fetch him to the garage to pick the car up on Monday.'

'And that's what you did?'

'Aye.'

'I don't suppose you know where he went when he left you?'

'I do, actually. You see, when he'd inspected his car wing and then been in the office to settle up with Mr Jameson, it was getting on towards dinner time and it was my half day, so, the long and short of it was...'

Mitchell spent the dramatic pause wishing he had let Mr Jameson sit in on the interview. He might have summarized this saga, regained the services of his employee and released himself to do more useful work. Even an officer considerably more loquacious than Magic would not have got more than an odd phrase in whilst walking upstairs with Mr Hunter-Brown. He extracted from the morass of words the information that Simon Denton had returned Hunter-Brown's favour and given him a lift for the short distance to his home. He had used his mobile phone ('While he was driving too! I wouldn't have told you that but you can't do him for it if he's dead, can you?'), first to ring his wife and say he wouldn't be back for dinner and then to ring somebody called Doreen to ask if, now she was doing a split shift, she could see him at nine o'clock in some pub or other.' Mitchell hoped that Nurse Shaw didn't object to his sex change.

'He couldn't have meant dinner at dinner time, could he? – same as you and me. He had a posh voice though. He was one of those that call supper their dinner.' Mitchell felt glad that the impression he gave now that he was a chief inspector still classed him with the plebs.

'So, any more calls?'

'Not by him, but somebody else rang him.'

'Remember any details?'

Hunter-Brown nodded happily. 'Somebody called Paul. As far as I could gather, there was a rumpus at work and this Paul needed to see Mr Denton – and Mr D said he'd got to see this Doreen about a personal matter. Do you want all this stuff?'

'Absolutely everything you can remember.'

'OK. So, this Paul on the phone arranged to meet Mr D in the Drum and Monkey and he said OK so long as he could make it to the Woolpack by nine o'clock. Yes, that was the pub, the Woolpack.'

There was a pause as Mitchell sorted out the pronouns. When he thought he understood this new information, he raised an eyebrow. 'Drum and Monkey?'

Hunter-Brown's smile widened. He could help yet again. 'Just up the hill from that stately home place in Cragvale. Greystones I think it's called. Didn't strike me as Denton's sort of pub – or his boss's either.'

Mitchell began gathering papers, which he took as his dismissal. 'Is that it then?' He looked disappointed.

'Just a minute. Did the person on the phone ask Mr Denton where he was?'

'Yes. He said he was in the car that he'd just picked up from the garage.'

'Did he mention that he had you as a passenger?'

'No.'

'Did you speak at all whilst Mr Denton was busy with his caller?'

'Course not. Garage hands do have some manners, you know.'

Mitchell had no time to soothe ruffled feelings. 'So the caller would have been unaware that you were there listening?'

'This bloke wouldn't have known, no. And, I wasn't listening. I could hardly help hearing. Hearing and listening's not the same. Anyway, I don't suppose the boss bloke would have cared. Didn't sound like private stuff.'

Mitchell made a valiant effort to be ingratiating. 'Everything you can dredge up is really important. Did you get the man's name?'

'I told you. Mr D kept repeating it – yes Paul, no Paul, three bags full Paul. It's what business people do to one another. Makes 'em feel important. Mr Jameson does it to folk he wants to impress or those he wants to do something for him.'

'Right. Well done. You're sure of the pub names?'

'Certain. Been in the Drum a couple o' times. Bit sleazy, actually. Bit o' dealing goes on now and then, so I've heard. Couldn't see Mr D being comfortable in there. Happen this Paul picked it at random and Mr D wouldn't know anything about it.'

'You didn't warn him?'

Hunter-Brown shook his head. 'Wasn't my place — and, for all I know, the pair of 'em might have been wanting to buy something. I don't know the signs of users. They could've even been selling the stuff.'

As the tortuous session rolled on, Mitchell prayed not. This collection of cases was quite complicated enough already.

Messrs Jameson and Hunter-Brown had departed, preening themselves on having abandoned their own duties in order to make such a valuable contribution to the maintenance of law and order. Mitchell remained at his desk, meditating on all he had learned since arriving at the station that morning. Some mysterious and possibly illegal doings were keeping Shaw and Lambert busy but he was not yet convinced about either what or why. He had brought the discussion at the briefing to an end before all their business was exhausted. His officers were restless, paying scant attention and eager for more action.

He had been right all the time about the death of Simon Denton being Cloughton's responsibility. He suspected, though, that there was business in Leeds that would have to be looked into before this case could be settled. The victim's spouse or partner was traditionally the chief suspect in murder. It was through no fault of his own that no member of his team had yet been allowed to meet her. If Louise Denton was not guilty, she must at least be helpful – and the same principle applied to Denton's adoptive parents.

This afternoon, whilst all these omissions were being made good, he would get on to the local fire people again. For the first time, Mitchell gave serious consideration to the idea that there might be a connection between the Yorkshire arsonist and their two current victims. What were the chances that he might have deliberately killed them? What about Mubarak Gupte? Could Simon Denton have discovered him setting fire to his ailing business and to his wife? Gupte could have attacked and dispatched Denton, and then added him to the bonfire. It left questions to be answered, of course. Why lug the body up to the first floor? That had to be asked whoever the killer turned out to be – and the most likely answer was that the media had told everyone in Cloughton about fire travelling upwards.

Mitchell ground his teeth, which had not received the same tender care as his victim's. How dare the superintendent, who should have been aiding and encouraging this investigation, hobble it with a ban on contacting important witnesses? He had not been slow to point out this injustice to Carroll himself. The super's defence – that Leeds had given them free access to the results of their own work on the case – was true, but not a sufficient answer. Did he consider himself and his team more astute than their counterparts in Leeds? Well, yes, he did.

Suddenly, Mitchell felt that he could not bear to be in his office a minute longer. Without pausing, either to justify or to resist his irrational urge to leave, he grabbed his jacket. Taking the back way, so as not to be detained by any other officer, he left the building. He needed to walk. He wished that he were fitter and more appropriately clad because running would be even better.

After a short while he looked around him and realized that five more minutes' brisk walking in the same direction would bring him to the Jacksons' house. They needed to speak to Cavill about Dorian Shaw. Suddenly, Mitchell felt better. He hadn't walked out on the job, just chosen to conduct an interview personally, and since his witness lived so close, to walk to his house. He wouldn't ring to check that Cavill was in. If he knew his quarry was unavailable, he would lose this pleasant glow of virtue.

Cavill was not only at home but also offering a substantial sandwich lunch. Mitchell's day was fast improving, though he shuddered at the noise coming from the king of all CD players in the living room. Cavill removed the disc apologetically. 'If it's any consolation, Caroline doesn't care for it either.'

'I always said she was a sensible girl.' Cavill found the case and stowed the disc safely away. 'Who is it, anyway? I'd better know so that I never get trapped at a concert with any of his stuff included.'

'I'm preparing a concert where the programme will be totally his stuff.'

'It won't be a hit.'

'On the contrary, I'm told it's a sell-out.'

Mitchell grinned. 'No accounting for how some folk spend their brass.'

'I've shelled out for the man myself. I assure you I didn't steal the CD.'

'No. I hope you didn't buy it from a young lad in the Woolpack either. It would still be stolen property.'

Cavill said, straight-faced, 'I don't think there'd be much call for Bartók in the Woolpack. Benny, I know you didn't come here for a musical interlude and I don't suppose you came to cadge a free lunch. What are you after?'

'Some gen on Dorian Shaw. How much did you see of him when you were involved with the opera group?'

Cavill chewed and thought. 'It depends what you mean. He was always around, but usually just as part of the crowd in the chorus.'

'Good voice, Caroline tells me.'

'Superb, but he'd never make a performer. He was always wanting reassurance. Most people who know they're good are either modest and say nothing or else they keep asking how they did in order to get heaped with praise. I don't know how to explain Dorian. He was good in his own opinion but he didn't trust that opinion. When he was given a brief solo, he'd go away after he'd sung it. Someone had to go and tell him it was fine before he'd mix in again.'

'I don't follow.'

'No. I didn't suppose you would.' Mitchell wondered whether he had just been insulted. 'He wasn't shy when he was actually singing. He was enjoying himself so much that he became unaware that anyone was listening. It was when he stopped that he worried.'

Mitchell frowned. 'And yet Caroline says he stays away from rehearsals to be with his woman.'

'He didn't when I was working with them but I don't think Becca was on the scene then. Caro knows because she still plays for them occasionally when their usual repetiteur can't.' Mitchell opened his mouth, then decided not to ask. 'I can't explain him and Becca. She's not pretty – she's not good to him, she's not especially clever though I think she's something of a sportswoman.'

'I didn't realize you knew the girl as well.'

Cavill got up and produced bottles of beer from the fridge. Mitchell, who had been to this house too often to be treated as a visitor, helped himself. 'Maybe he just likes letting people know he can get himself a girl, someone who's found something about him that it's worth staying with him for.'

Cavill sniffed. 'Depends what you mean by staying with him. From what I hear, she's quite generous with her favours. He's certainly generous to her – in the best sense. There's not much he wouldn't do for her.'

'You seem to know a lot about her.'

Cavill said, with an expression of distaste, 'She was a pupil of mine once. She plays the piano extremely well technically, but who needs mechanical Schubert? No mistakes and no soul describes her style. It was the mother who approached me about lessons.'

'How would you describe her in three words? Becca, not her mother.'

Cavill blinked at this question from down-to-earth Mitchell, then gave it serious consideration, his eyes shut. After some moments he opened them again and said, 'Manipulative, dissatisfied and just as insecure as Dorian.'

Mitchell nodded, then drained his glass and got up to go. 'Do you think, if the motive was strong enough, that either of them could gee themselves up to kill?'

Cavill said quickly, 'I don't think I want to take the responsibility for answering that.'

'That's an answer in itself.'

'Don't forget that several police officers in Cloughton once considered me as a multiple murderer.'

Mitchell gave an apologetic half smile. 'I'd forgotten that. I hope you remember that I wasn't one of them. None of us ever thinks about it.'

Cavill got up to show Mitchell out. 'Well,' he told him, with some bitterness, 'I do. Quite often.'

Shakila had received her CI's polite request that she should entertain his nephew with good grace. Rightly interpreting it as a command to keep the lad from hampering the morning's swift progress in their case, she went to meet him and listened with genuine interest to his account of how he had done the force's job of finding the driver who picked up Simon Denton outside the hospital.

When she had duly admired his keen observation and quick thinking, she found he was very keen on having the mysterious HOLMES explained and demonstrated. She hoped he would not be too conscious of how much was not being revealed.

Even though it excluded her from any active part in the morning's developments, she was content with her assignment. To play with computers as part of her paid work could not be grumbled at. In addition, she had been havering for some time about buying a bicycle. She was not happy with her fitness level lately. Cycling was less hard on the feet and the knees than running and she knew that Fran could give her informed advice on what to buy.

First, though, he must have his fun. She gave him a simplified account of what HOLMES would do and produced from it some sheets of information that compromised neither cases nor persons. Handing them over, she remarked that the room was close and stuffy and coaxed Fran into the canteen. There she rewarded his valuable evidence with coffee and doughnuts.

She set the tray of junk food in front of him, then broached the subject of cycles and cycling as he munched happily. '...I don't want the kind of machine you have, of course.'

Fran nodded and swallowed. 'No, I suppose not. What exactly do you want it for and where would you ride it?'

Shakila had not thought out her plan in any detail. She considered now. 'Cycling's not a very popular sport in Cloughton. Once you leave the town centre it feels as though you're going uphill at forty-five degrees in most directions. You said, when I talked to you before, that York was flat. Would you advise a few days' holiday there, just to get used to riding without wobbling?' She chattered on about the advantages she expected to enjoy and he listened approvingly.

Pushing away his plate, he added to her list. 'You see much more from a bike – you don't whizz past things so quickly, not if you're not racing, anyway.'

Shakila laughed. 'Not whizzing is definitely what I have in mind. You can advise me without finding I'm your rival in the Tour de France.'

Fran raised a warning hand. 'You can tease me, but I'm quite serious about that. You couldn't challenge me anyway. They don't allow women.'

Shakila wagged a finger back at him. 'Don't be so sure that that will always be. That's the next glass ceiling we women are going to crash through. Not me personally, of course. I'm too busy working towards

being the first black, female chief constable.'
She was getting very tired of this joke, but it
made the boy laugh. She changed the subject. 'Have you seen many of our local
beauty spots this week? I don't suppose
forty-five degree hills are a turn-off for you.'

He grinned, remembering. 'I did a short
tour with Uncle Benny on Monday. We
didn't get far and I wasn't looking at the
scenery. I was concentrating on him. I didn't
know which he was going to do first, fall off
or have a heart attack. You could advise me
now. Where do you think I should go and
what should I see?'

'Holmfirth's interesting. Been there?'

'I'm not sure. Could have been, I suppose,
but I don't think so.'

'You'd remember if you'd been. It's the
place where they filmed *The Last of the
Summer Wine*.'

'I don't watch much TV – except the news.'

'It's very pretty, anyway, and the best possible exercise. I'd guess the hills there go up
at sixty degrees, and you could boast to your
girlfriend that you'd eaten in Sid's café.'

'I haven't got one here and they won't
have heard of that place in Oz.'

Shakila pushed a little further. 'There's
plenty besides – fantastic views, interesting
old buildings connected with the textile in-
dustry, loads of arts and crafts and book-
shops...'

'And that indie clothes shop where you have to walk through a hardware store before you get to it.' Shakila stared at him. 'Yes, I remember now. I did go there. I had my sister with me. What I chiefly associate with that day is Maria being in a foul mood and refusing to take an interest in anything, so we didn't see it all. She went home on her own in a huff. Thanks for the reminder. I'll go again.'

Shakila glanced at her watch. Surely the CI would be through with his lorry driver by now. 'I'll have to go. We've a lunchtime briefing today, thanks to your evidence, and I have a phone call to make before then.' Making the phone call had only just occurred to her. She could see that Fran thought she had invented it to get rid of him, but she thought it could turn out to be a very important step in their investigation.

Jennifer arrived at Mitchell's office ten minutes before the briefing was due to start. 'I've got a request to make. Two, in fact.'

'You're usually reasonable.'

Jennifer took this as an invitation. 'I want to be the first to speak to Denton's widow.'

Mitchell nodded, perfectly understanding her reason. 'Granted. What else?'

'I want to take Shakila with me.'

'Refused. Sorry, but there are two reasons. We're still looking into Mrs Gupte's death, plus that of her child, and we're hunting an arsonist who destroyed a building, a business, a body and a live woman and who might be rampaging through the whole of Yorkshire with his pocket full of matches. I can't spare two officers from my regular team for one preliminary interview and we may need Shakila's Urdu to deal with our Asian family.'

Jennifer knew better than to argue. 'Can I have Smithson, then?'

'I wish. He's gone to London for the day, to his grandson's graduation. Leeds has offered us a female PC who's been to the house before. I'd like to accept this kind co-operation. We might need more of it before we're done.'

Jennifer nodded, accepting this. 'What do you want me to get from her? Louise Denton, I mean, not the PC.'

'Anything she'll give you. The flavour of her relationship with Simon would be useful, and the family circumstances in general. Try to get some idea of other people who could supply information, his employers, for example. Back off if she resists. No pushy questions that might alienate or upset her. We'll plan how to go on when we've assessed her.'

He looked up as Caroline and Clement came in together. 'Have you seen Shakila?'

Clement nodded. 'She's busy on the

computer again.'

'Is my nephew still with her?' Clement shook his head. 'Do we know what she's doing?'

'When I asked she said she could amuse herself how she liked as long as her work was done.' He had apparently been smarting from this retort but seemed mollified by the idea that Shakila had been bored by tiresome child-minding at the time. Mitchell felt that Clement had reason to be aggrieved. More than once, he had made an opportunity for Shakila to be incorporated into an investigation. It was unkind of her not to share whatever was the mysterious theory that was occupying her spare moments now. He deliberately did not look at Caroline who, he suspected, had been taken into her confidence. He determined to speak to Caroline alone before the day was out. He had played too many wild cards during his own career to resent Shakila following suit. However, he had to know that whatever she was up to would not jeopardize their main lines of enquiry.

Without waiting for her now, he gave the officers present an account of the satisfactory progress made that morning. They were impressed with the speed and efficiency of the dentists, both forensic and practising, and amused by Virginia's chase after the double-barrelled lorry driver.

Clement asked, 'What are we doing to find Denton's car?'

'Looking for it is my suggestion. Now we have an ID that even the super accepts, we're looking for a hell of a lot of things. Who benefits from Denton's removal?'

'The nurse,' Jennifer offered, 'except that he's set on committing financial suicide by giving information to his rival heir.'

'Did he have any choice?' They all turned to Caroline. Mitchell nodded for her to go on. 'Well, two people have said how kind Denton was to Margie. Your mother said it to you and Nurse Shaw said the same. The initial conversation with her may have been a kind gesture, but might he not have picked up clues from her himself? Maybe he asked her why she called him Davy. Maybe she had lucid periods when she told him things that matched up with what he'd been told about his parents. Perhaps Dorian Shaw was being helpful because it was all likely to come out anyway. If he had been helpful to him, Denton could then have been inclined to share some of the money.'

'If it was willed to Dorian, would Denton's claim have stood? Which would have been upheld in law?' They thought about Clement's question until he answered it himself. 'What matters as far as the case is concerned is what the two of them thought the law said.'

'Could we interview Margie?'

Mitchell liked Caroline's idea. 'Even if we're refused, or get nowhere with her, it would be interesting to see how Shaw reacts to the idea.' He made himself a note as Shakila opened the door and crept in, mouthing an apology silently so as not to interrupt the discussion.

Jennifer said, 'His wife might be glad to be rid of him for all we know.'

Mitchell sniffed. 'Well, don't ask her this afternoon.'

'Are we going to challenge Shaw and Lambert this afternoon?'

Mitchell turned to Caroline. 'You saw them last. What do you think?'

'I'd let them stew for twenty-four hours. They're both frightened. The girl's on something – to be precise, this morning she was coming down from something. I think his main concern was that I'd noticed but she was afraid of something else. They'll probably be planning how to support each other as we sit here, cooking up their stories again.'

'Is that good?'

Caroline nodded. 'I think so. She'll want to tell more lies. I think he's basically straight and isn't comfortable lying. Tomorrow could be interesting.'

Mitchell grinned. 'That's yours, then. You can have Smithson. Anything else you can tell us from today?'

'Not tell you, but I'll follow up what I asked about. I can see Lambert's GP about her supposed migraine, plus anything else he's prepared to talk about. Then I can see the friend she visited on Monday evening.'

'She'll have rung her already and warned her what to say.'

'Yes, I'll bear that in mind. Perhaps someone can see the darts player and check with the landlord of the Woolpack.'

Mitchell made another jotting. 'Let's find out all we can about Shaw. I've spoken to Cavill. Someone can go to see his hospital colleagues. Specially, we want to know all about this phone call that changed Denton's original plans. And someone can find his car. It surely won't be too difficult with a full description including the registration.' He turned to Shakila. 'Now, what's all this about Seddon?'

Shakila looked up soberly from her corner. 'He says a fat cow in a tracksuit chased him and his friends away from the doorway of the warehouse last Monday night. She came in a car and went back to sit in it when she saw the older blokes that the three kids hang out with. He thinks she'd come to buy drugs and he thinks that he'd recognize her again.' Having answered the question, she looked down again.

Dorian Shaw was not sure how long he had

254

been sitting in his armchair, mulling over his troubles, when he became aware that the noise from the bedroom was of Becca snoring. It meant that she was tanked up again and was unlikely to wake until well into the afternoon. He wondered what excuse he should offer to her employer. She had rung in herself yesterday to tell her company the touching but fictional tale of her mother's bad fall. That had been so that she could share his day off and continue her campaign to get him to buy Greystones.

If he thought that living in the gracious old place would really make her happy, he might be more willing to look further into the matter. Besides all the financial questions though, he suspected that the move would cut her off from all her friends. It could even be that the idea was really her mother's and that all Becca wanted was to placate the old trout and be left in peace.

Would the story of her mother's injuries do as a continued excuse for her absence from work? He was not going to lie for her about it. In fact, he was not going to lie for her ever again.

Carr Well House was one of those for which a name rather than a number was not a laughable affectation. Jennifer parked on the road outside its surrounding wall and surveyed it for a few moments without going farther than the gate. She could imagine how its stone mullioned windows, stone paved frontage and generous lawned gardens might inspire those minor poets employed by some estate agents. PC Pinder, wearing an eloquently impatient expression, waited for her in silence.

When she was ready, Jennifer moved forward and Carol Pinder followed. 'At least the woman's had the news broken to her already.'

The sergeant stiffened, then answered quietly, her voice expressionless. 'If you're thinking of Mrs Denton as "the woman", perhaps you'd better wait outside.'

Jennifer's heart sank. This officer had met Louise Denton when she was regarded as the wife of a missing man. Seemingly this had led to no rapport with her and Pinder apparently had felt no sympathy. What, the sergeant wondered, was Shakila doing this morning that was more important than the delicate task of obtaining information sensitively from a bereaved woman, whilst, at the same time, assessing the possibility that she might be in some way involved in his death?

She stepped forward and rang the efficient modern bell set into the stout and venerable door. The face of the woman who opened it to her was as closed and antagonistic as her present colleague's.

The Leeds force had informed them that Mrs Denton senior had arrived here the previous day and it was the older woman to whom Jennifer had spoken on the telephone earlier today. This one was younger. 'Louise Denton?'

The woman admitted to her name and ushered the two officers politely enough into a comfortable sitting room with cavernous chairs. Jennifer sank into the one she was offered. PC Pinder, choosing to express her resentment through martyrdom, sat on an upright wooden structure with gilded arms and no upholstery.

Jennifer melted her hostess's belligerent glare with her first remark. 'You must be very tired of sympathizers who tell you they can imagine how you feel. I asked to be the officer who came from Cloughton today. My husband was a policeman – in traffic division. He was blown to bits by a car bomb. I was pregnant at the time like you. It was some years ago now and the rawness has gone, but I do understand your situation a little.' She felt Carol Pinder shift behind her and hoped that she was uncomfortable in every sense. Louise Denton made no immediate reply but sat down herself and nodded her head slowly in acknowledgement of what she had been told.

Jennifer waited, giving the bereaved woman time and using it in trying to see

Louise as she would normally be. She was tall – taller, if Dr Holland was to be believed, than her husband had been – and raw-boned. Lean was the word she brought to mind rather than slim. Louise had an athlete's figure and a mannish face with well-marked brows and a prominent nose. Thick straight hair was pushed carelessly behind her ears. The teeth were large and well cared for. Jennifer suspected that she had worn a brace round them. She had noticed, in that kind of facial structure, the teeth usually protruded.

She guessed that Louise had been expensively brought up to believe that she had nothing to prove. Her clothes were casual – a polo-necked sweater, a knee-length skirt and knee-high boots. She wore no make-up. Either from fortunate carelessness or a good eye, she had presented herself in the best possible light. She was attractive because she was clean, healthy and confident.

She looked up at Jennifer now, half smiling. 'All right. I'm ready.'

During the long silence, the sergeant had noticed a photograph of a family group which included Louise and a man who was probably her husband. She reached out to pick it up. 'Are these folk some of your family? Tell me about them.'

It was a delightful study of man, wife and three children on a squashy sofa heaped with cushions. The tiny boy was standing, barefooted, on the woman's knee, her hands round his upper arms to steady him. The photograph was probably not taken professionally as the man's lower face was obscured by the waving arms of the small girl perched on his knee. All four were laughing rather than just smiling. In front of them, sitting on the floor and leaning against the man's knees, was a solemn, slightly older girl, posing responsibly and staring at the camera. Louise watched her without speaking.

Jennifer prompted her. 'Is this Simon?' The man was fair with regular features. His mouth – what could be seen of it – was smiling more than his eyes. His skin was reddened but not florid. Weather-beaten, she thought, rather than the result of high blood pressure or drink. Was that too much to read into a photograph?

'Yes, that was Simon.' Louise's tone was flat.

'With some of your nieces and nephews?'

'Oh no. They're ours. Elizabeth and Joanna are playing at a friend's house just now and Oliver is having his nap.'

Jennifer was puzzled. 'I thought this was your first child. The nurse in Simon's ward said–'

Louise held up her hand to stop the questions. 'You know Simon was adopted as a

259

baby?' Jennifer nodded. 'He got a way-out mother and a rock-solid father and he had a very happy chidhood with them. We fostered the three children and then decided that we might adopt the girls. It was to be Simon's payback for what he was given, and his compensation as well. He had mumps when he was a boy and we all, including the doctors, thought he was sterile.

'We've nothing against Ollie, by the way. It was just that he's taking a long time to settle with us and we want to be sure he'll be happy. Eventually we would have begun proceedings to adopt him too...' She stopped, seeming to lapse into her own thoughts.

'And then you became pregnant yourself.'

'Yes. It was a shock. Simon's mother even asked me if someone else was the father. I can assure you this child is Simon's. As soon as he knew about it, he started fussing about what sort of character traits the baby would inherit and whether he'd have any health problems.'

'I gather you didn't share his worries.'

'I'm curious, of course, but we don't know a great deal about the heredity of the three we're already looking after. I didn't like the idea of searching out his birth mother for several reasons. There'd be more people making a difference in their treatment of this fourth child – you know, an extra grandmother the others didn't have. And Simon might have found out things he couldn't cope with. Anyway, now the baby's already conceived, I don't see the point. It's different knowing about problems beforehand so that you can avoid them but why look for trouble when it's too late to avoid it? And then there's Kaya.'

Jennifer raised a questioning eyebrow. 'She's Simon's adoptive mother. Don't ask me about her. She indescribable. You'd have to meet her.'

'It's an unusual name. Is she foreign?'

Louise gave an unamused laugh. 'She was christened – with great ceremony according to her older sister – Kay Patricia. All through her childhood, she was known as Pat Meadows. She reinvented herself when she met Wynford. Her sister's always been plain Joan. She's nice and quite ordinary. You wouldn't think there was any connection...'

She stopped speaking again as they all heard the sound of a child's crying. Louise rose and made for the door. Jennifer got as far as, 'Will your mother not go...' before she had disappeared.

She returned moments later, carrying the small blond boy who appeared in the picture. He buried his face in Louise's sweater when he saw visitors. She said, apologetically, 'My mother has an agenda for me. It involves sending all three children to an-

261

other foster home "in the circumstances" – or maybe even an institution – and concentrating on her blood grandchild. She's gone home.'

Jennifer had the impression that the going had not been voluntary. She asked, 'Are you afraid that your husband's death will affect the progress of the adoption procedure for your two girls?'

Louise blinked. 'Oh, it hadn't really begun. Simon had made a first approach just as we discovered that I was pregnant. We thought about it and decided to wait. Simon said it would make them feel more secure as they grew up if they knew we had arranged their adoption after our own biological child was born. Now my mother's taking this attitude, I keep thinking that we should perhaps have got on with it earlier.'

Jennifer wondered how she could discover exactly whose suggestion this had been. She thanked her witness for the information she had given. 'It's all very useful background but could you face a few specific questions now?' There was no reply but she pressed on into the silence. 'What was Simon's job?'

'He worked for a small pharmaceutical company.' Shifting the child slightly to free her arm, she reached into a drawer and handed Jennifer a card printed with the details she needed. 'I worked at the same place before we were married. I was his assistant.' Her tone put this last term into inverted commas. Did she mean that she had been promoted beyond what her ability justified because a relationship had developed between Simon and herself?

The child evidently decided these visitors were not threatening. He wriggled round to survey them with huge eyes. Jennifer winked at him and he attempted to return the greeting, screwing up his whole face. The sergeant turned back to his mother and asked, 'Did you know where Simon was staying in Cloughton?'

Louise considered. 'I don't know the address, but I've got a phone number. I didn't use it because Simon had his mobile, but it's here somewhere from when he booked the place.' She set the boy down and rummaged more deeply in the same drawer. After a minute she produced the twin of the card she had already passed over. This one had a telephone number and a name written on the back. 'He got the place from the Cloughton Tourist Office,' she said, pushing the card across the table between them. 'Anything else?'

Her tone was dismissive, but Jennifer settled further back in her chair. 'We're rather curious,' she remarked, 'about why you didn't visit your husband when he was in the hospital for a whole week.'

'Is that a question?' Her hostility was back.

'Why didn't you?'

'Because I'd started bleeding. I thought I was losing the baby. The doctor wasn't as concerned as I was, but she suggested a few days' bed rest as a precaution. My mother took the three children and said she would ring Simon to come home, but then we got the message that he was ill and in hospital.'

'Leaving you lying in bed worrying.'

'Yes, I suppose. The news didn't surprise me though. Even without the infection his asthma's bad if he gets agitated. He was anxious to find his birth mother and about what she might be like and worried because his adoptive mother was angry. We thought if he knew about me it would take him longer to get better.'

'So how did you explain your absence?'

'He actually told me himself not to visit. This baby that he thought he'd never have was very important to him. He said it would be stressful to me to drive through the rush hour at visiting times and to hunt around for babysitters. He did suspect that something was going on though, because, twice, he asked to speak to the children and I said they were with my mother. He thought it was odd because she isn't fond of small children and she doesn't consider these three to be grand-children.' She added, inconsequentially, 'He wanted a boy. I hadn't told him it's a girl.'

'I'm a boy,' Oliver announced, proudly.

'You are and we're very proud of you.'

The child nodded in agreement, then fell to his knees and began to tug at a box of toys tucked under a small table. The two women watched him for a few moments without speaking, then Jennifer remarked, 'You've said very little about how you feel about what was going on.' This was received with silence. Jennifer persevered. 'Did you relish the idea of a second mother-in-law?' After a further pause, she added, 'Mine's an absolute godsend, but it's a risk I wouldn't care to take again.'

Louise nodded. 'Simon said he wanted information. He didn't seem to be planning to start up a new relationship with this woman if he found her. He was a soft touch, though. If she'd told him a sob story, he'd have fallen for it and then, who knows what we'd have been lumbered with?'

Jennifer began to feel that she might owe Carol Pinder an apology. She put the thought aside for a moment and pressed on. 'You referred to adopting the fostered children as Simon's payback and his compensation. What did the plan mean to you?'

For the first time, Louise looked Jennifer full in the face. 'To be honest with you, they were a cause of resentment at first. I didn't like being expected to give up my career for children who not only were not mine – they were not even his. Then they grew on me.

Now I love them.'

She bent to take up a spinning top with which Oliver had been struggling and set it humming. The child's eyes lit up and he reached out to it. Immediately, Louise stopped smiling and spoke sharply. 'How many times have I to tell you not to touch it when it's spinning?'

Oliver's lower lip trembled. He crawled under the table, but was not seriously upset. He poked his head out on Jennifer's side and made a second attempt at a wink. He seemed a nice child and she wished him a better future than to live with this woman. A few minutes later she took her leave along with a sullen PC Pinder.

As they walked down the drive the Leeds officer confronted her. 'You snubbed me for my attitude to Mrs Denton but I didn't hear you commiserating with her.'

Jennifer considered the accusation. 'I think I did, in my own way, but I freely admit your assessment was based on what she deserved. She isn't very nice, is she?'

Possibly PC Pinder was not used to apologies from senior officers. The smile with which she accepted this one was forgiving. Jennifer pushed her advantage. 'Time for a cup of something – somewhere cosy? We're grateful for what's been sent to us from your people, but there are a few questions I'd like to ask about your first visit to this house.

You were present when your sergeant looked round, weren't you?'

The cold wind showered the two officers with a sudden blast of icy rain which decided the question for them. Over tea and toasted teacakes, they compared their impressions of Louise and Jennifer listened to Carol Pinder's description of the token search that had been made of the house. 'The super didn't want us to probe too deeply. He was hoping we could pass the whole business over to you folk.'

Jennifer laughed and saw that she had no need to explain what had amused her. 'Your super's going to be happier than ours then. I've read what you sent us. I was interested in the bit about two versions of Simon Denton's piece of research.'

The Leeds officer shrugged. 'I was the one who found it – at least, I found the locked drawer. We opened it with one of an enormous bunch of keys that Louise produced. It seemed to be two versions of the same basic idea – not that I read it personally. They were both computer printouts, of course, but the handwritten annotations were in two different people's writing. I expect you'll have to find out who he was collaborating with. Our super thought, till today, that Denton would turn up when it suited him.'

The two women chatted for a few minutes longer before Jennifer excused herself. She had daughters she was hoping to see before their bedtime. She said goodbye quickly and was pleased that the PC waved as she drove away.

Mitchell had given DC Clement the task of interviewing Simon Denton's adoptive parents. Clement wondered whether Mrs Denton senior would turn out to be another of the old ladies that he was good with. Whatever his attitude to his orders, he had accepted them with good grace, remembering the CI's outburst the previous day.

The senior Dentons lived in Ripley, a village between Cloughton and Bradford on a hill where the wind blew constantly and postcodes were disputed. Clement found Town End Farm on the very edge of the village with green fields rising to the skyline behind it. Its back was towards Cloughton and Clement wondered whether that was the town it considered itself the end of. He thought not. Nor was it Bradford. Had Ripley itself once been considered a town? Certainly it was only a village now.

If this building had really been a farmhouse, Clement thought the farm must have been rather small. It was beautiful. There was a white wash over most of the stonework and it was topped with a roof of old slates. The gardens were neat but not painfully so, planned for use and enjoyment rather than show. There was no fashionable landscaping, just an extensive lawn with shrubs in the border and trees at the end, under which snowdrops grew in hundreds.

Clement stood on a small terrace of York stone flags and gravel, having parked his squad car alongside a Mercedes, gleaming but far from new. The door was opened before he rang the bell. Wynford Denton invited him in, introduced himself and informed Clement that his wife would join them presently. He spoke extremely quietly but his enunciation was so clear that nothing he said was lost.

They walked through a hall and into a sitting room over lush carpeting. Clement was ushered into an ordinary-looking armchair and realized its quality only when he sank into it. He looked around him, assessing the rest of the furnishings. Everything about the house, outside and in, was as understated as only the possessions of the very rich could afford to be.

His host made no conversation as they waited, but regarded Clement calmly. Clement returned the scrutiny. Wynford Denton's face was thin and mobile, his hair lank and receding, reaching to his shoulder blades in a pony tail. Over the crown of the head, the curl was dragged out of it by the tension of the elastic band that held it, but the tail behind looped in a miserable ringlet.

The man wore a good jacket over a shape-less T-shirt. Both were black, but the shirt, like his hair, was greying. When footsteps were heard outside the door the man rose to open it.

Kaya Denton came in carrying a tray. Having placed it on a low table, she settled herself on a cushion on the floor. Clement made a number of what he knew were sweeping judgements. She would most likely be deep into alternative medicine, meditation and some kind of weird religion. Why else would a woman in her late fifties sit on the floor? She would be guided by stones and symbols instead of common sense. What practical use would someone be who wore a couple of dozen metal bangles on one arm?

He turned from his hostess and surveyed her tray with some trepidation. All his judgements were justified. She was offering him some sort of herbal tea with honey and a wedge of heavy-looking cake with figs in it! There should be danger money for this.

Kaya Denton too was dressed completely in black. Clement felt that it was probably their custom rather than mourning. He commiserated with them briefly and un-comfortably. He always found it easier when bereaved people's grief was apparent. If they were not weeping already, he was afraid that anything he said might disturb whatever was holding them together. Besides, would this New Age couple expect the same conventional words on any subject as normal people?

The Dentons accepted the remarks they were offered calmly. Wynford refused cake – wise man. He put his tea, untasted, on the table and appeared to be meditating profoundly. His wife, rattling as she moved, fussed over her offerings. Clement counted the silver bangles. He had exaggerated. There were only twelve of them. Some of the percussion came from a necklace of pearlized discs strung on a cord. Her rings were silent, as was the hoop in her right earlobe, the size of which made up for its singleness.

Clement pulled his thoughts back to his duties and asked when they had last seen their son. They looked at each other for inspiration. Clement tried again. 'Did he get in touch with you whilst he was in Cloughton?'

This provoked an immediate response and an increase in the jangling. 'We didn't even know he was there until a couple of days ago. It seems that I was going to be replaced...'

Wynford placed an admonitory hand on his wife's shoulder. 'To answer your first question, it was three weeks ago when we got our duty monthly visit. We didn't know until then that Louise was pregnant or that Simon had any interest in his birth mother.'

'That's how it's been ever since he was

married...' The substitute mother continued to inveigh against her son's in-laws as she angrily clattered crockery, stacking plates crookedly back on to the tray. Clement allowed her to continue, waiting for any detail that his CI might appreciate. Anger was cracking the careful make-up which had not flattered her when it was fresh. Her eyebrows had been assisted to reach almost to her ears. The dark pencilling and crimson lipstick emphasized a hardness in the features. The hardness had been unalloyed even by the dazzling smiles to which she had treated him earlier, though the smiles had at least revealed a row of enviable straight white teeth.

Without speaking, her husband dropped his hand and placed it on her arm. As before, she responded, if reluctantly. The tirade stopped and she gave her whole attention to making her pile of crockery more stable. Clement revised his opinion that the woman was the leading spirit in their relationship and returned to his questions.

'We haven't been able to find out any details of Simon's adoption. Was it private?'

'Very. We put about a story that we were taking care of him temporarily because of family problems.' She produced a grim smile and another display of teeth. 'No need for the authorities to poke their noses into a simple act of kindness.'

She seemed to be acting a role and over-playing it, her tones harsh and loud, in striking contrast to her husband's. As though inviting him to take a part too, she went to sit beside him. When he failed to put a protecting arm around her, she took one herself and placed it around her shoulders.

Clement watched and felt sorry for her. He judged her to be older than her husband. Lines proliferated round her mouth and lower cheeks. Her forehead was relatively smooth, probably because her much hennaed hair was pulled back so tightly into its skimpy bun. She continued her tale. 'As he grew older, of course, there was inter-ference, but by then he had become our son by custom. Everyone testified that he was happy and so the court case that followed went in our favour. Anyway, there was no one else wanting him. There were rumblings about precedent, but the main principle was what was in the child's best interests.'

'So how old was Simon when the law intervened?'

Kaya glanced at her husband and he answered. 'It was when he was seven and we sent him to prep school. It was a conscien-tious one that asked a lot of questions. It was also at a time when the social services were getting a lot of earache about child abuse and everything was being tightened up.' He removed his arm from his wife's shoulder and cleared his throat. Anticipating the next question, he said, 'It was because we had never asked for any money that we had never been challenged before. We didn't claim family allowance or apply for any tax concessions. It's surprising what can be swept under the carpet if there's no money to fight about.' He stopped speaking and returned to his meditation.

Clement debated whether he would learn more by asking further questions or by letting his interviewees fill the silence. He waited, his eyes on the man's face. It was hardly lined. The blue eyes were keen and told Clement that the man would keep his own counsel. He had the impression that this extreme degree of reserve was not usual for Denton and it occurred to him now that the man was genuinely overcome with grief for the horrific death of his unconventionally acquired son.

He turned back to the wife who was more concerned with her in-laws' infringements of her rights. 'So, you must have known Simon's real mother well.' He realized his mistake too late and met her glare apologetically.

'I'm his real mother!'

'In every way that matters, of course you are – and, as his mother, you'll want to cooperate in every way with our search for his killer.'

Her expression softened and she set herself to answer Clement's implied question. Clement understood that the change of attitude was not effected by his placatory remark. It was her response to her husband's replacing his arm, voluntarily this time, round her shoulders.

'No, I don't know her at all. She was a close friend of someone I went to school with. She was called Freeman – well, she was at school anyway. She married a Robert Shaw. I went to school with him too.' The pronouns were getting inextricably mixed. The longer Mrs Denton talked, the less Clement would understand about the relationships of all the people who had had a hand in Simon Denton's having been brought up in this household.

He noted carefully all the names and the odd clear fact from the muddled story. He could read up the Dentons' court appearance. He could possibly ask Jennifer whether Louise Denton could throw any light on the situation. He could almost certainly persuade the CI to call Wynford Denton to the station without his wife. Not displeased with the facts and impressions he had obtained, Clement put away his pocketbook and made his farewells.

His plan to prowl around Leeds for an hour, revisiting old haunts, was scotched by a call from his chief inspector. Could he go to Baker Pharmaceuticals and speak to Simon Denton's immediate superior, Simon Pollard?

'Was that an order you gave me? It sounded as though I had a choice.'

'You have, so long as you make the right one. Oh, Adrian, cheer up. I don't think any of them will be past retiring age.'

Dorian Shaw's day off was evaporating around him as he continued to sit in the same chair that he had occupied since Becca had left the room. His mind, though, had been busy. Mentally, he had confronted Becca about the drugs, about her responsibilities, about the way she valued everything in financial terms. He had terminated each conversation, as it played itself out in his head, before it could reach its inevitable and disastrous conclusion.

What he must do, though, since she had reneged on her responsibilities towards it, was to see to next door's cat. In this freezing weather, she spent the nights shut in their garage. She was a clean creature and by now would have been shut up for sixteen hours or more. She would certainly be in some distress and anxious to be let out.

He was not particularly an animal lover and he hoped he would not end up assisting at the birth of Bunty's kittens. Reluctantly he took the neighbours' keys from the row of hooks by the door and a bottle of milk from the fridge. He ran down two flights of concrete steps to the ground floor of their block of flats. Cutting through the side gate into the garden of the first of a row of semi-detached houses, he pressed the disc on the car key and the up-and-over door of the garage rolled up smoothly.

Bunty shot out in a flash of tabby stripes and squatted on a flower bed. Dorian averted his eyes as he would have from a patient on a bedpan. Having relieved herself and tidied the flower bed with her paws, the cat set off immediately back to the garage. He thought she looked thinner. He hurried round the Robinsons' pale blue Bentley to peer into the blanket-lined box and found it full of bodies. They were so small that he could have held two in the palm of his hand if their heads had hung over the edge. They lay across one another but he thought he could count five, fully furred in assorted colours with their little umbilical cords chewed off roughly and already beginning to shrivel. Why had he thought kittens were born pink and bare? They had been licked clean and dry. Their eyes were tight shut and their ears folded down, not yet pricked. They made little mewling noises as they sought Bunty's teats.

For a whole minute, he stood entranced, all his worries forgotten. The proud mother raised her eyes to him, half suspicious, half beseeching. He wasn't the usual source of food, but nor was he a stranger. She was anxious for her new family but very hungry.

The bench to his left held three clean saucers, several tins of supermarket cat food and a tin opener. He poured milk, then found a plastic lidded tin, half its contents used. He used the opener as a fork to push the meat on to another saucer and placed both offerings beside the box.

He wondered about the temperature. The garage was cool but not draughty. Bunty would curl herself round the kittens when she had finished her late breakfast. The feline family would survive now until Becca could be woken up. He stood watching the little creatures for a few moments longer, knowing that soon he would have to face up to all the problems of his own family life, if a family was what they had ever been. In fact, the time for decisions was now.

This time, he made no plans to discuss things with Becca, to try to explain his point of view to her. She was not going to change. The decision he had to make was whether their nights of passion and his pride in being seen with her were worth the grief she was causing him. He wondered if the passion might be somewhat one-sided, or whether perhaps Becca's passion was for what he would inherit rather than who he was. He had to work out whether he could continue to give his affection – no, his love – with no return except the pleasure of pleasing her. For the first time, it occurred to him to wonder how she had learned the expert techniques she used in bed.

What she had given him – no, she had given him nothing. What he had gained for himself, apart from sexual pleasure, was a reason for his existence. He was there to protect her from the law and, in his professional capacity, from some of the physical results of what was fast becoming an addiction. Were his patients then not another reason to justify his being? Not, he thought, in any personal way.

He had better go home. He looked around the garage checking that he had left everything tidy, then stopped and frowned. He didn't think that the car was in the same position as it had been the last time he had had to feed the cat. That was worrying – though it was possible that Becca had moved it to leave more space round the cats' box. He knew she had parked it after driving the Robinsons to the airport and she wouldn't use it again until she picked them up there next week. He would check with her later whether anyone else had keys. If any harm came to the car they would be held responsible.

It was extremely dirty and splashed and

there was something caught under the rear off-side mudguard. Curious, he went to pick it off. It was a photograph, just a passport-sized shot, stuck to the metal by a clod of mud thrown up by the wheel. He tore it slightly in pulling it out. He took it over to the window to examine it in the light. The man smiling from the picture, his arm round the shoulders of a woman, presumably his wife, was Simon Denton.

At Baker Pharmaceuticals, Clement was received by a rather worried-looking managing director. Was Robin Chalmers, the DC wondered, not comfortable with interviews that he did not conduct and control himself? Or had he, perhaps, something to hide?

The man demanded officiously that Clement should observe the company policy to record all interviews with its employees, from himself down to the cleaners. Clement was amused by Chalmers' understanding of the structure of society. He said, 'But you could alter it. That's not an accusation, just a statement of fact.'

The man smiled with surface charm. 'You'll have your copy before you leave. You can supervise the making of it if you like.'

Was the recording a spur-of-the-moment idea to put him off his stride? If so it wouldn't work. Clement told him, 'I can and I will.'

Taking that as agreement, Chalmers switched on his machine. Clement sat back, quite content. Under the agreed circumstances, the tape would probably be of more benefit to the investigation than to Baker's. He asked his first question. 'What, precisely, was Simon Denton's job here?'

Chalmers cleared his throat in preparation for this demonstration of his sharpness and fluency. 'Our headquarters are in the States but Baker Pharmaceuticals is a speciality pharmaceutical company that develops and commercializes products mainly for clinical skincare. In addition to our discovery-to-development research programme, we have global marketing and sales capabilities in over a hundred countries. We have a workforce of over four thousand people and—'

Clement had had enough. 'Now you've got the propaganda out of your system, could you answer my question?'

Chalmers blinked and drew breath. 'We have a distinct company strategy focusing strongly on the development and marketing of speciality products.' He stuttered to a stop, noting the warning in Clement's eye.

'We shall do our homework and read the account of your company on the website that you are quoting to me. Did you write it? Or perhaps Simon Denton did?'

'Neither. Denton's expertise was originally in the development of topical products for dermatology. In recent years we have begun building new competencies in the design and clinical investigation of oral drugs.'

Clement was becoming increasingly grateful for the tape. All these terms could be looked up later and he needn't waste time and dam up the flow of information by asking about them now. He was following the drift so far though. 'Are you trying to tell me that Simon Denton was trying to adapt stuff that used to be in creams and lotions to pill form?'

'Basically, yes.'

'Let's keep it basic then, shall we?'

'All right. Simon was working on oral formulations for severe cases of psoriasis. Do you know what that is?'

'I do, but my boss may not.' Too late, Clement remembered that his boss would listen to the tape.

Deciding that this inaptly named managing director either would not or could not tell him what he needed to know, he asked to speak to Simon Pollard, Denton's immediate superior. He soon discovered that, if it were possible, he liked Pollard less than Chalmers, but this man at least spoke plain English. Denton had worked in the company's 'Product Research and Development Pipeline' and had apparently almost finished a detailed monograph on a particular aspect of his psoriasis topic. It explained his research and the potential practical application of it, providing also a five-year sales forecast for his prospective product. Certain technical terms floated past Clement's comprehension but he felt he had a basic grasp of Denton's plans and achievements.

At one point, the door of Pollard's office opened and a head appeared round it. 'There you are, Poll,' it said. 'Can you just come–'

Pollard shook his head. 'Later. I'm helping the police, in the person of this officer, with their enquiries.'

'About Denny? OK, I'll sort it myself.' The head disappeared and the door closed.

Clement asked, 'Does everyone call you that?'

'We don't stand on ceremony and use surnames, but there are four Simons in this section. Denton and I are two. The other two even both have the initial E as surname. Eventually each of us answered to a corruption of our family name. Denton became Denny. Endicott is, unoriginally, Endy. You'd do well to speak to him. Denny worked for me but largely he worked with Endy. I'll send for him when you're ready.'

Pollard finally came to the end of his remarks with a fulsome testimonial to Denton. 'We'll have an awful job, trying to replace him.'

Endy, when he appeared, was a man after

Clement's own heart, producing just the kind of information Mitchell would want – pure gossip. As he chattered on, the DC wondered whether the man was aware of the 'company policy to tape'. He wondered whether Simon Endicott should be warned, but dismissed his misgivings. He had no wish to hamper his own enquiries.

Questions were hardly necessary after the opening one: 'Did you make any contribution to Mr Denton's monograph?'

'Denny's monograph! I didn't need to. It was nearly finished when he took it over, though none of the big cheeses know that.'

'Who did the donkey work then?'

'Louise Merton, his assistant. It wasn't part of her work. She was bright and was doing it as a kind of hobby. She used to work on her laptop after hours and on her days off because she'd got excited about one of the components of some stuff Denny was experimenting on. She was his research assistant. Well, he called her an assistant. Most people at our level knew that she did a lot of the work and he collected the credit for it. The gossips say that the reason he married her was because she was proving to be cleverer than him and she was beginning to show him up. They also say that she accepted him because he was rich and she thought they would go on working together. Then he lumbered her with three ready-made kids to keep her at home.'

'Right. Louise Merton is now Louise Denton.' Endicott nodded. 'And was the gossip accurate?'

'Don't know.' He shook his head virtuously. 'You'll have to speak to those who started it.'

'Does the gossip say anything else?'

Endicott shrugged. 'It's always saying something. Some folk think Poll was sweet on Louise. He was in the States when she and Denny got engaged. He was certainly gob-smacked when he came back and heard about it.'

When Clement could bear no more, he reached over and switched off the tape recorder. He enjoyed the horror on Endicott's face as he was dismissed. It was a good thing, he decided, that he had issued no warnings.

At the Mitchells' house, Saturday evening supper was a cheerful occasion at which they normally ate a takeaway meal of some kind. Before the days of Virginia's cookery course, this meal was eagerly awaited by the family from Sunday morning to Saturday evening each week. Fare on the Mitchells' table had improved vastly over the last year.

'Now Mum can cook a bit, we'll have to find something else to laugh about,' Declan had once remarked. Virginia had objected to

285

'a bit' but had taken her elder son's joke in good part. Tonight it had been Sinead's turn to choose the treat. The pizzas had disappeared down to the last crumb and all seven of them were greasy-fingered and replete.

Virginia took the twins upstairs to be bathed, Caitlin had been sent to wash up the plates and Declan had gone to start his homework. Mitchell looked across at his nephew. 'I think you can go back to your chess games with Mr Cornish now. I have to ask you, though, for reasons I'm not able to explain right now, to arrange to play them here rather than in Crellin Drive. You'll find it has advantages. You're not at home in Ripon any more but you are reasonably comfortable and relaxed here, aren't you?'

'Yes. It's good here.'

'Your friend will be off his home ground here. You'll be putting him at the same disadvantage as you were at yourself when he first beat you.'

'I suppose so, but I don't want to beat him now. I want to learn his tricks.'

'I'm sorry. It's here or not at all.'

Fran scowled. 'But he'll think we're snobs. He'll think we consider his street dangerous or run down – somewhere where I wouldn't want to be seen.'

'I thought you would prefer it to not playing with him at all.'

Fran's face was set. 'Well, I don't.'

Virginia came back into the room. 'I've left them to their water play for five minutes. If you see waves coming downstairs, Fran, just warn me.' She took note of his sullen expression but made no immediate comment. After a minute or two, Fran announced that he was going to clean and oil his bike ready for a long ride the next day.

'No church then?'

'Do I have to? Oh, you mean Declan might not want to go if I don't?'

'That's up to him. As Father Xavier remarked to me earlier this week, Declan doesn't need anyone's protection to meet with his Maker. Where are you thinking of riding to?'

Fran shrugged. 'I'll wait for the weather forecast and then decide.'

When he had wandered off, Virginia asked, 'What's bitten him?'

'I said he could play chess with Cornish again, provided it was here. He took exception to it on Cornish's behalf. I sympathize with him. It's not easy to explain something tactfully when you don't understand it yourself.'

Virginia nodded. 'So, Cornish is half off the hook. He didn't make away with Simon Denton but he still might be an incendiary.'

'That's it exactly.'

Mitchell waited for his wife's objections. Instead, she said thoughtfully, 'I had a bit of a barney with Fran myself on Thursday morning.'

'What about?'

'I hardly know. Something and nothing. He's small for his age and still physically adolescent, he's in limbo here with no company of his own age and no structure to his days. You put the boot in on his chess. He must be fed up. I'd suggest he tried to get a part-time job of some kind. He could save up the money to buy something for the bike – but who'd want him when he might suddenly have to up sticks and go?'

A shriek from upstairs accompanied by much splashing prevented her from hearing any suggestions Mitchell might have had.

## Chapter Eight

In the Mitchell family, Sunday morning was sacrosanct. Barring crises or significant family occasions, nothing was ever arranged. Weekdays and Saturdays were for work, school, music lessons, sports fixtures and personal commitments. Virginia was adamant that the children's week should leave some 'messing about time' and this was it.

This particular Sunday, after a lively family breakfast, Caitlin had chosen to reorganize her bedroom. Sinead, when last checked on, was dancing in the sitting room to music from the radio. Michael was adding to a sizeable castle of Lego bricks, begun the previous weekend and already seriously impeding progress across from the door to his bed.

Fran had departed, in full cycling regalia, to Beverley. Declan, not quite daring to ask if he could go too, had set off on a less ambitious ride. His parents had demanded details of his intended route and assured him that, if he seriously intended to become 'a real cyclist like Fran', he would certainly be provided with the appropriate gear that he had requested. Bemoaning his own lack of messing about time, Mitchell glanced at his watch and departed in haste.

As Clement debated with himself how to engineer a meeting with Wynford Denton, without the distraction of his wife's complaints, the problem was solved for him. His 'Morning, Magic,' was answered with, 'Customer waiting.' He turned and saw his quarry, an empty coffee cup in front of him, seated on the padded bench in the foyer.

Denton senior seemed to be wearing yesterday's clothes under a black leather coat, unbuttoned now, in the warmth of the building. He looked as though he had not slept. Clement offered him a canteen breakfast but the man shook his head. 'I must make this brief. My wife is not aware that I'm here.'

Clement sat beside him. 'So, what can I do for you?'

Denton looked down at his feet for some moments and, when he spoke, it was not to give a direct answer. 'I loved my adopted son, Constable Clement, but I was not blind to his faults. Yesterday, Kaya was less than fair to his wife and I want to redress the wrong that we did her. Simon was always very charming but he liked his own way and was determined to get it. People didn't always realize that. He was a Jacob, not an Esau...'

'What?' Clement vaguely associated these names with some early book in the Old Testament. He was surprised. Wynford Denton looked as though he would know more about the Druids than the Bible.

'Jacob was a smooth man. So was our son in every sense. He was quite bright mentally, but quick to pick things up rather than an original thinker. He was sharp enough to know which brains to pick. I had the impression that his wife would have risen higher in the pharmaceutical business than Simon would. I think he borrowed Louise's ideas for his own work and decided that having her at home would facilitate and also conceal this deception.

'The marriage was becoming less happy as Louise saw what was happening. She was shocked and disillusioned when she found out that their lovely house had been bought with our money and she resented being expected to care for Simon's "waifs and strays". That was how I once heard her refer to the children. She hadn't realized that I had come into the room. The two girls are rather waif-like, Elizabeth especially. I don't know what will happen to them all now, nor what, if anything, I can do for them.'

Denton gave his shoes a further close examination, then looked up again. 'Louise is strong-minded but Simon was extremely manipulative in a subtle way. I could never decide whether it was done consciously. Kaya thinks it was because of Louise's antipathy towards us that he visited us so seldom, but I fear it was not.'

Clement listened patiently to more in a similar vein. Though no new facts emerged, he was interested in what the man had had to say, alternately feeling profoundly sorry for and then suspicious of him. He had plenty to think about as he ran upstairs, hoping not to be late for the morning call.

Half an hour later, the morning briefing was under way. Mitchell checked that his team members were all aware of the scraps of information that had come in in the last few hours. 'There's a call out for Simon Denton's car. It's not the family one – he left that for his wife. He was apparently going to hire one here but ended up buying an old banger with which he seems to have demolished his landlady's gatepost. I thought it would have turned up before now but joyriders may have taken a fancy to it.'

'So, it might be anywhere.'

Mitchell glared at Clement. 'Confine interruptions to what's useful.' The rest of the team took note of the CI's mood and let him continue. 'Dorian Shaw has been to the station to bring us a picture of Denton with a woman.' He held it out to Jennifer. 'Is that Louise?' She nodded.

'It's filthy because it was caught in a clod of mud, stuck to the underside of the mudguard–'

'Who owns the car?'

This question was answered, unchallenged. 'Dorian Shaw's neighbour. Lambert was on cat-sitting duty. She also drove the owners to Manchester airport ten days ago and is due to meet them there on this coming Wednesday. He'd gone in to feed the cats because she was stoned.'

'Did he say that?'

Mitchell opened his mouth to reprimand but closed it again. Caroline's question was fair. 'He left a note at the desk, with the photograph. It's in the file – just says he offered to do it. The rest is my brilliant deduction. He's shopping her. Bit of a change of policy on his part.'

Caroline interrupted suddenly. 'Shakila, can you get your friend Pat Seddon to take a look at this muddy car?' There was no response. 'Shakila!'

The DC started and blinked, obviously unaware of Caroline's question. Mitchell felt he had been patient with her for long enough. 'Shakila!! Go home now. That's an order. First thing tomorrow, get yourself back here, either fit to do some work or prepared to tell me exactly what's wrong with you.'

Biting her lip and with head bowed, Shakila stumbled out of the office. Caroline rose to follow. Mitchell glowered at her, then reached for the telephone and requested that a driver should deliver his DC to her house.

Quite calm again, he turned to Caroline. 'What will get us further with Shaw, frightening the living daylight out of him or appealing to his better nature?'

Clement suggested, 'A bit of both, good cop, bad cop?'

Mitchell grinned. 'Which are you, then?' Clement seemed to give the question serious consideration as Mitchell turned to PC Smithson. 'Bring him in when this powwow is over. I'll scare him myself. You can stay to pick the pieces up. We've got to decide quickly whether those two miseries are worth all the time we're spending on them.' He switched his gaze to the two remaining women. 'You've talked to them. Well?'

Caroline said, 'I don't think Shaw has either the guts or the motivation on his own account. If he was scared of losing his inheritance he'd hardly have been so helpful with Denton's searches. He has seemed completely in thrall to Lambert though. It's extraordinary – she's got very little to recommend her. She's rude and she's scruffy – though I've seen her when she was under the influence. She's definitely on something that's doing her no good. She might clean up quite well if she felt like making the effort.'

Jennifer added, 'She's tall and muscular and she's fond of having her own way. I could see her cheerfully disposing of anyone she considered to be an obstacle. She'd probably be strong enough to lug and drag the body about if she's county standard in chucking a javelin.'

Clement asked, 'Is Shaw becoming less blinkered? He must see that that photograph might implicate her in some way. According to what she says, she hasn't even met Simon Denton. Why did he bring the picture to us?'

Mitchell considered but only produced another question. 'Who went to check her friend out, the one she visited on Monday night?'

PC Smithson raised a hand. 'I didn't get much. Name's Hannah Webb. She said Becca arrived later than expected, around nine, but she wasn't watching the time. She'd been going to give Hannah a lift to the pub because she'd broken an ankle. Becca said she didn't feel well and they stayed in.'

'What was she driving?'

'Dorian's car. Hannah said she looked a bit windswept. They stayed together till about eleven. Apparently she always made a fuss over minor ailments but she looked rough this time and Hannah was sympathetic.'

'Did she make any comment on the woman in general, or her relationship with Shaw?'

Smithson gave his CI a hard look. 'It's all in the file. She said Becca had an eye to the main chance, which we'd gathered for ourselves.'

'Did that mean Shaw's expected inheritance?'

'I expect so. She said he wasn't anybody's dreamboat but he was a nice guy. Hannah herself seemed shallow but sharp.'

'Worth seeing her again?'

'Can't think what we'd ask her at present. Maybe, if there's something specific we want to know later.'

'Why,' Clement asked from his corner,

'did Shaw bring us the photograph? Does he think Lambert killed Denton and took him out to Cragvale in the Robinsons' car?'

Mitchell shrugged. 'I'm not a mind reader. I do think it probably dropped out of Denton's pocket when whoever did kill him carried him into the warehouse. Lambert could just have driven through the mud and thrown it up. Actually, we don't know for sure that Lambert was driving it.'

'We might have been on the way to answering that question if you'd let Shakila answer mine.' Caroline tossed her head and ignored Mitchell's glare.

When he felt he had quelled her sufficiently, he continued. 'She's the likeliest person unless either Dorian Shaw is being extremely devious or some other person has any of the Robinsons' keys. We'll get uniforms on to that.' He glanced at Smithson whose hand was raised.

'There's a note in the file. One of the PCs on the knocker talked to a Mrs Smithson – no relation so far as I know. She saw the Robinsons' car leaving the garage in the dusk at the beginning of the week – Monday or Tuesday, she can't be sure. It wasn't light enough for her to see the driver. She rang the Robinsons' number to see if anything was wrong that had brought them home early. She got no answer.'

'Becca didn't know that Denton was going

to ring.' They turned to Jennifer. 'She might not even have known at that point that Dorian was risking losing his money. If she intercepted Denton, dispatched him in some way and took him to Cragvale, where did she get the fuel to start the fire and the stuff to make the rope or trail with?'

'The Robinsons' garage? She could have replaced them later.'

Jennifer nodded. 'All right, but then, how did she get him down all the stairs from the flat? She could have dragged him across the ground from the flats to the garage, I suppose – and from the car to the warehouse door. She wouldn't have been expecting to find all Seddon's little friends at the warehouse...'

'Wouldn't she? Maybe they were her suppliers. She could have been there for drugs and have no knowledge of Denton's death.'

'Whatever. Anyway, she'd have had to carry the body up to the first floor. Denton was slightly built and only average height – and she's a tough cookie, but even so–'

'No, she wouldn't!' Mitchell was remembering his night at the fire and his scramble to lug heavy hosepipes up all the stairs. 'There's a lift. The firemen wouldn't allow people into it, of course, but it's big. It was originally meant to haul bales of wool up and down when the place stored them till market day. There was no machinery, just a rope pulley. She could most likely have folded Denton up into it, pulled him up, secured the rope, then walked upstairs. No wonder she was looking a bit ragged when she arrived at her friend's house...'

'So could anyone else. That last bit doesn't implicate Becca.'

Mitchell understood that Jennifer was defending the girl because she disliked her. 'True. Let's give some consideration to Louise Denton, then, if only because the spouse is the traditional suspect.'

Clement raised his hand and briefly described his early session with Wynford Denton. Jennifer paid close attention. When he finished, she produced from her pocket the family photograph she had borrowed from Louise. 'I thought, at first glance, that it was a happy family scene, but look again.' Clement took it and looked. 'The bigger girl at the front – I think that's Elizabeth – is sitting close to the others but she's making no physical contact, nor is she paying any attention to the game that's going on behind her back. She looks anxious and excluded. Louise seems to be concentrating very hard on her game with the little boy.'

Caroline was peering over Clement's shoulder. 'That's right. And the distance between Simon and Louise on the sofa is strange. Most people would move in close together, if only to make things easier for the photographer.'

Mitchell was unimpressed. 'It all sounds a bit airy-fairy. The two younger children are laughing. The older one might well hate cameras or be sulking because she's been in bother. Or she might have problems that have nothing to do with the rest of the people in the picture. Don't forget these children are being fostered. It's quite likely that they've got problems from their past. None of this social worker stuff would cut any ice in court. We should think about what Adrian picked up from the folk at Baker's, though.'

There was a pause whilst they did so, but when Clement spoke, it was on another topic. 'I'm still trying to work out what Denton senior was up to this morning. He seemed genuinely upset at having to reveal his son's less pleasant side...'

'But he didn't have to.'

'Precisely. So, what was he up to? Did he come to plant as much suspicion of Louise as he could, lining up for us all her resentment against him – all the ways he'd hobbled her and used her?'

'Perhaps he killed Simon himself and was throwing up a screen.'

Mitchell wondered how seriously Caroline's suggestion was meant. 'It seems odd how cut off from each other the Dentons were in his last week. She let him come over here on his own–'

'Well, she didn't want him to find his mother. In any case, it wouldn't have been very convenient to have brought the family as well. Not cheap either.'

Mitchell ignored Caroline's interruption. 'He's taken into hospital and she says he told her not to visit. She hasn't seen the car he was driving. She didn't tell him about the baby scare. I begin to doubt whether that really happened.'

Caroline was persistent. 'It's not so strange. He was ill. She was pregnant. They were protecting each other.'

Mitchell was beginning to feel that the discussion was no longer serving a useful purpose. 'Any other contenders for chief suspect? One of the parents, because he was an ungrateful son? No? We'll get the show on the road then.'

'Have we dropped Mubarak Gupte?' Smithson asked.

Mitchell smiled at him sweetly. 'We haven't dropped anyone yet. Let's get busy.' He handed sheets to Jennifer and Clement and a stack more to Smithson to distribute to the uniformed officers.

Caroline asked, 'Where am I going?'

Mitchell looked at her, unsmiling. 'Wherever I send you, you'll go straight to Shakila's house. You might as well do it with my blessing.'

As the rest of Mitchell's family were happily enjoying their various leisure activities, other Cloughton residents were less relaxed and content. Caroline had thought that Shakila's problems might be easily solved once she had been persuaded to make a clean breast of them and accept her friends' help.

Now, though, there were two worried officers. Between them, the two women were considering all the evidence that supported Shakila's disturbing theory. Shakila was brewing tea as Caroline made an orderly list of the facts. They had decided together that a consultation with Beardsmore might help to clarify the situation. They would consult him before taking any irrevocable steps.

Wrapping up against the bitter weather, they left the freshly brewed tea to go cold.

Being in the habit of rising bright and early every morning to set about the day's tasks, Sylvia Townsley saw no reason to spend the first hour of the Lord's day lying in bed.

Simultaneously, she was checking that her little house was immaculate in every nook, and keeping a constant watch on any comings and goings outside. Neither activity lessened the efficiency of the other. If DC Clement called again, she would not have a great deal to tell him, but it would be a very accurate account of the non-events.

Fran Mitchell was well pleased with the way his training had progressed since he had been staying in Cloughton. Having no parents, brothers, sisters or teachers to distract him with their demands, he had been able to tackle a long ride, over very varied and often usefully steep territory, almost every other day. The rest day between gave him a chance to be a good guest, give a hand in the house and generally fit in with his cousins.

He felt a bit guilty for ignoring Declan's hints this morning that he would like to have ridden together with him. However, today's ride had been particularly successful. He was pretty sure that he was going to arrive in Goole at least ten minutes sooner than he had estimated. When he got there, he would take things easy up to Selby, give his legs a rest and enjoy the scenery. He hoped he would not lose all this fitness when he was back to school, his own family and whatever demands were made on him in the new life in Oz.

Dorian Shaw was being interrogated once again, though he supposed that the word was an unfair description of the gentle questioning that Clement was subjecting him to. He was on the late shift today, going into the hospital at one o'clock, so he wouldn't finish till at least nine tonight. He was beginning to resent spending so much of his off-duty coping either with Becca or with the police.

He felt no better for knowing that he had only himself to blame for the continued police attentions. The main topics of Clement's questions were the Robinsons' car and the photograph he had removed from its mudguard which the police would not even know about if he had kept his mouth shut.

After some time, there was a switch to his evening in the Woolpack on the evening of the Cloughton fire. He described his visit yet again in all the detail he could recall, even including what was drunk and whether he or his darts opponent had paid. He couldn't imagine how that detail could help.

'And there's nothing else you can remember, no other tiny details?'

Dorian shook his head. 'Nothing that can have any bearing on firing a decrepit warehouse or doing away with one of my patients.' He felt a stab of alarm. 'You don't think...' He stopped. No need to give the police more suspicions than they seemed to have already.

Clement did not press for the sentence to be finished but just shook his head mournfully. 'You don't know what's important. Neither do I! Just give me every scrap of information, however trivial.' He waited hopefully.

Dorian wanted to be helpful, short of getting Becca into more trouble. He searched his memory again. 'When I was riding in – on the bike – I overtook an old friend. I don't suppose he recognized me in all my leathers and helmet. I was at school with him, the run-down comp up the hill from Greystones and close by the Woolpack. Near that warehouse too. The school used to be bigger in our day – took all the valley kids outside the Cloughton boundary. My friend does live in Leeds now, but don't get excited. So do a hell of a lot of other people.'

Unable to contact Beardsmore, Shakila had left a message at the station asking him to make contact with her. When her cell phone rang, she fished hastily in her pocket. Instead of Beardsmore's voice she heard Patrick Seddon's, whispering so that she hardly recognized him. 'I'm in the Brown Cow coffee place, miss.'

'Not the sort of place you usually hang out.'

'I crep' in, miss, because I saw the fat cow in the track-suit through the window. She's all tarted up now, o' course. She's with one of the gang – them whose names I don't know. Could be their new place for dealing. Wouldn't think o' looking there for him, would you?'

'Has he seen you?'

'Don't think so, miss. They've got their backs to me now they're inside and they're a good way from the door. They're having soup and stuff brought – early lunch, like. Should be here a while.'

'Give me ten.' Shakila made the journey in only seven minutes. She had planned an oblique approach but, as she entered, Seddon sprang from his hiding place to offer his puny muscle. Nevertheless, the confrontation was satisfactory. When the woman turned, Shakila saw the whites of her eyes.

Early in the afternoon, Roger Cornish put away his mobile phone and signalled to move out of the convenient lay-by where he had drawn in to answer it. He was puzzled. Worried wasn't perhaps too strong a word. Bob Beardsmore knew perfectly well when their next game was to be played. Even if he had forgotten, he surely didn't need to check it in the middle of what was a working day for both of them. Was he a suspect? What exactly did they think he'd done?

Both Caroline and Clement had suitably thankful hearts as they made their way to 'evening prayers' on Sunday. Caroline's satisfaction was marred slightly by the problem of having to keep Shakila's secret for a further twelve hours. She knew that, if nothing came out in the course of the debriefing, Mitchell would keep her behind and ask her direct questions.

For the immediate present, she relied on reporting on the day's success and avoiding her chief inspector's eye. Mitchell gave her the first slot, keeping his eyes on her face as she spoke. How was she to mention the presence of Becca Lambert in a cell downstairs without mentioning Shakila's involvement? She had no wish to make trouble for a colleague who had virtually been ordered not to work for the rest of the day. Even to say her name would invite questions.

There wasn't a solution. She would just give the facts and their explanation, as briefly as possible. '...so Shakila was called to the café by Patrick Seddon. She's suspected that the woman he saw last Monday was Dorian Shaw's partner but she had never questioned or even met her, so she sent for me.'

'And?'

'Lambert was obviously terrified. I thought for a minute that it was because she thought Seddon might be a witness to her killing Denton. I think that's wrong though. She seemed more than willing to accompany me back to the station. I told her she wasn't under arrest and she said she'd come anyway.

'I've left her downstairs to worry. I suspect

she's scared of the man she was with. He'll get back at her for letting us get a good look at him. Seddon says he saw drugs change hands, though how he recognized them and what value his evidence has is anyone's guess. The chap was only drinking coffee, so, beyond taking his name and address and refusing to answer his questions, I ignored him. What do you want me to do with her?'

'Nothing. We'll try Smithson on her later.' Mitchell grinned and turned to Clement while Caroline, relieved to be out of the spotlight, sat back to listen. 'I can see you can't contain yourself any longer. What have you got?'

'A lot of ideas and theories that you're going to pour cold water on because I can't prove them.'

Caroline was intrigued. Clement, sent, for once, to deal with matters central to an enquiry instead of to his old ladies to obtain confirming evidence, had used his opportunity. His words to the CI had been negative but his tone was upbeat and confident.

Mitchell's response was encouraging. 'At least get them off your chest.'

'Right. First, I think that Hunter-Brown's Paul, who rang Denton whilst he was in the car, is Simon Pollard, Denton's boss. You've heard on the tape about sorting out the four Simons. Hunter-Brown heard Paul for Poll. I think he came over here on Monday and killed Denton.'

'And that's all your evidence?'

'No. You told me to pull Dorian Shaw in again this morning. You didn't tell me what to ask him so I bored him into a semi-coma by repeating all the questions we'd asked before and challenged him to produce a piece of fresh information, however trivial. Bingo! Near the Woolpack, on the way – so he thought – to meet Denton, Shaw overtook an old friend. Pollard and Shaw went to school together at Cragvale High. Apparently, it was a respected going concern then. Pollard would know the lie of the land.'

'Did they stop and speak?' Clement shook his head. 'This was going on for nine o'clock on a January night. Pollard's car was coming down from the Drum and Monkey where, according to Hunter-Brown, he and Denton were meeting. Shaw was driving slowly because the roads weren't really fit for biking. Pollard's car had to wait at the bottom of the hill for him to go by. There are streetlights on both sides of the road at that junction. I went to look.' Clement gave Mitchell a tentative grin. 'Anyway, I decided to go out on a limb for once. I won't claim overtime if I'm proved wrong but I went back to Pollard. I told him we were interested in Shaw and that Shaw thought their recognition might have been mutual. I told him he was hoping that Pollard might give him an alibi.'

'And Pollard said Shaw was mistaken?'

Clement nodded. 'He assured me, though, that Shaw wouldn't lie. He was just mistaken.'

'What was his own alibi – or didn't you ask?'

'I didn't but he volunteered that he was making a concerned visit to the pregnant wife of his sick colleague. It shook him when I told him we were taking in his car.'

'Louise backs him up, I suppose.'

'Give me a chance, sir. I haven't got wings on my feet.'

'Adrian, are you after my job?'

Clement grinned. 'Yes, sir.'

When Mitchell arrived home, he was unsurprised to find Virginia deep in a book. He did a double take when he saw that it was an atlas. 'I know. You're following our son's first intrepid cycle ride. How much is it going to cost us?'

She blinked. 'What?'

'The gear, better helmet, psychedelic elastic shorts, not to mention–'

She held up a hand to stop him and closed the book. 'Nothing, so far. He's a bit short of staying power. He got as far as the park where he met a crowd of his friends. He had a rest whilst Jack and Nathan fetched their bikes. They spent the rest of the morning racing each other round the cycle track at the back of the playground.'

Mitchell grinned and settled himself at the kitchen table. 'I hope he rang you with the change of plan.'

'No, but I've dealt with that.'

'So, where's everyone?'

'Twins in bed, Fran and Declan playing chess, Kat out to tea and a new DVD with her friend Daisy. Have a good day?' She placed a loaded plate in front of him.

Mitchell grabbed his knife and fork and began to eat. 'It's just improved. It wasn't bad anyway. I've discovered a new side to Adrian. He came back with a tape of his three interviews at Baker's. I wondered for a while if he'd engineered that for himself but, apparently, it is their company policy. He was very crisp with the bumptious MD and quite subtle in getting Denton's new assistant to gossip.'

He explained Clement's theory to her. 'It's quite plausible, actually. It'd do a lot for his confidence if he could prove it.'

'What does he think this Pollard's motive is?'

'Well, rumour says he was sweet on Louise. Denton snapped her up whilst he was abroad. Denton is supposed to be sterile from mumps, so Adrian thinks that Louise's baby might be Pollard's.'

Chin on hand, Virginia checked over the

story mentally. After some moments, she offered, 'From what you've said, now and before, I think Louise is a likelier candidate. She was tricked and flattered into marrying – was she a lot younger than her husband?'

'You'll have to ask Jen.'

'You will, you mean. He pinched her research, landed her with damaged kids while she was still feeling clever to have married the boss – and while she was still too young to cope with their problems.'

'Jen thinks she was too selfish too.'

Virginia ignored the interruption. 'He couldn't give her kids of their own and – didn't you say that Denton senior bought their house for them?' Mitchell nodded. 'Probably, then, she thought Simon was richer than he actually was. Check whether the parents had any ideas about everybody having to make their own way and leaving all their money to Greenpeace or the Third World or some society for growing organic crops...'

Mitchell put his cutlery neatly across the middle of his empty plate and sighed with satisfaction. 'Great. I hope there isn't any more. I wouldn't be able to resist and you've been bullying me to lose half a stone.'

'And then some!'

He pulled a face at her. 'I'll get Adrian to follow up some of those suggestions. Louise is genuinely pregnant, though. We've seen her GP, who, incidentally, knew nothing about a threatened miscarriage. She wouldn't be hauling bodies about.'

'I didn't say she'd done it herself.'

'You mean, what if Pollard is as much under Louise's thumb as pathetic Shaw is under Lambert's? It's a thought.' Another one occurred to him. 'What were you really doing with the atlas?'

'Just checking something.'

'For an article you're writing?'

Virginia looked up and caught sight of the clock. 'Tell you later. It's time for the news.'

'Shall I call the boys?'

She shook her head. 'Let them finish their game.' She had seen and heard an earlier graphic description of the afternoon's fire in the small East Yorkshire area of Hessle. Three children had been playing in the row of derelict cottages that had been destroyed. So far, none of them had died but all had high percentage burns and would presumably be at least frightfully hurt and disfigured. Her own dreams would disturb her tonight. She didn't think she could cope with Declan's.

# Chapter Nine

Arriving, as was his habit, at his second-floor office just before seven on Monday morning, Superintendent Carroll was astonished to see DC Nazir waiting outside the door. His heart sank. Until now, the two loose cannons in Mitchell's team, one of them being the CI himself, had appeared to work together surprisingly well. When the young constable overstepped the mark, Mitchell remembered his youthful sins and was usually her defender.

The superintendent had been vaguely aware of yesterday's contretemps but had expected both sides to see that it was sensibly resolved. The last thing he had expected was that the sparky DC would bring her grievances to his level in both senses.

As he contemplated her without speaking, DC Caroline Jackson arrived at the top of the stairs and came purposefully towards them. Would her presence improve or worsen the situation? If she felt that Nazir needed her support, then the rift with CI Mitchell was deep. On the other hand, Jackson could be depended on to apply common sense in dollops. Neither DC appeared to be indignant.

After contemplating them for a moment longer, the superintendent greeted them, invited them into his office and offered them armchairs. Then, he waited. If they wanted to involve him in a petty squabble that should have been resolved on the corridor below, he was not about to pave the way for their stream of resentment.

What Nazir eventually said was not what he had been expecting to hear. 'We think, sir, that we know who the arsonist is.'

Showing no reaction, he asked, 'The Cloughton one?'

DC Jackson shook her head. 'We don't think so. He has an alibi for last Monday evening.'

'You're here because you think I'll support a theory that your chief inspector has rejected?' He saw at once that he was wrong. Nazir was on the verge of tears and Jackson looked solemn and uncomfortable.

Nazir took out a notebook. 'Sir, without giving you a name, can I give you the evidence in the order that I discovered it and worked it out? You're more likely to believe it with the evidence first.' He nodded, seeing that the girl was overwrought. If he altered the way she had prepared herself to tell her story, he might well have hysterics to deal with. He noticed Jackson move her chair closer to Nazir in support.

'This man lives in North Yorkshire, has his own transport and I know that he travelled to the site of some of the fires at the relevant time. He was in Cloughton when the fire in Holmfirth happened last autumn at the end of September. I've made a chart with dates and–'

'Constable Nazir, we're none of us still in the nursery. Can we stop this melodrama?'

'Let her do it her way. It's the way she can manage it. It's not easy.' Jackson's tone was admonitory rather than appealing.

The superintendent hid a grin, then saw that she was right and stopped smiling. 'All right, Shakila. Carry on.'

The use of her forename seemed to change the atmosphere and encourage her. She handed over her dated list of fires. Carroll put it on his desk, keeping his eyes on her face. 'I read Dr Morton's book – and some others – and got an idea of the sort of people who light fires.' Her face lightened for a moment. 'His profile seemed to describe a good many people I know. I don't offer you the profile as evidence, except that the man does belong to a family too large and busy to spend time with him. He is a loner and he has been in a difficult situation lately.'

The superintendent bit his lip hard, then allowed himself to laugh. 'This sounds like the denouement of an Agatha Christie story. Look, I'm interested. I'm listening. Just give me the facts you have without trying to justify them all.'

Both women relaxed visibly and Shakila's manner became more businesslike. 'Sir, I'm talking about the chief inspector's nephew, Francis Mitchell. He's a phenomenal cyclist, seriously intending to ride in the Tour de France as soon as he's old enough to enter. On Wednesday I met him, after the Rotherham fire. He said he'd ridden to Skipton that day, but he smelt not only of sweat but of smoke and urine. Dr Morton said–' Carroll indicated that he too had read the profile.

'I'm not mistaken. I offered Fran a bar of chocolate and I leaned towards him to tuck it into his saddlebag.'

Anxious to support her colleague actively, Caroline put in, 'I thought that she could have been mistaken at first, sir. Then I remembered last year when Shakila recognized a particular perfume a woman had used, even though her body reeked of vomit and alcohol.'

Carroll nodded, remembering the occasion himself. 'I'm wondering why you've taken so long to come to me. I suppose it was the personal involvement and the furore it would cause, especially if you were proved wrong.'

Now Shakila was indignant. 'No, it wasn't. It was because I couldn't see how even Fran could have covered such a distance as he'd have needed to if he was responsible for the Rotherham fire and yesterday's at Hessle. Then it occurred to me that he might not have been where he said. I thought I had evidence for that. He'd bought chocolate teddy bears for CI Mitchell's twins. He showed me them poking out of the bag with the confectioner's name and the address on the street in Skipton where the market is held. However fast he rode, he couldn't have been in Skipton and Rotherham on the same afternoon. In the end, I tried to destroy his evidence. If he'd been in the shop they would surely remember his bright blue kneelength clingy shorts. I decided to ring, pretending he'd lost something and was trying to retrace his steps. I couldn't get through. In the end I tried both the computer and the local force. The shop closed down last summer.'

'He'd kept a bag and used it for an alibi. Clever.'

Caroline said, 'Maybe he has a whole collection of objects to make people think he was somewhere he'd never been.' Shakila nodded.

The superintendent was moving on. 'What about yesterday? You're not telling me the boy cycled from Cloughton to Hull and got back in time for tea?'

'No, but who is the CI trying to nail for these fires?'

'You tell me.'

'Roger Cornish, who's played chess with Fran Mitchell and drives a lorry freelance. He went to Sheffield and Nottingham on Wednesday, a stone's throw from Rotherham. He went to Hull yesterday.' Shakila, almost perky now, held up a hand to prevent the superintendent's interruption. 'Beardsmore is checking that Fran and the bike went with him on both occasions, but we don't need that now. Last night, Caroline saw the pair of them lifting the bike down from the back of the lorry.'

'Where?'

'In a pub yard – The Grapes on Finch Road.'

'So, you think they're in it together?'

The women exchanged glances and Caroline answered. 'I doubt it. I don't think they knew each other until Fran came on this current visit. Probably Fran just asked him to take him farther afield so that he could vary his routes by having a lift into new areas and just cycling back. Unless he's stupid, Cornish might be putting two and two together by now and wondering if he dare point a finger at a chief inspector's nephew.'

Shakila sighed. 'He isn't the only one, is he?'

Mitchell was exceedingly annoyed when, at

318

eight thirty that morning, neither Caroline nor Shakila had arrived in his office. When the call came from Superintendent Carroll, apologizing because he had delayed them and asking if they could be spared a little longer, he was no less annoyed but considerably more puzzled. 'What do the rest of you know about this?' he bellowed as he slammed down the receiver.

Jennifer, Clement and the various uniformed officers were glad to be able to deny all knowledge, beyond having noticed that something was troubling DC Nazir. Beardsmore felt a little uncomfortable with his silence, but he had only asked a couple of questions on Shakila's behalf and passed the answers back to her. He was no wiser than anyone else in the room about their purpose.

Mitchell watched them settle, resignedly waiting for his bad temper to work itself out. He felt annoyed with himself, but angry now only with his three colleagues in the office upstairs. He grinned shamefacedly at his depleted team. 'Right. Let's talk our own secrets down here. Adrian, I enjoyed your tape. Good work yesterday. You produced a very plausible scenario but you've a vast amount of checking to do. I've made a list on your sheet. If anything else occurs to you, feel free to use your initiative.' He saw that Clement's cup was full and running over.

'Smithson, see if you can work your charms on the Lambert woman. I honestly think all she can tell us about is the mini drugs ring that our arsonist has temporarily deprived of its headquarters. Tell her we'll be sympathetic so long as she'll give us some names. Jennifer, dig Seddon out of his pit. Tell him Lambert's spilling the beans to a colleague. You can do the reverse, Smithson.

'Since Shakila hasn't seen fit to be here to cross-question me, I'll volunteer that I'm going to hassle the forensic team until they guarantee to examine our impounded car today. Don't get excited, Adrian. Denton has probably ridden with Pollard dozens of times for quite legitimate reasons.'

Clement shook his head. 'Not as many as that. I'll have to check the dates but that car is very new. I'll check the garage first for a delivery date, before it occurs to Pollard to suggest to them a date convenient to himself. He won't find the hospital so easy to bribe. With luck, we'll find that delivery of the car was after Denton was cosily tucked up in his ward.'

As he listened, Mitchell had been arrangng action sheets on the table by the door. 'They're all in alphabetical order,' he told his team. 'Pick up your own and get cracking.'

Having his CI's permission to use his initiative, Clement ignored his action sheet for the present and made a telephone call to a garage in Leeds. It was listed as Roberts & Son, but managed by a Stuart Kent who assured him that Mr Pollard had taken delivery of a new Mondeo just over three weeks ago on 29th December. So, if traces from Denton were found in the new car, Pollard could claim that they had driven together before his colleague departed for Cloughton. Pity! Clement sighed. Now he would have to go over to Leeds. Perhaps he'd better attend to at least some of Mitchell's instructions first.

PC Smithson felt that swallowing his antipathy to Miss Lambert had paid dividends. Making the strange condition that she should not be released from her cell until the four men she would name were in custody, she told him a story that would be of great interest to the drugs squad. As he had, just the previous evening, struck a bargain with a Mr Anil Kelu, which had produced evidence to put Gupte behind bars for several years, Smithson felt extremely pleased with himself. He had never thought of himself as an ambitious man but, if he were twenty years younger, he might be demanding a transfer to CID.

Twenty minutes before the 'ring-round' was due to begin, Mitchell had presented himself, as requested, in Carroll's office. Now, he felt increasingly colder as he listened to the superintendent's even tones enumerating the various pieces of evidence against his nephew. His features felt immobile and his facial muscles were refusing to respond to what he was hearing and feeling. He wished he could think of a suitable expression for his features to adopt, and that he could force them into it.

Carroll probably thought he was angry, imagined his chief inspector disbelieved the facts that were being laid out systematically before him. If that was what Carroll thought, then he was wrong. Mitchell took a deep breath and tried to relax. Mentally, he was making his own additions to the list of damning evidence against Fran. He realized now why the boy had not wanted to play all his chess matches at their own house. He knew too why Fran had accepted the ban on his playing away only on condition that he himself could make the phone call that cancelled the previous arrangements. He had not dared to have Roger Cornish speak to either of his temporary guardians. Mention would very likely have been made of the trips the two had made together. Fran had been using Cornish's lorry to take him further distances than he could have cycled within a day, and, at the same time, sheltering behind the suspicions Mitchell himself had that Cornish was lighting the fires. The superintendent's revelations also accounted for Fran's extreme reaction when Ginny had questioned the provenance of the chocolate bars.

Mitchell had no doubt that all the accusations being levied against his nephew could and would be justified by investigation. His mind turned to contemplate the possible results. Some of them were certain. Fran would be given a custodial sentence. Even as the superintendent was speaking, a car was most likely bringing the boy to the station. How would Ginny be feeling and reacting? And how would his mother, newly out of hospital, cope with the news?

His own position would become very awkward, both in the family and at work, though that was not of importance now. Sean and the rest of his family would not be able to leave for Australia unless they were prepared to leave a son behind. He thought sadly that Sean might do just that. Sean might blame him for some of what had happened – but then, Sean had always blamed anyone but himself.

Mitchell knew that he would be allowed no part in the forthcoming procedures. He wondered who would be in charge of them. Were Caroline and Shakila afraid that he would consider their accusation to be a personal attack? At least he could set that right.

Having even this small positive plan loosed his tongue and unfroze his face. He looked up as the superintendent paused. 'I realize that this is as difficult for you as for me. I hope and expect that this case will not affect my other investigations. I would like your permission to take one hour's leave to go home and speak to my wife. If, by any chance, you haven't yet arrested my nephew I'll wait until he's out of the house. Would you please tell Constables Jackson and Nazir that, not only do I not feel their work is in any way a personal attack, but I commend their keen observation – and their tact.' With as much dignity as he could muster, he stood up and left the room.

Back in his office, he grabbed a pair of scissors and hacked at the various ivies, so beloved of the office cleaner, until hardly a leaf remained. Next, he opened the file and began to make a list of the parts of their current investigations he would still be allowed to work on. He had to keep busy until a call from Superintendent Carroll told him his nephew was safely in custody and he was free to take his hour at home.

In a few minutes, the call startled him even though it was expected. The voice though was unexpected. It was his wife's, calm but urgent. 'Benny, the police have come for Fran. He went up to his room after breakfast and didn't come to tell me he was going out. The bike's gone, and his helmet, but none of the other gear. He isn't here.'

DC Clement was, he decided, in transports of delight. He turned the phrase over in his mind. Yes, 'transports' was very appropriate. He had surveyed Roberts & Son from the opposite side of the road and made his plan. Ignoring a gleaming year-old Merc and an almost new Celica on the forecourt, he had walked to the far end where a couple of aged Minis were starred as 'This week's BARGAIN!!!'.

As he had expected, the young apprentice had been sent out to attend to him. Mr Kent would not expose himself to the weather for such a small return. The apprentice was a chatterer. Amongst questions about mileage, number of owners and the availability of parts, Clement volunteered that his friend Mr Pollard had bought a new car from here at a bargain price, so he was hoping to get a similarly low price.

The boy shook his head and grinned. 'No chance. Mr Pollard's price was because he's Mr Kent's brother-in-law.'

Clement nodded sagely. 'Ah, that'd be why he got his delivery rushed through before the New Year. He was hoping it'd come in time to impress his folk at the family party.'

The boy's grin became wider. 'Well, that didn't come off. We couldn't get it till 7th January. He didn't seem to mind actually.'

Clement did a rapid calculation. By then, Denton would have been safely in hospital. Trying for a casual tone he remarked, 'Might drop in on him while I'm over here. Is he still at Brooksby Road?'

'I don't think that was the address. I'll just go and look in the book.' He returned in short order, bearing the information on an oily piece of paper in a remarkably neat hand. Clement thanked him, fed the information into his satnav and set off again.

Arriving at the prestigious address, he was a little disappointed to find no one at home. It would have been good to go back to Mitchell's early afternoon check-in having the intended confrontation to report on. Fate, however, had something better in store for him. Peering through the side window of Pollard's double garage, he saw, reared up against the opposite wall, the number plates of the car that Simon Denton had bought in Cloughton.

Niamh Mitchell came back from her kitchen into her sitting room and handed her grandson a tall mug of drinking chocolate. 'You'd better drink that if you can't eat anything.' When he made no move to take it, she placed her offering on the small table beside the chair she had put him into when he had arrived at the house in a state of semi-collapse.

She had heard his account of his mis-doings and of the crisis that had precipitated his flight to her accepting hospitality and capable ministrations. Her voice was calm. 'Now then, I ought to telephone your uncle and aunt, your father and the police so that a lot of people can stop worrying at least about your physical safety. First, though, I'm waiting for Father Xavier to arrive. He's on his way now. When you've made your confession to God, you'll feel braver about making it to mere mortals.'

Fran sat staring at the opposite wall but seeing, she suspected, the ravaged bodies of the three children whose presence in the derelict cottages he had not anticipated. He confirmed it. 'Have any of them died? Will the doctors be able to help them?'

She was not willing to comfort him with lies and answered with a lift of her shoulders. She asked him, 'Did you sleep at all last night?'

He answered, bitterly, 'Yes. Like a log. I wasn't called down for the news. I didn't know about them till I listened to the headlines on the little radio in Declan's bedroom after breakfast. I was looking forward to hearing all the details of the fire.'

Niamh willed the priest to hurry. She had tried to be all things to all six of her own children but could think of little to say that would console or help this grandson, the firstborn of the one child of her own whom she had failed. She blamed Sean for many of Fran's troubles, but did that not lead logically to her own responsibility for Sean's failings as a father? She pitied Father Xavier who must have been many times given the responsibility for dealing with the results of the sins of his flock.

She saw Fran's shiver of fear as his knock sounded. She remained in her chair, knowing that this family friend would let himself in, take over responsibility for dealing with the wickednesses committed by her family and release her to give the practical help that the other members would need.

The Mitchell children had been fetched out of school. It was important that they should be given their parents' version of events before being exposed to whatever their schoolfellows had understood from the comments their parents had made. They had accepted the news of Fran's guilt phlegmatically, concentrating on its practical aspects. After all, Fran was almost an adult and there sometimes seemed neither rhyme nor reason in adults' behaviour.

'Will Fran be in prison for ever?' Caitlin

had asked.

'It's not a prison. He'll go to a special boarding school to help him to stop lighting fires and to understand what harm it does. Then, he will probably come home again.'

'Will I be able to go and play chess with him there?' Declan wanted to know. Mitchell was pleased that one of his children seemed to be happy for Fran still to be accepted as family. Without waiting for an answer, Declan continued, 'When he comes out, might he come here and make a fire in our house?'

Sinead grabbed Mitchell's arm. 'If he does, will you ask him to get my fairy doll out first?'

Mitchell picked her up and sat her on his lap. Michael, keeping his usual considering silence, went to sit on his mother's.

Caitlin had rallied already and was considering how to deal with the difficulties the news brought them. 'Who's going to visit Fran when Uncle Sean and the others are in Australia?'

Her parents exchanged glances. So, this child shared their assumption that Fran's father would treat his son, in these new circumstances, much as he had done since the boy's birth sixteen years ago. Virginia said, 'I expect we shall as soon as we're allowed.' Satisfied that all of them were curious rather than anxious, she sent them upstairs to their own devices. They could go back to school after lunch.

Mitchell began making coffee. It was what he always did when his immediate future was undecided. By the time he came back into the sitting room with his steaming jug, the therapy had worked again. 'I'm taking the time off that the super has offered. We've got Gupte slammed up, Clement seems to have nailed Simon Denton's death firmly to Simon Pollard, Shakila has unmasked our arsonist...'

'Carroll wanted it sorted out on his patch, didn't he?'

'But not, I imagine, in the way it's turned out. He suggested that I look for promotion elsewhere, thinks life will be easier if I start afresh...'

'Well, he offered just the reason for going that will persuade you to stay. I won't start packing yet. When did you ever take the easy option?'

Fran Mitchell sat quietly in the small room where he had been incarcerated. He was not sure of the room's status, but he didn't think it was a cell. Nor was he sure whether or not the young man who was keeping a careful watch over him was a police officer.

When Fran had asked him for paper and some soft pencils, he had used his cell phone to pass on the request. The pencils that arrived were only HB and the paper was lined, but the man had done his best. Fran had covered two of the sheets with cruel caricatures of his parents. They had afforded him almost as much relief as the fires.

His minder had asked if he wanted anything more. Fran had a long list of requests but none of them could be supplied by anyone here. He hadn't bothered asking. He wanted his father and mother not to visit him here. He wanted to talk to Auntie Ginny. He knew that Uncle Benny wasn't allowed to see him yet. He wanted to see the little, dark DC Nazir and thank her for pulling him out of the downward spiral he had been caught in.

Later, he would ask if he could see Father Xavier again. They would probably allow him to come – and Granny Niamh wouldn't let him down. She had arranged for him to see the priest before she had turned him over to the police. And Father Xavier had pointed out to him that she and Grandpa, like his own parents, had brought up six children, born in quick succession. Sean, his father, like himself, had been the eldest. Like himself, he would have had unwelcome responsibilities thrust on him. His father's parents, like his own, would have had little time to listen to his problems, his frustrations, his resentment. But shouldn't he have learned from his own experiences that six children were too many?

Fran felt too tired right now to think it all out – but there was one small thing he could do. He picked up his two portraits and ripped them into small pieces. Taking the remaining blank sheet, he began to draw again.

After a minute or two, he surveyed his second attempts. Not right – but then, he was going to have plenty of time to work on it.

The publishers hope that this book has given you enjoyable reading. Large Print Books are especially designed to be as easy to see and hold as possible. If you wish a complete list of our books please ask at your local library or write directly to:

**Magna Large Print Books**
Magna House, Long Preston,
Skipton, North Yorkshire.
BD23 4ND

This Large Print Book, for people
who cannot read normal print,
is published under the auspices of

**THE ULVERSCROFT FOUNDATION**